Tales of Ambergrove

Realm of Chaos

Dragonwolf Trilogy Book Two

H. T. Martineau

authorHOUSE®

AuthorHouse™
1663 Liberty Drive
Bloomington, IN 47403
www.authorhouse.com
Phone: 833-262-8899

© 2021 H. T. Martineau. All rights reserved.

No part of this book may be reproduced, stored in a retrieval system, or transmitted by any means without the written permission of the author.

Published by AuthorHouse 10/01/2021

ISBN: 978-1-6655-4010-0 (sc)
ISBN: 978-1-6655-4011-7 (hc)
ISBN: 978-1-6655-4013-1 (e)

Library of Congress Control Number: 2021921046

Print information available on the last page.

This book is printed on acid-free paper.

Because of the dynamic nature of the Internet, any web addresses or links contained in this book may have changed since publication and may no longer be valid. The views expressed in this work are solely those of the author and do not necessarily reflect the views of the publisher, and the publisher hereby disclaims any responsibility for them.

Some dreams are worth having more than once.
For anyone who doesn't think they can achieve their dreams:
You can. You will. You will again.
Onward to the next adventure.

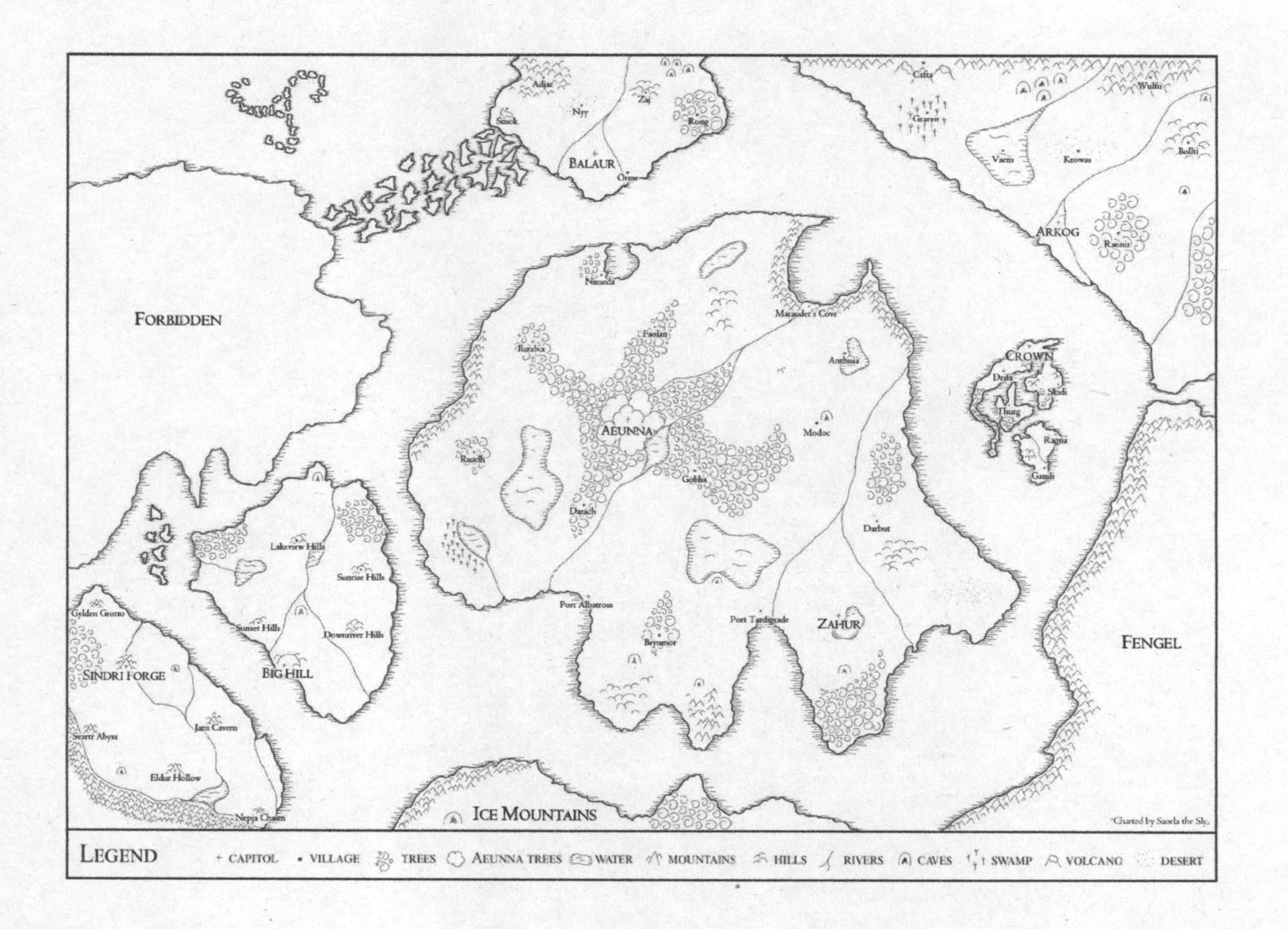

FORBIDDEN
Smok
Adjar
Nyy
Zaj
Rong
BALAUR
Orins
Cafta
Grarvtt
Wulfu
Vaem
Krowas
Bolfti
ARKOG
Rannir
Nimeda
Maraduer's Cove
Faolan
Barabia
Anthusa
AEUNNA
Modoc
Ruadh
Gobha
Darach
Darbut
CROWN
Drifa
Skidi
Thurg
Ragna
Ganali
Lakeview Hills
Sunrise Hills
Sunset Hills
Downriver Hills
BIG HILL
Gylden Grotto
SINDRI FORGE
Jarn Cavern
Svartr Abyss
Eldur Hollow
Nepja Chasm
Port Albatross
Port Tardigrade
ZAHUR
Brynmor
FENGEL
ICE MOUNTAINS
*Charted by Saorla the Sly.
LEGEND
+ CAPITOL
• VILLAGE
TREES
AEUNNA TREES
WATER
MOUNTAINS
HILLS
RIVERS
CAVES
SWAMP
VOLCANO
DESERT

Contents

Chapter One

Keena's First Voyage

A blue sail rippled from *Harrgalti's* mast as the ship pressed along the coastline of the forbidden lands. Teddy stood at the helm, his red beard rippling and the sun glinting off his bald, green head. He stood alone on the deck, stoic and determined. The forest dwarves had always been taught to fear the old cities—he was no different. Now, on the orders of the goddess Aeun herself, his niece and her companions had to venture right into the heart of that land and face its evil.

Teddy sighed and placed the pin in the wheel to keep it sailing true before looking over his map again. He'd spent a lot of his time the past couple months poring over it, trying to select the perfect docking island so he could keep the young ones as safe as possible.

As he scanned the cluster of islands to the south of the forbidden lands, a shriek from below reached his ears. Sighing heavily, he rolled up his map and strode to the stairs leading below deck.

Down in the belly of *Harrgalti,* a motley crew surrounded a large galley table. A sea elf sat at one end, smirking at his companions while he combed through a book. Next to him sat a gnome—his total opposite. Whereas the sea elf, Finn, was tall and slender with blue skin and long, green hair, the gnome was short and stocky with earthy-brown skin and a bushy, black beard. The gnome, Kip, was also much more amused by the commotion on the other end of the table.

Mara, their leader in name if not always in deeds, a young woman with fiery red hair wrapped up in a caged bun, sat at the table eating a sandwich—well, some of it. A mass of fur and wings bounced around on the table and nipped at the sandwich as she took each bite.

"Don't let her ruin your sandwich!" a russet, toddler-sized bear called disapprovingly to her friend. The bearkin, Ashroot, had made the sandwich—as she made most of the food—but she was amused despite the potential waste.

The pup was an awkward creature, tripping over its wings, unable to maneuver its large paws, and whipping itself with its tail—a danger due to the spade that was hidden in the hair at the tip. This terra cotta fluff ball was no ordinary creature. She was a dragonwolf—one of the last of her kind. As a young pup, she wasn't much more than a ball of cuteness now, barreling around the table, but she would be a sight to behold when her horns grew in, and she was old enough to fly and breathe fire.

"Keena, Keena, Keena!" Mara called to her dragonwolf, in rapid succession as if it were all one long name. She took another bite of her sandwich and left part of it sticking out of her mouth.

Keena yipped and nipped at Mara's mouth, sticking her tongue out as far as it would go, trying to get at the sandwich. Ashroot shrieked, Finn snorted and shook his head, and Kip laughed a deep, belly laugh. Right as Keena successfully snatched the bite, growled playfully, and gulped it down, Teddy reached the doorway to the galley.

Mara sat and giggled, holding a hand over her mouth as she chewed the rest of her bite. When Keena licked at her chin, Mara jerked her head away and laughed—until she saw the look on Teddy's face.

"You shouldn't do that, Mara," he told his niece. "It would be a wasted year for all of us if you were killed because you were playing too much with a wild animal."

"Sorry, Teddy," she replied quietly.

Kip scoffed. "Nonsense! She's a sweet baby!" he said in a childish voice. He rapped on the table a few times, and the dragonwolf jumped into his arms. In one swift motion, he flipped her over to cradle her like a baby, rubbing her belly and making faces at her. He rubbed his beard on her snout and she sneezed, snorting a little puff of fire into the scraggly hair.

He made an involuntary noise, dropped Keena, and began patting out his singed beard.

"See?" Teddy said disapprovingly, stroking his own beard.

"She's just too young to talk right now, Teddy," Ashroot offered. "Once she gets older, we can talk to her—train her—and she'll be just as behaved as I am."

There was a clatter at the far end of the room as Keena started pawing at cabinets and yipping. "Maybe not quite as behaved," Finn muttered.

"She'll get it, Finn," Mara said, grinning at the wild look on Kip's face as he checked and triple checked to make sure his beard no longer smoldered.

Teddy crossed his arms and said, with feigned gruffness, "Perhaps if you have all this time to get the ship burned to cinders, I should be giving you something useful to do."

"Right, like you didn't already have a plan before coming down here," Kip joked.

"That may be true," the dwarf replied, grinning and holding up his rolled-up map.

Mara groaned and Finn nudged her. "Time for you to get back to the helm," he said seriously. "There's more at sea than just the Dragon's Teeth."

Mara opened her mouth to retort, but Teddy cleared his throat and called loudly, "Alright, young ones, gather 'round." He pulled a chair to the center of the table and sat, spreading his map.

A few weeks later, Mara stood at the helm of Harrgalti, sailing, checking the map, and periodically tossing a wooden ball across the deck for Keena. Kip had carved a few of these toys for the dragonwolf pup—another each time the previous one was chomped beyond recognition.

Teddy had tasked Mara with most of the remaining sailing toward their next stop. He'd explained what he believed was the best way for them to undertake the daunting task set by Aeun. Before they began, they would need to sail to their brothers in the mountains—the mining dwarves. The mining dwarves lived far away from most of the world, surrounded by the forbidden west and the frozen south.

Not wanting to deal too much with their grumpier brethren, Teddy had planned to visit a settlement called Gylden Grotto. This network of caverns rested at the northernmost tip of the mining dwarves' lands, demanding only a quick sojourn into their territory. Mara had only seen mining dwarves once before—when they stayed in Port Albatross. She was surprised, on her arrival to Ambergrove, to learn that the small, gruff, mining men she'd read about in her stories and played with in DUNGEONS & DRAGONS were really only half of the dwarves that existed. Teddy called them the miserable half.

Mara was his great-niece, but she had only recently met him and the other forest dwarves. She'd spent much of her life on Earth, and it was still difficult for her to divide what she thought she knew growing up from what had become her reality.

Keena yipped and skidded into Mara before pawing at her leg and growling softly. Mara twisted the slobbery ball out of her pup's mouth and tossed it again down the length of the ship like a bowling ball. Keena chased after it with glee, barreling right into Finn as she ran. The sea elf smirked as she snorted and yipped at his legs before continuing to bound after her ball. "She's a fireball, isn't she?" he called to Mara, before meeting her at the helm and staring out across the water.

"Have you decided what you're going to do?" Mara asked.

"Mmm."

She looked over at her friend. His emerald eyes were cloudy, guarded. "Ash is going to stay below deck," Mara ventured. When he didn't respond, she continued, "Kip is going to stay with her. His people have a pretty tense relationship with the mining dwarves, too, bec—"

"Well, his people didn't put them here, did they?" Finn snapped, crossing his arms.

It reminded Mara of the sort of attitude her sister Kara used to get when their dad told her to eat her vegetables. Though briefly amusing, it was hardly the same. "I'm sure it wasn't like that …" she replied quietly.

He chuckled wryly. "Oh, it was. Haven't you met my mother? I assure you, grandfather, great-grandmother, great-great-grandfather … none of them were great. They were conquerors with the people in the forbidden lands, driving others out and marauding in the seas, causing many to retreat to land to keep safe. The dwarves may have found a nice mountain home, but it was only after they were driven from everywhere else." His face twisted to a grimace. "Those dwarves will hate me, and rightly so. I think I would be a detriment to the stop if I went along. It's best if it's just their kin—you forest dwarves."

"I'm sure you're more their kin than I am—since you've been in Ambergrove all your life and I've only been here about a year—but okay. I'm sure Ash will love your company."

Finn pursed his lips for a moment before uncrossing his arms and throwing his hands in the air. "There's no arguing with you." He sighed. "But one day you'll see how much you belong here. … And Ashroot is a natural-born mariner. I enjoy her company." He nudged Mara. "Maybe she can try teaching me how to cook again!"

Mara grimaced. Finn had made a valiant effort last time he tried his hand at cooking, but none of them had been able to choke down the meal he'd prepared. "Practice makes perfect, I guess."

A deep chuckle met her ears. "No, practice makes acceptable. It does still take a certain amount of skill, dedication, and love to make perfect." Teddy emerged from below deck, grinning ear to ear, adding, "I'm sure you'll make acceptable meals eventually."

Finn glowered at him and then shrugged in acceptance. Although the two men had had a rocky start—Teddy thought Finn had a hand in a near-death experience of Mara's at the hands of his mother, the queen of the sea elves—they had bonded over the months at sea together, and now Teddy was like a father to the young elf.

As Teddy approached the helm, he glanced at the horizon and went on, "We should be able to see the dwarven lands within the hour. Once they're in view, it's just a few hours to port at Gylden Grotto. We should be there for supper—which is a real treat with the mining dwarves. They have this way of curing meats in the mines that—" He saw Finn's face fall and changed course. "Well, we'll get some meats from them, and you and Ashroot can surely make us a fine meal out of it."

Finn nodded and turned to scan the horizon, and Mara met her uncle's gaze. He rapidly gestured a hand in front of his neck and dropped his head to one side with his tongue out, making it clear what he actually thought of Finn doing anything with the delicious meats. Mara giggled, and Finn looked back to see Teddy looking a little too innocent.

It was just getting dark when they made it to the port at Gylden Grotto. There were lights out for travelers and two guards there to meet them at the docks. As Teddy spoke with the guards, Mara and Kip prepared below deck. After unsuccessful coaxing, Finn decided to stay behind with Ashroot, and although Kip's people had an aversion to mining dwarves, Kip himself did not—he'd just planned to stay behind so there was someone to keep Ashroot company. He cheerfully joined Mara in preparation to meet the outside world for the first time in months.

Teddy had told them the dwarves favored warriors and good weapons and were prone to breaking into brotherly brawls at any time. Fierce melee weapons were encouraged. Kip had a rig to carry his hammer on his back, and, although it was easy enough to draw the hammer from it when needed, it did take two people to get it strapped up for travel.

Mara helped Kip with his hammer, and he helped her with her battle axe for good measure. Since meeting Kip, the gnome had lugged around his giant hammer—his weapon of choice. While Mara had a variety of weapons courtesy of Teddy, her favorite was her dragonwolf battle axe, with the head of a wolf at its tip and stylized wings for blades.

They both wore their armor—Kip his scale mail from his time as a Big Hill soldier and Mara her rusty, blue and purple elven chainmail. Finally, Mara grabbed her two small axes, slipping them into rings at her hips. After she'd survived the Serpent's Gauntlet only by the clever use of small axes, she'd told her uncle she didn't want to go anywhere else without them. Mara wrapped her hair into her fancy bun cage—dragon dome and wolf's head pin—and they were ready.

They met Teddy on the dock and saw him point back at them and draw a hand across his chest in a clawing motion before continuing his conversation with the dwarves. Mara looked sheepishly over at Kip. He'd joined their journey after they'd left Port Albatross on *Harrgalti,* but he and Finn had still missed Mara's first trial. Whenever she was able to display the scars from her test with the Great Silver Bear, Mara made sure they were visible. That single paw swipe across her chest proved her to be a true forest dwarf.

When Mara and Kip made it over to them, the mining dwarves nodded in Mara's direction and one addressed her in a gruff voice, "Welcome dwarf. You and your uncle are our kin, and you are welcome to any supplies you would need from our city. We have lived under the shroud of the forbidden lands for too long, and we are happy to aid you in any way we can." He smiled warmly at Mara from under his coal-black beard. He definitely looked like the dwarves she was used to before coming to Ambergrove—he even reminded her of her father's DUNGEONS & DRAGONS character, Dalzi, and she was hit with a pang of sadness to be seeing her father's character and not the man himself.

The other guard scrunched up his nose and gave Kip a severe look before adding, "Your *gnomish* friend," he spat the word, "is welcome to accompany you, though he will have to pay for his supplies."

Kip nodded respectfully to the dwarves. "I understand. I thank you for allowing me to visit your mountain."

Mara gave Kip a pat on the shoulder. She could see little beads of sweat forming at his temples. His people had never really gotten along with the mining dwarves, and gnomes were brought up to fear them. Never mind that Kip had a young nephew who was half mining dwarf, and whom he loved more than anything in the world. He wouldn't try to justify himself to them. As the dwarves led them to the edge of the docks and down toward their mountain entrance, Mara lagged behind and caressed the wooden trinket around her neck. She hadn't yet figured out what the symbols meant, but Kip had carved the necklace and given it to her the morning she was to face the gauntlet, and she hadn't removed it since. She watched his back as they descended into the home of the mining dwarves.

Hundreds of little tunnels were dug into the mountain. The guards led them down past home after home to a wide, tall chamber. There were various shops branching off into the mountain or set in stalls in this area. Raucous laughter came from a place that was clearly a tavern, and just as they passed, a friendly brawl spilled out the front doors. Without so much as a glance, the guards led them straight back to an entrance with an intricately carved doorframe, and Teddy had to steer Mara away from the spectacle of a real-life friendly brawl.

"Wait here," one of the guards ordered. He entered the room, and they could hear murmuring conversation for a moment before he emerged with another dwarf. This dwarf was shorter than the others, but stouter with meat and muscle. He had golden beads braided into his long, black beard, and he wore a red and gold tunic and dirty, black pants.

The dwarf walked up to Mara and held out a hand. Mara reached out her right hand to clasp his and bit back a gasp when he grabbed her arm and twisted it down to reveal the dragonwolf on her bracer. The dwarf looked up at her, and Mara could see something strange in his hardened eyes—respect. That was good. She remembered all too late that the last time she'd greeted a leader like the men did, Chief Sokti of the gnomes had all but thrown them off his land.

"You are Mara, Dragonwolf of Aeunna," he said. It was not a question.

There were scattered gasps and whispers around her. Mara glanced around to see a crowd had begun to form. "Y-yes," she answered.

The dwarf laughed a deep guffaw and released her arm, giving her a few hard claps on the back. "Welcome, welcome!" he bellowed. "You bested the champion of the sea elves and sailed your ship through the Dragon's Teeth *twice!* I am honored to have you in my halls."

"How could you possibly know that?" Mara asked, bewildered at the idea that word had traveled so far.

"Lass, when you do things that have not been done in centuries, people tend to notice," he explained, winking before stepping back and bowing respectfully to Mara. "I am Hodd. I am the leader of the mining dwarf community of Gylden Grotto. Your people will eat with us and rest for the night, and we will give you any supplies you require in the morning. I will be glad to assist you in getting rid of the scourge of the forbidden lands however I can. Follow me."

Hodd led them across to the tavern and Mara shared an incredulous look with Kip. He rubbed her arm gently before stepping into the tavern behind her, while Teddy beamed behind.

They awoke the next morning on hard bedrolls. Teddy had explained that they should never refuse the hospitality of the mining dwarves, even if it didn't seem so great to them. They'd eaten an amazing dinner—roast mutton and potatoes in a savory bread bowl—and listened to the mining dwarves tell stories. Mara even had to hide her delight when they got involved in a tavern brawl, instigated by Kip and ended by Mara's small axes. When she hooked the axe blade on the mining dwarf's sword and joked that he'd lost to the same move as the sea elves' champion, he'd guffawed and ordered them all more drinks.

When it was time to rest for the night, the barkeep had led them up to this room. It was made for occupants the size of the mining dwarves, and there was just the one room for all guests—living under the shadow of the forbidden lands, they never really had many.

They'd all stretched out together on the floor. For all three of them to fit, Teddy, who was by far the tallest, had to stretch out along one wall and Mara and Kip lay perpendicular, with their heads at his knees. When Mara woke the next morning, she felt a weight on her waist. Kip was snoring softly behind her and had wrapped an arm around her in his sleep. Softly, she slid her hand up to cover his. The snoring stopped briefly, and Mara's heart hammered for a moment.

Teddy, much too old to spend the night cramped on a hard floor, had barely slept a wink. He watched this little exchange unfold and saw Kip's eyes snap open when Mara covered his hand with hers—and saw him pretend to snore again when Mara tensed, thinking she'd woken him. *Kids,* Teddy thought. He remembered being so young. Being so awkward around the person he cared about. So unsure. His eyes burned as he thought of his dear Freya. It had been over a year since he'd seen her face, felt her warmth, and touched her fondly as those two did now.

Teddy patted his chest. He'd written a letter for her every week. They hadn't been anywhere they could send a message for a while, so he had a hefty bundle wrapped up and ready to send out before they left Gylden Grotto. He hoped his letters were helping her to cope without him. It had been a long time since he'd left her alone for so long. Unfortunately, because they didn't really stay in one place long, he hadn't heard from her since they left Port Albatross when they were just a few weeks into their journey.

Kip made a particularly unconvincing snort, so Teddy rolled his eyes and decided it was time for them to get started. With a soft chuckle, he groaned and rolled over, bonking both of them in the head and snorting awake just as unconvincingly. He peeked down and saw both of them jerk their hands back as he rolled to sit up, beckoning for them to do the same. He looked at their flushed faces and grinned under his beard. *You'll get there young-uns.*

They gathered their belongings and had a nice breakfast in the tavern before heading to the market. The barkeep gave Teddy a handcart to load up and sent them out together with it. The market was dimly lit, despite the hundreds of lanterns strung through the halls. To Mara's surprise, they first piled ropes, huge canvases, and iron spikes into the cart. Teddy hurried around, oblivious to his companions, gathering various construction materials and tools. When they made it to an armorer, Teddy got four helmets and, when the burly man had glared up at Kip, told the armorer it was always good to have spares.

Hodd met them at the armorer's booth and handed Teddy a large, clattering bag. "These will help you when you venture out into the evil, brother," the mining dwarf rumbled. Teddy clasped his arm, they nodded to each other, and Hodd winked at Mara before venturing off down one of the tunnels in the mountain.

Teddy assured Mara they could come back again to further explore and learn more about her brethren, but for now it was time to go, so after piling the rest of the cart with food supplies, they bid farewell to the mining dwarves and headed back to the ship.

A few hours later, *Harrgalti* was on a steady course north, and Teddy stood at the head of the table in the galley. The table was loaded up with the prizes from Gylden Grotto, and the others sat around it. Mara held Keena's sleeping form and gently stroked her ears—the pup had not left her side since she'd returned—and they all waited patiently as Teddy divulged his plan.

"Foremost, we cannot stay on *Harrgalti* for this step in our journey. We need to preserve the ship for darker times ahead, and we need to make sure we aren't spotted and put the ship in danger—because then we'll have nothing. The first step is simple." Teddy rolled out one of his many maps and pointed to an arrowhead-shaped island at the top of the cluster of islands between them and the forbidden lands. "We will dock the ship here in this tiny cove, bring her in at high tide and get her up on land. She'll be safe then from water creatures. We'll build our camp on this island."

Teddy went over and patted on some of the supplies—rope and canvas. Mara thought back to some old cartoons—whenever she was faced with something new in Ambergrove, she'd tried to relate it to something she knew. "So, we're going to build an exploration base camp—something like on a survivalist island." She imagined Tarzan's lost family's refuge and Nim's elaborate island.

Teddy nodded. "We'll build our camp here, and I've gotten enough supplies that it can be run like a rudimentary homestead for the time we're here, and we can return to Gylden Grotto for more as needed. Ashroot, there are many supplies for you to help in the kitchens—for preserving foods and trapping fresh. You may even want to put in a garden if we settle in. You'd have everything you need here."

Ashroot grinned her little bear grin. "Great! It's been so restricting to cook on the ship. We'll have some good food now!"

Mara, who'd always thought Ashroot's food was good, just shook her head at her friend. Finn held up one of the helmets and asked, "And what about these?"

"Ah." Teddy grabbed one of the other helmets and held it up. "The enemies here will not fight fair. We'll need some protection when we go out there, and these are the best helmets in Ambergrove. They are made to protect most of the head while still leaving full visibility." The helmets were all the same. Simple, blocky things like Mara had seen dwarves wear in movies. This would protect everything but the nose from a sword swing.

"Um, Teddy?" Ashroot asked quietly. "Why are there only four helmets?"

Teddy stared at her a moment before replying gently, "Well, dear … that's because you aren't going to need one. You aren't coming with us." He paused, waiting for some sort of argument or interruption, but none came. Teddy continued, "The forbidden lands are nothing like any of us have ever seen before. It will be dark and dangerous. It will be there that one of us is lost."

Mara looked down and fiddled with her cuff. This was the worst part of the whole journey. Fate dictated that one of them would not make it home, and she was certain if the bearkin went into the forbidden lands, she would be the one lost. "I agree, Ashroot." Mara said, turning to her friend. "You are here to make sure we are taken care of. You wanted to come with me to help, and you wanted to talk to Aeun. You can help the most here by staying at camp and keeping everything ready for us when we come back. I don't think you should set foot in the forbidden lands."

The others nodded, looking fondly at the bearkin. She gulped and nodded back.

"Alright then." Teddy pounded a fist lightly on the table. "We'll be into the cove by nightfall. We'll sleep here tonight, make camp first thing in the morning, and prepare for our first trip out into the wilderness."

The pounding fist startled Keena awake. Thinking the noise had somehow come from the supplies, she yipped and jumped up onto the table growling at one of the helmets with all her might.

Chapter Two

Questhaven

Keena, dang it, get off of that. You're not helping!" Teddy shouted, waving a hand frustratedly at the dragonwolf.

As the crew was using ropes to haul *Harrgalti* onto the beach, Keena growled playfully and jumped up, trying to catch them. Teddy slackened his rope and pulled it tight as Keena chomped on it, flinging her back away from the work and into Ashroot's arms. Ashroot took her back a dozen yards to where their supplies lay stacked on the beach and held her, struggling, in her arms until the others had completed their task.

They'd chopped down some trees and made a grooved runner to hold *Harrgalti* on the beach. They pulled the ship up the grooves and secured it to a few nearby trees. Although it was difficult to pull the ship into place, Teddy explained that this would allow them to simply cut the line to release the ship, and the weight would drive it back into the water at high tide.

Grumpy and sweating, they all plopped down on the ground near Ashroot, who released the struggling dragonwolf. Keena yipped and barreled over to each of them in turn before finally settling in Mara's lap and licking the sweat from her face.

"What's next, old man?" Mara panted, laughing.

Teddy glared at her for a moment and sighed. "We'll start by pitching tents. We'll get the main tent set up first, and then everyone will have their own tent to set up," he explained.

"Ah, I get my own room?" Finn exclaimed. "I don't have to listen to that one's snoring anymore!"

He gestured to Kip, who threw a stick at him and laughed.

"You can pitch your tent anywhere you like on this side of the island, as long as it's sheltered from view from the sea," Teddy explained, raising a hand to catch the stick as Finn threw it back at Kip.

"Come on, you couldn't let me get him *once*?" Finn asked grumpily, as Teddy chucked the stick out of reach and into the water.

Keena yipped and ran in after it, shoved her whole head in the water, and ran back. Placing the stick in Teddy's lap and shaking herself dry, she coated the men in seawater, wagged her tail, and waited. Teddy grabbed the stick and made a theatrical throwing motion before pressing the stick into the ground behind him. Keena ran back into the water, splashing and dunking her head in every so often in search of her prize.

"W-what next?" Mara managed, stifling her laughter.

"Once the tents are set up, we'll split up. Two of us will help Ashroot get the supplies all organized and ready, and two of us will head out and explore the island."

"And then?" Finn asked.

"Then we'll come up with a plan to head into the forbidden lands."

Thunk, thunk thunk. "Here you go, Finn." Kip pounded in the last of Ashroot's tent stakes and handed the elf his mallet.

"Ow! Are you kidding me? Get. In. There. You. Stupid. Thing. Argh!" Kip turned to see Mara kneeling next to a mass of canvas and ropes. She threw her hammer behind her and Keena ran after it. Kip walked over and patted his legs as Keena emerged from behind a bush. Seeing the great toymaker, Keena bounded over to him and gave him the mallet.

Kip scritched Keena's nose and produced a wooden ball for her. Then he walked over to Mara's hunched form and bonked her on the shoulder a few times with the hammer. She sighed heavily and hissed, "I don't want the stupid hammer, Keena!"

"Now that's just not nice."

Mara turned, startled, and Kip booped her on the nose with the hammer. She sputtered. "Oh, Kip!"

Kip grinned at her and said, "I see you're having troubles with your tent. Did you want some help?"

She sighed and rubbed her face. "Yeah, if you would, please."

"Alright, up you get, dwarf." Kip offered her a hand, and she took it, allowing him to pull her up. He booped her with the mallet again before handing it to her.

"Alright, you!" she said in mock irritation, snatching the hammer from him. Mara grinned and took the mallet around to the back side of the tent.

Kip heaved the tent frame up and pulled the rope tight so Mara could hammer the stake in the right place. Stake two, stake three, five, eight. Mara walked to the front of the tent next to Kip, who opened the flap and peeked inside. "Yep, that's a tent," he said.

"Good observation," she replied sarcastically.

Kip helped her move her things into her tent—her trunk, her bed, weapons—and they headed out in the direction of similar shouting and cursing to find Finn fighting with his tent.

"Need a hand, sea elf?" Mara asked.

"Or two or four," Finn grumbled, not looking up.

"Well, then you're in luck!" Kip replied.

When Finn looked up, Mara and Kip had their hands outstretched in front of them—the mallet in one of Kip's. "That'll do," the elf agreed.

With three working on Finn's tent, it was up in a few minutes. When they were done, and Kip walked around to the tent flap and opened it, Mara rushed up behind him and covered his mouth with her hands. "Yeah, yeah, we know," she said, laughing.

He wriggled out of her grasp and laughed. "Alright, then why don't you help Teddy finish up his tent while Finn and I haul in his stuff?"

Mara nodded and headed toward the sounds of a mallet in the distance, and as she walked away, she heard, "What makes you think I need your help, then?" and "Fine, then why don't you try it yourself, eh?" She grinned as she left her friends to their work.

Mara crested a small hill and found Teddy standing up in front of a perfectly-pitched tent. "Of course," she muttered.

Teddy turned to her and smiled. "Hello there, lass. Could you help me with these things?"

Mara nodded and walked over to her uncle's tent. He had bed, trunk, and weapons, like the rest of them, but he also had a small stool and a writing table. Mara tripped when carrying the table into the tent, and the drawer flew out, spilling the contents. As she murmured apologies to Teddy and they both gathered the scattered papers and supplies, Mara pulled a piece of paper out from where it had fallen under the bed and smiled softly. Greying hair, smokey eyes, and a pleasant smile—it was a portrait of Teddy's wife, Freya.

When Mara turned, her uncle sank to the bed and ran a hand along his scalp. She handed him the picture. He looked longingly at it before saying quietly, "Ah, yes. I look at her when I write her letters, and … and before I close my eyes each night." Teddy kissed the picture lightly and his lip quivered.

Oh no. *Oh no, oh no, oh no. Not this,* Mara thought. She didn't want to see her uncle cry. A single tear streamed down his cheek and into his russet beard. "Hey, Uncle Teddy, it's okay," she murmured.

"I-I'm sorry, Mara," he stammered, sniffling. "I'm supposed to be the strong one. I don't know what's gotten into me."

"Hey." Mara lifted Teddy's chin and wiped the tear. She looked into his eyes and shook her head. "Love is not weakness. Sadness is not weakness. Even the strongest man feels pain, and it'll destroy you if you hold it in. Let it go."

Teddy smiled faintly. "That sounds like something Freya would say," he whispered. He looked into Mara's eyes for a moment, and then he burst into tears.

Mara sat on the bed with him and hugged him as he sobbed.

When Mara left the tent awhile later, promising to come back to check on him before lunchtime, Teddy collected the scattered papers and returned them to the drawer. He'd kept supplies for letter writing during their entire journey, regularly writing updates and sending them to his lifemate in bulk whenever they'd stopped in a town.

When they stopped in Gylden Grotto, he had quite a stack accumulated. He didn't dare send any letters from the sea elves' lands, but he'd last left some in Nimeda. He'd sent a letter as soon as Mara had pulled through the first night there. He hoped then that they would finally be in one place long enough for one of his letters to get to her, and for her reply to reach him, but up to then he'd never received any replies.

In his most recent stack of letters, his first left at Gylden Grotto, he had told Freya about Mara's voyage through the Dragon's Teeth and what the final trial would be. He told her how Mara had fearlessly taken them through the Dragon's Teeth *twice* and how they'd found another companion—a real dragonwolf pup. He'd told her that they were going to plan to stay on an island until they'd been victorious, so if she was receiving the letters—if she did finally receive them—he would be nearby long enough for a reply to Gylden Grotto.

He picked up Freya's picture and traced her features. Although it was a true likeness, there were little things that the artist couldn't capture. The single tiny freckle on her nose. The wispy smoke of her lightening hair. The twinkle in her eyes. How her lip curled slightly when she smiled. Each wrinkle that told the story of their lives. He kissed the picture gently.

"Soon, now, my love. Soon, I'll hear from you. It's been so long," he whispered. He opened the drawer back up and removed some of the supplies. "Until then …"

He began another letter, telling his lifemate about their visit to Gylden Grotto.

Finn and Kip had set the table from the galley in the center of the main tent. They and Ashroot were setting the chairs around the table and putting out food when Teddy and Mara joined them.

"Come, sit for lunch!" Ashroot called brightly.

As Mara sat, she noticed Finn was staring oddly at her. Teddy and Kip began talking, and Mara was just turning to Ashroot when she felt a light kick under the table. She looked up to see a pointed glance from Finn. He nodded his head slightly in Teddy's direction and raised his eyebrows. He must have come over to Teddy's tent and heard the old man crying. At least it seemed he didn't consider it a weakness either. She raised a hand slightly and teetered it side-to-side, as if to say "so-so." Finn nodded and gave her a small smile, and then they turned to the others' conversation.

"… but you had us beach the ship, so how are we going to get there?" Kip asked Teddy.

"Thanks for volunteering!" Teddy replied, clapping Kip on the back. "You and I are going to stay behind after lunch and make a raft, while Finn and Mara scope out the rest of the island to see where we are."

Kip made a face, glaring comically into the middle distance until Ashroot placed a large sandwich in front of him, and he began to scarf it down instead, mumbling, "Thanks, Ash."

"Keena, Keena, Keena!" Mara called. Ashroot handed her a bowl of cubed meat along with her sandwich. The dragonwolf pup came running into the tent and jumped onto the table near Mara, who pet the pup, scritched under her chin, and held out a cube of meat for her. When Keena snapped at the food, Mara pulled her hand back and said, "Ah, ah, ah. No. Nicely. Nicely, Keena. No. *No.*" After a few tries, the pup gingerly took one cube at a time until the bowl was empty.

Kip produced a wooden ball from one of his pockets and threw it to the edge of the tent for Keena as Mara dug into her own sandwich. Teddy rose and rifled through some things in the corner of the tent before returning to sit at the table with the clattering bag from Hodd in tow.

Finn swallowed his last bite of his sandwich and asked, "What's all that?"

"This is a special gift from the leader of Gylden Grotto," Teddy explained, tapping the bag. "Before we split up, I want to teach you how to use them."

"Let's get started, then," Mara mumbled before swallowing a bit of her sandwich.

"Alrighty then," Teddy replied, grinning in a way that made his companions uneasy. "Once we begin our journeys into the forbidden lands, we will need to have a way to contact one another if we're separated out there. Ashroot, you will still need to find a way to call out to us while we're on the island, even if you aren't going to the forbidden lands. For you, I have this."

Teddy pulled a drum out of the bag first. It looked like a small bodhrán, with a shoulder strap and a drumstick attached to it. Ashroot squealed, slipped the strap over her shoulder, and admired the drum.

"Give it a go, will you?" Finn told her with a little nudge.

"It's pretty self-explanatory, Ash. Hit it as hard as you can," Teddy added.

Apprehensively, Ashroot grabbed the drumstick and beat the drum once. The sound reverberated through the tent. She beat it a few more times for good measure, grinning her bearish grin. "I love it," she cried.

Keena ran around in circles yipping at the commotion.

"Alright, alright, that's good." Teddy chuckled. "We'll get you some practice with that so you can send messages with different rhythms. For now . . ." He turned to the rest of the group as he stuck a hand back in the bag. "Yours won't be as easy to use as that little drum."

"Why *not*?" Kip whined theatrically.

"Because you need both hands free to use a drum, and *you're* not likely to have both hands free when you need it," Finn answered.

Teddy nodded.

"Just show us then!" Kip said, sighing.

"Yeah, come on, old man!" Mara added.

Grinning broadly, Teddy pulled his hand out and showed them a large horn with a strap looped onto it. Mara recognized the concept from the tragedy of Boromir, but it was more commonly known as a Viking horn. She'd always wanted to try using one of them. Excitedly, she swiped it out of her uncle's hand and pressed it to her lips, the horn curving upward. She puffed out her cheeks and blew with all her might . . . and all that came out was a hard breath and a faint, spitting fart sound.

Teddy threw back his head and cackled, beating a fist on the table. "Th-that's not how you do that!" he managed. Kip and Finn joined in on the laughter, and Kip even tipped over out of his chair.

"Why don't you try it then, big man?" Mara asked Kip accusatorily.

Teddy laughed a few more times, more slowly, and composed himself before saying innocently, "Yeah, Kip, why don't you try? I'm *sure* you'll do better."

Kip stood and Mara handed him the horn. Out of the corner of her eye, she saw Teddy smirking right before Kip blew. Kip's tactic, it seemed, was to yell into the horn. He took a deep breath and a muffled, humming shout came out instead. It sounded to Mara like a child's imitation of Tarzan.

This time, Teddy fell out of his chair with laughter. He rolled on the ground cackling, and Keena jumped up on top of him, thinking it was playtime.

Mara snorted and took the horn back from Kip. After a few minutes, Teddy sighed and stood, dusted himself off, and took the horn from Mara before sitting back in his chair and wiping his eyes. He took a deep breath and began, "Alright, kids, let me teach you how to use these." He took the other horns out of the bag and distributed them. As he explained, he demonstrated. "You want to pucker your lips, make a small opening just enough that your mouth is actually open, but your lips create a seal on the hole. Keep your cheeks tight. You'll blow like you're trying to cool hot food, only blow as hard as you can. You're going for short bursts of air. Let's try it."

They all tried at once. Teddy's horn made the proper sound, but his was the only one. After a few tries, Finn was able to get a warbling sound from his, and after a few more, Kip and Mara followed.

"You'll get it with time," Ashroot offered.

"Pfft—yeah, I guess," Mara panted after another try.

"That's good enough for now. You don't want to try too much and wear yourself out today—then you can't signal for help if you need it tomorrow," Teddy explained. He snapped his fingers and added, "Now, why don't we move on to signals?"

Teddy explained the different signals they would use if they were separated. Three short bursts was a distress call. Two short bursts was just a locator—for if someone was lost. One short burst was a warning to stay away. They could repeat the signal with a moment's pause between rounds, if needed. He demonstrated these on his horn and had Ashroot try on her drum.

Satisfied, Teddy clasped his hands together and said, "Now it's time for the real work."

Mara slung her new horn on her back next to her bow, shouldered an empty pack, and slid her small axes into the loops at her hips. She turned and saw her dragonwolf puppy wagging her tail. "Wanna go for walkies? Walky? Walky-walks?" Mara asked her excitedly, patting her legs.

Keena yipped and twirled on the spot before bounding outside the tent. Mara shook her head and chuckled before striding out of her tent toward Finn's. She found he was just as prepared as she was. Although he didn't have any ranged weapons, his weapons of choice were twin dirks—and some sparring time on the ship had shown her his skill with a blade was as deadly as any of his kind.

"You ready, dragonwolves?" Finn asked.

"Let's do it to it," Mara replied.

Teddy met them at the edge of their little camp with a map, blank except for the outline of the island. When they approached, he handed it to Mara and explained, "We made our camp in the safest possible area of the island, but we still need to know what's out there. Take this and chart what you find. Forageable food, fresh water, cover for a storm … and beware—we may not be the only ones on this island. Be cautious. Yes?" He raised his brows expectantly. Mara nodded. Teddy turned to Finn and repeated, "Yes?"

"Yes, sir," Finn replied.

"Alright then." Teddy rubbed his hands together excitedly. "Time to teach Kip how to build a raft." He laughed all the way back to the main tent, and Finn and Mara left to explore the island.

The first thing Mara did was mark the camp on the map. "What's that?" Finn asked, poking his head around to look at the map.

Mara had labeled the map in cursive writing, giving the camp—and the whole island, really—a name she thought was apt. "That's the camp's name," she mumbled embarrassedly.

Finn squinted at it, reading slowly, "Questhaven. Hmm … I like it. It's nice. Peaceful."

"That's what I was thinking," she replied. "It's a nice, safe place, a home while we're here. That's what I thought anyway." She shrugged. "I like it."

"Well then, I'm sure the others will like it too." He smiled gently. She'd learned that was meant to be his sincere face.

"Yeah," she replied, smiling back.

He sighed. "Alright, let's get started on the rest of it." He beckoned her to follow him into the island.

To begin with, it was easy. They'd found a small waterfall and a freshwater pool not too far from their camp. Mara drew a little circle with squiggles for the water and was making the shape of the tree when Finn stepped over to admire her work and chortled.

"What's so funny?" Mara asked sternly.

"That looks like broccoli!" He burst. He gestured in mock conversation as he continued, "'Oh, what did you guys find on the island?' Well, Teddy, we found magical broccoli falls! This island is the nightmare of all children! We—"

"Alright then!" Mara shouted. "Let's see what else there is around here."

Keena splashed behind them as they walked along the bank, and Mara marked the various berry bushes lining the pool. Finn inspected the berries more closely as Mara drew, telling her that one of them was actually poisonous. She drew a skull and an X over that marker on the map.

As they rounded the waterfall, they entered a forested area. Mara marked the edge of the forest on her map. "There seems to be a path here," she told Finn, pointing. "Do we follow the path or follow the edge of the forest?"

"Your guess is as good as mine." Finn shrugged. "What do you think, Keena?"

The dragonwolf looked at him a moment, panting and wagging her terra cotta tail. Then she ran over to him and circled his legs, whipping him with her tail as she looked around. After a moment, her ears perked up, and she looked at something only she could see. She bounded off down the path, so Finn and Mara rushed after her.

Suddenly, Keena skidded to a stop. When Mara came up behind her, she heard raised voices. She motioned to Finn, and they crouched behind a nearby tree and crawled in the direction of the sound. In the distance, in a small clearing, they saw a giant wolf lying in a pool of blood. Mara recognized the yellowed skin of goblins as a few of the creatures roped the wolf's puppies and dragged them over to one of the many cages on the far side of the clearing.

Although she'd seen and read about all kinds of goblins growing up, the sight of the Ambergrovian goblins—real and dangerous—turned her stomach just as much now as they had in her first encounter. They had yellowish, sickly-looking skin hanging off their bony bodies, oversized noses and batlike ears riddled with piercings, and radioactive-looking hair—acid green, poisonous purple, or light blue—in spiked or unkempt styles. Balls of fury that they were, they still barely came up to Mara's chest. Despite their size, the pups had to put up quite a fight as the goblins pulled them away from their mama.

"We have to do something," Mara whispered.

"Yes, but what can we do? We don't know how many of them there are or what weapons they have," Finn replied.

One of the puppies refused to leave its mother. The goblin tugged on the rope, and the pup dug its heels in and coughed as the rope pulled on its neck. "Enough of this," said one of the goblins in their wicked, scratchy voice. He pulled a bloody spear out of the mother and whipped the pup's rump with the handle. Mara started, but Finn held her back. She wasn't the only one who needed to be restrained. There was a growl and a rustle next to them as Keena bounded into the clearing. The young dragonwolf charged the armed goblin and chomped down on the spear handle, growling as fiercely as she could.

That was it. They had to fight. As Mara drew her axes and charged into the clearing, Finn pulled his horn off his back and blew.

Chapter Three

First Blood

As he knelt on the beach, Kip tightened a rope on the raft, half listening to Teddy's instructions. "Lash that one there. Yep. That's it for the base. Next, we need to—"

Kip looked up. Teddy had been bracing the logs so he could lash the base of the raft together. He'd stopped abruptly and now stared out into the middle distance, brows furrowed. He jerked his head to one side and then stood and bolted up toward the main tent. Kip followed and caught up with Teddy as he made it to where Ashroot stood in alarm.

"Teddy! Did you hear—" Ashroot began.

They all turned to look inland as three sputtering horn bursts met their ears. Kip ran toward his tent for his hammer, shuddering. *What if she's in trouble and we don't make it in time? What if something happened to her and I never got the chance to—*

"Come on, Kip!" Teddy bellowed as three more blasts sounded.

Kip grabbed his hammer, making a mental note to keep a weapon nearby in case this happened again, and he raced with Teddy toward the feeble distress call, clutching the hammer to hold his composure.

Sometimes you have to kill the monster, Teddy said. The last time Mara had faced goblins, she'd been too afraid to kill them. She'd barely fought at all. But she'd been through a lot since then. She'd killed dozens of spiders to save Kip's sister and nephew and rid the Big Hill of a scourge. She'd faced sea monsters, defeating the kraken with the help of her companions. She'd made it through the gauntlet of the sea elves and fought for her life. Now she needed to fight for Keena's life and the lives of all the wolf pups.

Mara charged the nearest goblin—the one whose spear Keena had chomped—and neared him just as he jerked the spear to one side and flung Keena away into the brush behind him.

"How *dare* you?" Mara screeched, swinging her axe. The goblin brought the spear up just in time to block her savage swing. "How *dare* you attack these wolves?" She chopped again, gouging a chunk from the spear shaft. "How *dare* you take these puppies?" She chopped again, snapping the spear in half. The goblin looked up at her, wide-eyed. "How *dare* you throw my baby?" she screamed, chopping again and splitting the goblin's skull.

She wrenched her axe away and spun to face the next nearest goblin—the one who held the rope of the poor wolf pup who wouldn't leave its mother. She drew one of her small axes and threw it toward the goblin. She missed, but she got his attention. He dropped the rope and struggled to unsheathe his sword as she charged. The wolf pup took the opportunity to run to its mama. As the pup passed, dragging the rope behind, Mara slipped on the rope, fell into the goblin, and crashed to the ground.

The goblin shrieked and clawed at her face. It had been unable to unsheathe its sword before she'd fallen into it, so it was defenseless. Mara lay on her remaining small axe and had dropped the battle axe when she fell, so she was in the same situation. She struggled to roll where she could defend herself.

The goblin clawed at her face again, and she felt the pain and the trickling blood. She didn't have claws, or even moderately long nails, so she made a fist and hit the goblin repeatedly as she rolled to free her small axe. It worked. The goblin let out an ear-splitting shriek as she rolled over on top of it and pressed her axe into its chest with both hands, using her bodyweight to drive the axe to its mark.

That's why you never leave home without the little axes, she thought triumphantly.

By that time, the other goblins had mustered. Mara scrambled to her feet and rushed for her other axe as a spear came flying past her head. Fully armed, she turned to see a line of goblins. Finn was right—they had no idea how many there were, or even if these were the only ones. Finn rushed up behind her, giving three final bursts on the horn before tossing it aside.

"Ready?" he asked, drawing his dirks.

Mara turned to him and nodded. They charged.

There was a flurry of metal as Mara and Finn fought. Because they had sparred two-handed together, they knew each other's styles well enough and were able to fight as a unit. Teddy and Kip reached the clearing to find a dozen goblins lying on the ground and more still coming.

"Friends behind!" Teddy shouted as he bore toward the fray.

Finn and Mara twisted to see Kip and Teddy, and then glanced back at each other and nodded before tucking and rolling—Mara to the left and Finn to the right—to make way for their companions to join the fray. Since the men had evened the odds, it wasn't long before all goblins had fallen.

Before anything else, Teddy ordered Kip to help him check the bodies. Finn strode to the cage of whimpering pups and released them. As they all ran toward their mama. Mara disappeared into the brush, shouting, "Keena, Keena, Keena! Keena!"

She found her beloved pup tangled in a briar bush but otherwise okay. Keena yipped and gnawed at the briars, whimpering, and Mara's brain went out the window at the sight of her poor, trapped baby. She grabbed the thorns with her bare hands and ripped, trying to free Keena from this pain as quickly as she could. "It's okay, Keena. You're okay now. You're okay. You're safe, my girl," Mara murmured, wincing but otherwise ignoring the thorns shredding her hands.

In a few moments, the pup was free. Keena jumped on Mara, knocking her down, and licked her wounded face and hands. Mara lay there a moment, hugging and petting her beloved pet. "I thought I'd lost you," Mara whimpered. Keena yipped as Mara hugged her, and Mara heard *Ma. Ma. Ma-ma.*

Mara gasped and squealed, hugging Keena even tighter, tears streaming down her face. She knew that eventually Keena's yips would become words, but she was absolutely floored to find that her first word had been "Mama." She *was* Keena's mamà, and she would do anything to protect her baby—from goblins or anything else, as any wolf mama would do. Then it hit her. *Wolf mama.*

Mara gave Keena one more tight squeeze and jumped up, rushing to the giant, unmoving form of the wolves' mama. The pups yipped at her as she neared them, and Mara said soothingly, "It's okay, babies. I'm here to help." When Keena yipped at them, they obediently made way for Mara to approach their mother.

It wasn't good. When she first saw the draft horse-sized wolf in a puddle of blood, Mara had assumed the worst. She'd been butchered. There were countless broken spears in her sides, and blood streamed from her nose and mouth. With a hopeful sigh, and a pleading glance to the sky, Mara took one of her small axes in both hands and raised the flat of the blade to the wolf's mouth. Mara held her breath and waited. After a moment, there was a slight fog on the blade. *Yes.*

"She's alive!" Mara shouted. She patted the wolf's brow gently and smiled. "We'll take care of you, mama," she murmured. With another gentle pat, Mara turned back to the others and shouted again. She heard Teddy say something to Finn, and her uncle appeared at her side.

"Let me see," he said, gently running a hand over some of the wolf's injuries. His brows furrowed as he caressed her snout. "We'll be using that raft sooner than we thought."

"What?" Mara asked, wondering what those had to do with each other, but Teddy had already turned back to the men.

"Kip! Finn! Come with me!" he ordered. Before leaving the clearing, he turned back to Mara and gestured to the wolf. "Stay here with her. We'll be back soon, and we'll carry her back to camp."

Mara nodded and turned back to the wolf as they disappeared. "Hold on, mama," she whispered. Mara sat by the wolf's head and pet her gently, and the puppies huddled around their mother and licked her wounds as they waited for help to return.

The men returned a little while later, awkwardly carrying the half-made raft. Ashroot shuffled behind with a bundle—some small fish to lure the wolf pups back to their camp. The wolf was massive, so even using the partial raft as a litter, her legs would still be hanging over the sides. Mara and the men worked together to gently lift the wolf onto the raft. She didn't stir. They made sure her head and body were fully supported, and then Mara and the men each took a corner and lifted the raft, taking the injured wolf back to camp, making frequent stops to adjust the weight or take a moment's rest so they could be sure to get her back without dumping her on the ground due to their own exhaustion.

The puppies followed without worry. Whether due to concern for their mother, Ashroot's bait, or Keena's encouraging yips, they only needed some nudging. It was a miracle they were able to get her all the way there without mishap. When they got back to camp, Kip watched the puppies and kept them occupied, while Finn fetched fresh water, and Ashroot started a fire to boil the water. Mara and Teddy worked together to begin tending the wolf's injuries.

As the forest dwarf gathered materials, he explained, "We don't know yet if we'll be able to talk to her. We'll need to clean and cauterize the wounds, just in case we cannot continue to help her because she's too wild. We'll have to be tactful and quick." Teddy paused and rested a hand on Mara's shoulder. "Are you ready?" he asked her.

Mara nodded. They began by removing the broken spear tips. Once Finn had brought the water and it was heated, they cleaned each wound thoroughly. Teddy had some special gut thread that would be good for interior wounds, so he stitched up the deepest trouble spots and prepared the wounds to be cauterized.

Cauterization was a nasty business. Effective, sure. Best for a wild animal who may not allow her wounds to be tended again later, certainly. But the smell of burning flesh is one that lingers, and Mara couldn't help but wonder as Teddy prepared if they would just be causing her undue pain. Teddy used some of the leftover daggers from the sojourn through the Ice Mountains, and Finn ran back and forth to bring him fresh daggers as needed for him to have blades hot enough to complete the job.

Mara held the wolf soothingly and pet her face as Teddy began placing the flat of a blade against each wound until it had sealed. One after the other, he burned them closed. The wolf only stirred once, but weakly. When he'd finished, Teddy and Mara both took bowls of poultice and massaged them gently over each wound before laying a blanket over her to prevent the pups from licking the poultice away. Once done, all they could really do was wait and hope for the best.

Finn and Kip gathered sticks and some leftover canvas to make a shelter around the mama and her pups, and Teddy turned to Mara as the pups rushed to pile on their mother. "Your turn," he said.

So much had happened so fast, Mara had forgotten about her own injuries. None of the others had so much as a scratch as evidence of their fight with the goblins, and Mara hadn't sustained a wound in the battle besides the cuts to her face—not counting her foolishly shredding her hands when it was over. She sat obediently and allowed Teddy to clean her face. There would be no need for stitches, but two of the cuts were surely deep enough to scar. Thankfully, they were just to the right of her right eye, so there wasn't any real damage.

He took his time with her hands, pulling out the remaining thorns and digging out the ones that had become embedded, smacking Mara when she struggled—she'd never been good with splinters—and then he applied some of the poultice and wrapped them. Satisfied, he went to meet Kip and Finn. Since the wounds had all been tended to, before long the men all headed back out into the forest on Teddy's orders to clean up the bodies, investigate, and to make sure there were no more stragglers who might find their camp.

Before leaving, Kip stepped over to Mara and placed a hand on her face, just under the deepest claw marks. "I'm glad you're okay, Dragonwolf," he whispered. With a quick sideways glance, he leaned in and kissed her lightly on the forehead before hefting his hammer and heading back out to the forest with Teddy and Finn, leaving Mara utterly bewildered.

"That's the last of them," Finn said, as he and Kip tossed a goblin onto a pile.

"Alright, then. Thanks, lads," Teddy replied, wiping his hands on his pants and glancing around. They stood on the deck of a ship. It was small, smaller than *Harrgalti*. By the looks of it, the goblins were pirates. *Not anymore,* he thought, looking out at the pile of dead goblins. The rest of the crew had been so surprised when, instead of their own, a motley band of angry men had come stalking through the woods to meet them.

The ship was docked in a little cove at the northernmost beach of the island. Only a handful of goblins remained on the ship, so Teddy and the boys had defeated them pretty easily. A quick assessment below deck told them that the whole crew had been accounted for—there were thirty-four hammocks strung below deck and one extravagant bunk in the captain's cabin. One-by-one they'd dragged the bodies of the goblins from the forest and back to their ship, piling them on the deck.

Finn wiped his hands on his pants and looked around. "That's it. Let's finish this," he announced. He strode to the helm of the ship and turned the wheel to face the open sea, tying the wheel to keep it true. Then he and Kip unfurled the sails while Teddy lit a torch and tossed it onto the pile of goblins. As the flames grew, Kip swung his hammer at the anchor chain, releasing the ship, and they went back to the beach. They watched as the ship slowly listed out into the open water, flames licking at the rigging.

"Tell me again why we did it like this?" Kip asked Teddy.

Teddy gestured offhandedly toward the ship. "Ship goes up in flames on the open sea and the whole crew is lost. Doesn't seem suspicious wherever the wreckage may end up. Nothing points to here, and nothing will be found here. This is to keep us safe," he explained.

"We do still need to check the rest of the island, just in case there's something else here to contend with," Finn added.

Kip nodded in agreement, leaning on his hammer as he looked at Teddy.

The forest dwarf rubbed his scalp before looking at the others in turn. Teddy sighed. "Let's split up. Finn, I know you can sound that horn enough for help. Kip, how do you feel about it?"

Kip looked out at the flaming goblin ship for a moment, and then looked determinedly back at Teddy and replied, "In need, I'll make it work."

"Good enough for me," Teddy replied. "Kip, you head down this coastline through the east side of the island and back to camp." He gestured down the beach. "Finn, you take the west. I'll zigzag here through the middle, and we'll all meet back at the camp. You find anything—anything—untoward, you sound your horn, and we'll come help you. Got it?" The younger men both nodded. Teddy patted them on the shoulders. "Alright, let's go," he finished, heading away from the beach and the doomed ship without a backward glance.

Finn lit a torch and walked away from the beach into the forest. The further he walked, the more bored he became. He walked to the northernmost tip of the island and met a steady river. He could see the sea peeking through the trees on the other side of the river, so he decided to just follow it south. He listened to the bubbling and watched little fish swim and jump out of the water. He watched bats flying overhead and listened to owls hooting and other chittering wildlife around him.

As he made his way through the forest, that was all he found. Trees, water, and animals. He wondered, not for the first time, how the dwarves knew what animals they could talk to. If he were a forest dwarf, would he be able to talk to the fish or the bats? Or an owl? The opossum or the raccoon that darted by?

Each time he saw a creature flee as he passed, he was sure to say, "I mean you no harm, animals. I'm just passing through."

But they couldn't understand him. He knew it didn't work that way. If only Teddy had come this way instead of him. He'd probably at least have been able to learn something from the animals. All he could say is that there was a water source and lots and lots of trees. He made it to the southern tip uneventfully and popped out where the cliff overlooked their camp. In short order, he followed the ridge around and down to the right level and made his final trek back to the camp.

Teddy tiptoed through the forest near the stained ground where the wolf mother had lain just hours before. Somewhere, he knew there had to be a den. He hoped he'd find someone there who was alive and willing to be reasonable. Deep in the brush was a huge cave with rocks sealing the entrance—though, it seemed, not for long. Teddy watched the rocks shifting and listened as something large and groaning slammed into them.

He approached slowly and shouted, "Great wolf!"

The rustling stopped, and there was silence for a moment. Then, from within, a savage growl, *I will rip you to pieces for what you have done!*

The pounding continued more fervently as Teddy raised his voice again, "We have not done this to you, great wolf. We have not. They were goblins!" The pounding stopped. "You can smell them, can't you? They came and attacked your mate and tried to take your pups."

Where are they?

"Your family is at our camp. Your mate was gravely injured, and we have tended to her. Your pups are safe and resting with her. The goblins are all destroyed and burning. They have paid for what they did to you."

Good.

Teddy waited for more pounding, but none came. He continued, "If you will allow me, I will help you free, and I will take you to our camp so you can be with your mate. You will see then that she is safe."

If she is not . . . neither will you be.

"That's fair," Teddy replied as he began moving rocks.

Kip walked north along the coast and quickly found himself in a valley. The sea disappeared behind a small mountain ridge, and the land rose to a ten-foot cliff to his right. Through the valley, all was barren. He hummed to himself as he walked, swinging his hammer absently before flipping it behind his head, across his shoulders, and hanging his arms casually over it as he continued along. He could see the moon shining brightly above and gazed up at the sky as he walked. Mara was okay, and the threat had been eliminated, so he could breathe easily. The sky above was cloudless, and the stars shone brightly, so he searched for his favorite constellations—Goli's Hammer and Baerk, god of the earth and patron god of gnomes. Recently, each time he looked at the sky, he'd begun searching for Aeun as well.

He smiled as he saw the forest dwarf goddess spread across the stars. Growing up, he'd never been interested in the forest dwarves. They were too large, too far-fetched to ever come into his scope before. But now he'd met them. Now he'd met *her*.

He sighed and smiled as he came out of the valley and into a forested area. The stars faded away, but the forest itself was beautiful—all willow trees of varying colors. He reached up and touched the branches as he passed, and then he entered a small clearing. Near the center of the clearing, he stumbled and swung his hammer down to keep from falling. Then he looked down and grinned.

When Kip returned to the camp, he found all his female companions curled up in a pile of puppies, tucked up against the wolf mama. Keena lay mixed in with the other pups, discernable only by her wings and the small spade of her tail that poked out of the pile. Ashroot seemed to have fallen asleep petting two of the pups, and Mara had her hand on the mother's neck as though she'd fallen asleep while caring for the wolf. He smiled warmly at the sight. Then, not wanting to disturb them, he went into the main tent and added what he'd found to Mara's island map—most of it anyway.

A little while later, Finn returned to the camp, added his own part to the map, and discussed the creatures and plants he'd found with Kip. Before long, they heard howling, and the camp erupted into activity. Finn and Kip rushed out of the tent to investigate, Ashroot ran to hide, and the pile of puppies wiggled and yipped. They tumbled over each other and ran toward the sound.

Keena stayed behind as the pups ran around and away, and Mara stood with one hand on the wolf mama's side. A colossal wolf, whose size Mara could only compare to that of an elephant, burst out of the forest and toward their camp, carrying Teddy on his back. When he made it to the edge of the camp, he skidded to a stop, flinging Teddy off his back as his tail wagged and he excitedly greeted his pups. After a moment, the wolf met Mara's gaze, and he made his way over to where she stood.

When he reached her, the wolf leaned in close, snarled, and sniffed Mara's face. She felt his cold nose graze over the scarred claw marks on her chest. *You are forest dwarf, like the big one.*

"Yes, I am," she squeaked, trying to stay still. "I'm the one who found the goblins attacking your family. They will not again."

The wolf bared his teeth in a similar grin to that of a bearkin before passing Mara and nuzzling his mate. She stirred, but not much. Mara slapped her leg and clicked her tongue at Keena, and they left the wolves in peace. As she and her pup walked back to the main tent to join their companions, Mara turned back just once. The giant wolf curled up next to his mate, and the pups came to pile up beside them.

Mara smiled. It had been the first time she had willingly entered a battle. Although blood had been shed before she'd found them, *she'd* been the one to draw first blood when she'd entered the forest. She'd had quite a few reasons to fight once she'd gotten to Ambergrove, and this wasn't her first time reuniting a family. *There's no better reason to fight,* she thought, smiling to herself as she entered the tent.

Mara awoke the next morning with Keena curled up next to her on her bunk. She stretched her hands out to pet her puppy, and she felt the ache ripple through her fingers. *Worth it.* She scritched Keena's ears and poked her horn nubbies until the pup woke and started wagging her tail. "You ready for some breakfast?" she asked. Keena licked Mara's nose and yipped, thumping her tail on Mara's leg. "I take that as a yes," Mara murmured, laughing.

When Mara made it across the beach to the main tent, she found Ashroot already there, making breakfast. "Good morning, Ash!" she called.

"Morning, Mara!" her friend replied. "Have a seat and get you some breakfast."

She gestured to the table where some casserole steamed from a pot. Eggs and cheese, potatoes, and some of the meat from the mining dwarves. There were also some other colors in there that Mara couldn't quite make out. She sat at the table and scooped a healthy serving onto her plate and another onto a small saucer, placing it on the ground beside her for Keena.

Mara took a large bite of her casserole. It reminded her of something her dad used to make that he called a mountain man breakfast. It was so good. "Mmm … So, what has you up so early, Ash?" she asked.

"Well, Finn is out fishing for food for the wolves, and Teddy wanted to be up early to give the mama wolf a once-over, so I wanted to have breakfast ready when they got started. He should be up soon. Kip is sleeping in a little, though. He stayed up late making copies of the map for everyone. There's a stack there." Ashroot gestured to the edge of the table, so Mara pulled one over to look at as she continued her breakfast. "I wanted to make breakfast and get some other stuff ready in the daylight today," Ashroot finished.

Mara nodded and perused the map. At least, it seemed, the island wasn't overrun with monsters. They'd have a lot of resources to work with during their stay. She choked on a chunk of egg when she saw that Kip had labeled the maps *Questhaven,* because it was very clear that, whatever gnomish schooling entailed, cursive writing was not part of it.

She put the map back on the stack and was just finishing up her breakfast when Teddy walked into the tent. "Morning, ladies!" he said brightly. He plopped down to sit next to Mara, scooping a healthy serving of the mountain man breakfast and beginning to shovel it into his mouth. After inhaling most of his breakfast, he turned to his niece and asked, "Mara, are you about ready to help me out with the wolves?"

She took one last bite and set her plate down on the ground for Keena to clean up. "Yep, let's do it," she replied as Teddy set his plate down next to hers.

Ashroot passed Teddy a pot of boiling water and some cloth, and he and Mara headed over to the wolf cuddle pile. They all still slept, but the male stirred as they came near, jostling the puppies and waking them all up when they tumbled away from him. As their father stood and stretched, the pups all rushed up to mom to nurse.

Gently, growled the colossal wolf. *Your mama needs you to be gentle.* He pawed at the pups until they obeyed, then he turned to Teddy and Mara. *Are you here to check her condition?*

"Yes, we are," Mara replied.

Proceed, then. The colossal wolf stepped out of their way.

Mara walked over to his mate's face and began to run a hand down her side. Teddy began at her tail, and they both worked their way to the middle. The cauterized wounds were healing nicely. They took the cloths and warm water, and they cleaned away the old poultice from each wound. After a few moments of this, the wolf stirred.

Mmm . . . so painful, she began.

Her mate came around and nuzzled her snout. *Moon? Moon, are you alright?* he asked.

Fang? she replied quietly. *Is that you? Wh . . . What happened?*

You were attacked by goblins, my love. These dwarves and their companions have given you care and protected our children.

Wh . . . what? She stirred and turned to face Mara, who paused in her cleaning.

"Moon?" Mara began, resting a hand on the wolf's side to steady her. "How do you feel?"

You saved my children. That's all that matters, the wolf replied. *Whatever you need of us, we will give it. You are welcome on our island for as long as you need.*

Agreed, her mate replied, nuzzling her neck affectionately.

"Thank you," Mara said with a smile. "I'm just glad you're all okay. Your wounds are healing well, so we should be able to get you back on your feet soon."

Good . . . Moon dozed back to sleep as they continued dressing her wounds.

Soon after, Finn met them with a large basket full of fish, Teddy and Mara finished applying the poultice, and then they left the wolves to their breakfast.

A little while later, Mara and her companions all sat around the table in the main tent.

"What's needed still for the raft?" Mara asked.

"Just a sail," Teddy replied.

"And then is that everything we need?" Kip asked.

The tent went silent. Teddy turned to each of them before replying. "Yes, that's everything. We just need a sail and then we can make our way to the forbidden lands."

"Well, almost," Mara interjected. Teddy raised a brow. She continued, "We need to stay until Moon is in good enough condition to go without us. When she can return to her den with her family, we can leave the island."

"Agreed," Kip said. Finn nodded.

"Alright, then." Teddy sighed. "While we're here, we may as well do some extra preparations. Weapons training and horn-blowing practice each day. Some of us," he scratched his right brow pointedly, "have gotten rusty and need to get back to practice." Mara made a face. He continued, "Make sure you're packed and ready, so we can leave as soon as we're able. Make time for anything you'd want to do before we head off." Teddy tapped the table a few times and stood, heading back to his own tent.

The rest of the group dispersed—all but Kip. He unfolded his copy of the island map and glanced down at it. His map was the only one that was complete. When he'd gone around to explore the island, he'd found something he wanted to keep to himself, at least until the time was right. He glanced back up to Mara as she walked away toward her tent, baby talking Keena as she went.

He pulled his own dragonwolf out of his pocket—the carving he'd worked on for his nephew, Loli. He glanced over at the family of wolves and back to Mara. They'd become a family over the past year, once Mara had saved his own family. With any luck, they'd be more of a family by the time everything was said and done. Time would tell.

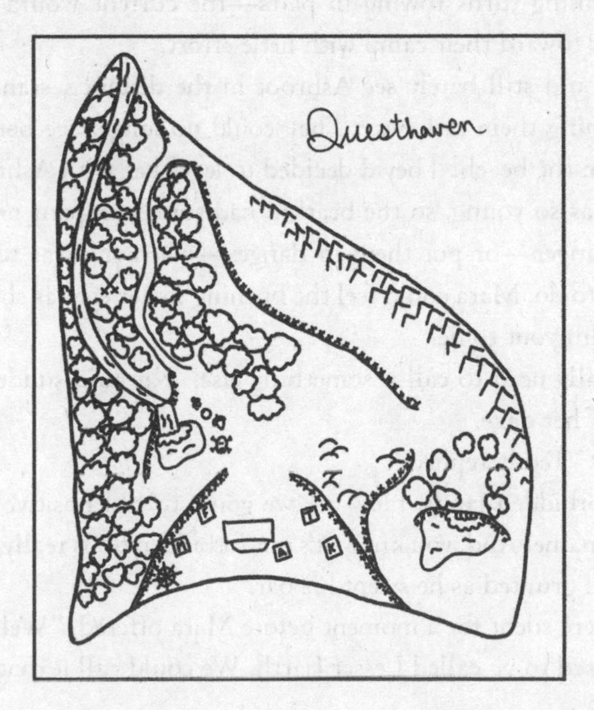

Chapter Four

The Fallen City

Mara pulled her rope, tightening a knot, and then lay a hand on the mast of their little raft. Their small sail was unfurled, Finn sat with his back against the mast looking through supplies, and Teddy and Kip stood on either side, working together with oars. Teddy explained that this would be the best transportation at the start, because they did not yet know what they would face when they made it to the forbidden lands, and although it would be bitter work to get the raft to their destination—they would be taking turns rowing in pairs—the current would bring them swiftly back toward their camp with little effort.

They could still barely see Ashroot in the distance, standing on the beach watching them sail away. They could no longer see her, but Keena howled from the beach. They'd decided to leave her with Ashroot, at least while she was so young, so the bearkin had some company and so Keena wasn't in danger—or put them in danger—when she was too young to know what to do. Mara could feel the burning in her eyes as she listened to her pup calling out to her.

"We really need to call it something else," Kip said suddenly, pulling Mara out of her daze.

"What?" Teddy replied.

"The forbidden lands. How are we going to feel positive going there with such a name? And, you know, it's not forbidden to us really." Kip shook his head and grunted as he swept his oar.

They were silent for a moment before Mara offered, "Well, Aeun told me that it used to be called Lesser Earth. We could call it that."

Teddy laughed a great boom. "Well, that's certainly not as scary as the forbidden lands, but how ridiculous!"

The men all laughed for a moment. Mara smiled. Finn threw up a hand and pressed, "Okay then what should we call it?"

Silence.

"Well," Mara began, "What would you call it, Kip? It was your idea."

"Me?" Kip asked, chuckling. "My people live in hills and every name has hill in it. You don't want me giving it a name."

"That's very true!" Finn agreed.

"What would you call it, Mara?" Teddy asked, turning to look at her before making a great sweep with his oar.

"Yeah, Mara," Kip agreed. "You came from Earth. What would you call it?"

Mara fiddled with the rope for a moment. What would she call it? In the year that she had been in Ambergrove, she had used her recollections from books and movies to relate what she'd seen to what she knew. However, as she had felt more a part of this new world, she'd thought back to Earth less and less. She stared out into the open water and made a face.

"That difficult, is it?" Finn asked.

"Well, I …" She paused, and then it came to her. "I think we should call it Chaosland," she said, smiling to herself. It sounded like a theme park, but none of them would know what that meant if she told them.

"Hmm … Chaosland," Teddy mused. "Why?"

"Well, most old countries on Earth have 'land' after their name. Scotland is the land of the Scots, England is the land of the English, and Chaosland is the land of chaos."

"Interesting. Though, here, we would probably say 'realm' instead of 'land,'" Teddy replied.

"I think it's better that way," Finn interjected. "According to Mara, we're fighting darkness from Earth, so it's only right to give it a name that they would give it."

"I agree," Kip said.

"Alrighty then. It appears I've been outvoted. Chaosland it is." Teddy made another large sweep with his oar, and he and Kip pushed them slowly forward toward their dark destination.

It took a few days before they made it to the southernmost tip of the forbidden lands—now Chaosland. By the time they were dragging the raft up the bank and hiding it in the bushes, Teddy had begun arguing with them rather than telling them to stay quiet. A few days at sea with no shelter and no time apart had made them all very cranky. They were lucky to have made it to a deserted area.

None of them had the energy for sensible pursuits. They made a small fire, and each slept on a different side of it without another word to each other. Finn and Teddy both had their backs to the fire—and to each other. Mara lay on her back, caressing each of her tokens in turn. She twisted the friendship bracelet from her sister. The little pink, blue, and lavender strings were worn and faded but still remarkably strong. She traced the little peg branches on the Aeunna tree embossed on the silver bangle from her father. Her hand came to rest on the bindrune necklace, a carved token from Kip, before she closed her eyes and went to sleep, unaware that Kip was facing the fire, and her, grinning ear to ear.

The next morning, once they had rested as well as they could on the hard ground, they were all calmer when they awoke. Teddy had woken early and hunted a hare, and they all had breakfast in silence. It was an apology, and they all knew it. Nothing more need be said. As they finished their breakfast, it was Finn who broke the silence.

"What's the plan now?" he asked Teddy.

Teddy looked up at him and grinned a devilish grin. "Why, you boys are so *good* about volunteering!" he said brightly. Finn groaned as Teddy continued, "Well, it is only fair. Kip made the map of our island, so you can make the map of Chaosland. As we make our way through this land, we need to note the places we find, the resources, and the enemies. It will take some time to traverse this land and find the leader—to cut the head off the snake—but one thing we do need to do is make sure we're prepared."

"Great," Finn muttered, sore about the upcoming chore of mapmaking.

"Then what?" Kip asked Mara, taking a final bite of his breakfast.

Mara stared at him, wide-eyed. "Um, why are you asking me?"

"He's right, Mara," Teddy agreed. "Although I can provide advice and sensible planning, such as our making a map, this is your duty. We follow your lead."

Mara reddened. *Of course.* She chewed her hare slowly, turning it practically to liquid before swallowing and replying, "Well … we need to make our way up. We shouldn't leave Ashroot too long, and we'll need more supplies from her sooner rather than later." Teddy nodded. She continued, "So I think we should get as far as we can, sail back to Questhaven to regroup, and then come back and try a different place. We need to explore as much as we can of this land. See what makes it tick. See what enemies are here. Find the leader. But we also need to take care of ourselves along the way."

"Well said," Kip declared, patting Mara on the shoulder and grinning behind his grizzly beard.

"Agreed," said Teddy. "You have the head of a leader." He winked at her.

"Well then, no time like the present!" Finn sighed, went to a pack, and whipped out a large piece of paper and a pencil before plopping back down and writing Chaosland at the top.

Their first sojourn through newly-dubbed Chaosland began rather uneventfully. There were bushes and trees for miles. They walked for a full day and didn't run into a single creature, nor hear any. Teddy was just saying that it would soon be getting too dark to press on, and they should probably think about stopping to make camp, when Finn gasped and swore.

Finn had been behind at the beginning, chasing the others doggedly while trying to mark on the map. After a few hours of nothing but trees, he began to hurry ahead so he could stop and mark things down instead. At this moment, he had crested a hill that none of the others had even begun to climb.

"What is it? More trees?" Mara whined.

"No, trees aren't that bad," Kip groaned. "Probably an impassable river."

"Well, it can't be enemies, or a sensible man would also have turned around and told us to be quiet!" Teddy hollered pointedly.

Finn didn't turn his head. "Just come see," he muttered barely audibly.

Mara nudged Kip with a hand, saying, "Race ya!" before lunging up the hill ahead of him.

"No fair!" he called behind her, running as fast as his short legs would carry him, and still just matching Teddy's long strides.

Mara's cackle broke abruptly as she met Finn on the hill. "What the—" she gasped and then swore herself. "T-that looks like . . ."

But how could she voice a comparison to her companions? What it looked like was something out of an apocalypse movie. Down in the valley was a town—or maybe a small city; she was never clear on the distinction. At least, it used to be a town or small city. Every building she could see was crumbling. It looked as if there had at one time been skyscrapers, but those were now no more than a few stories high.

It didn't look like a city from Mara's time—the twenty-first century. Neither did it look like something plucked out of time. It was a ruined frankencity, made over time by those with different experiences from Earth. There were simple houses, more intricate buildings that looked Old German to Mara, makeshift skyscrapers, and crumbling smokestacks attached to what looked like factories. Like the rest they had seen of Chaosland, however, it appeared to be totally deserted.

"It's a ghost town," Mara whispered.

Finn rubbed his face and muttered, "Yeah, and I don't really want to meet them."

Mara laughed. "No, no, not actual ghosts. Ha! No, that just means that it's deserted," she explained.

Finn was spared the need to respond as Kip and Teddy made their way up to stand between them. "Blessed Aeun," Teddy whispered. "Never in my wildest dreams did I think I'd see one of these."

"What is it?" Kip asked.

"It's a city. They're terrible places they have on Earth. The cities are breeding grounds of evil. My mother used to tell me stories about them," Teddy explained.

"Well, they're not *all* bad," Mara reasoned quietly. "Um … so I've heard." Mara hadn't actually been to a city before. Big towns, sure, but nothing like this. Although she'd heard terrible things about cities, she wouldn't exactly call them hives of evil.

"These are," Teddy muttered. He turned and looked seriously at the others. His eyes were hard, and the darkness there made Mara wonder what he'd been told to make him feel so strongly. He continued, "Keep on your guard. We don't know who calls this place home, but it is probably our best place to find shelter for the night." Mara nodded. Teddy finished, "Right then. Let's go."

They made their way slowly down into the valley, and as they neared the outskirts, they saw a city limits sign. Mara squinted at it. "What does that say?" she asked.

Kip laughed a deep, belly laugh and cried, "Well, I guess Chaosland isn't that ridiculous."

"What?" Finn squinted at the sign and read slowly, "New Swit-switzerland? … What's a switzer?"

"Probably some Earth demon," Teddy grumbled. He turned to Mara. "Yes?"

Mara snorted. "Well, no. Switzerland is the country of the Swiss people."

"Then why don't they call it Swissland?" Finn asked.

She paused, pondering. "Um, I don't know. But it doesn't make sense for them to call it New Switzerland anyway."

"Why is that?" Kip asked.

"Switzerland is pretty notoriously neutral. It doesn't make sense for a bad city in the midst of all this awfulness to be called Switzerland." Mara explained. She glanced out at the skyline. "I wonder why they named it that …"

"I guess we're about to find out, aren't we?" Teddy grumbled.

"Right, right …" Mara replied before heading closer toward the sign and the ominous town. She gazed into the middle distance, looking at the skyline but not really seeing. Why was it New Switzerland? Maybe they'd had it all wrong. As they neared the sign, Teddy swore. *I guess it is his turn,* Mara mused. They were doing a lot of that today. She looked up at the sign and gasped.

It couldn't be dried blood, because it was clearly old, and something like blood wouldn't have lasted in all weather, but across the city limits sign, written in what looked eerily like blood—and was the size of the swipe of a hand covered in it—was one word: F E A R.

"I guess they didn't like Switzerland either," Kip muttered after a moment.

"It makes sense though, doesn't it?" Finn replied. "They were the people who didn't fight. Why wouldn't they fight? Because they were afraid, most likely." He shook his head.

"Well … it's not as simple as that," Mara began, remembering how Switzerland figured into Earth's history and its world wars.

"Maybe the new people here just don't take too kindly to the idea of peace," Teddy interjected.

"Maybe." Mara walked up to the sign and wiped a hand across it. It was dirty but not much else. Nothing sinister.

As Mara looked at her hand, her uncle rested a hand on her shoulder. "Why don't we head in and see what we're working with?" he asked.

"Yeah, let's do that," Mara replied quietly.

The city limits sign was right at the edge of the city, so after a few steps, they were in the shadow of the first building. Mara stopped and stared, starting violently when she felt a hand swipe across her cheek. She turned to see Teddy looking at her with concern. She wiped another tear from her other cheek.

"Does it remind you of home?" he asked quietly.

She stood quietly for a moment. "Not *my* home, but Earth. It reminds me of some places I used to visit, and some buildings I saw in school." She sighed, and then turned and pointed to the nearest building. "Like that. That looks like the buildings I saw in my research project for German class." She'd learned these were referred to as half-timbered houses, and she'd always liked them. Next, she pointed to the building beside it, adding, "And that looks like one of the old buildings in the town next to ours—like an Old West general store."

Teddy didn't know what any of this meant, so he just nodded. As far as Mara was concerned, she'd done pretty well in school. She wasn't particularly athletic or involved in things until coming to Ambergrove, but she paid attention in class—if only to absorb all she needed so she could do her work quickly and get back to reading. German class was no different, but the tottering, old teacher still had a way of pulling in history and culture that made learning the language just a bit more interesting.

One of those things was teaching them about historical German cities, using pictures largely from his own travels. The buildings seemed so unique to Mara, she was enthralled. Each building was tan or white, usually with simple, paned windows and a standard roof for the period in which it was built. The charm was in the geometric wood patterns on the exterior. It gave the homes a Hansel and Gretel look. It seemed the original New Switzerland planners had shared Mara's opinions.

The streets were cobblestoned, but they were still streets all the same, like Victorian city streets, and much more advanced than any roads Mara had seen in Ambergrove—except perhaps in Port Albatross. Sidewalks even lined each street with streetlights stationed at every other house. It seemed many domestic buildings were half-timbered houses, and many of the buildings seemed plucked out of the wild west, but the city also sprawled out to reveal many different buildings that were impossibly modern. Some of the buildings in the distance reminded her of earliest skyscrapers from the industrial era, like she had been thrust in time to a Jack the Ripper movie. The feeling worsened as she looked down the deserted streets. She pulled one of her little axes from its ring at her side.

"Should we explore the city then?" she asked.

Teddy looked apprehensively ahead of them and up at the sky. "Why don't we wait for that until tomorrow?" he replied. "We can spend a quiet night on the outskirts and start fresh with the morning light." The men murmured their agreement, and Teddy beckoned Mara to lead on into the first Germanic-looking building.

As she entered the building, Mara noticed every small detail. The brass doorhandle with a deadbolt—thankfully unlocked—opened to a narrow hallway. A coatrack hung on the wall nearest to them, and a leather duster hung from one of the pegs. Down the hall, Mara saw photographs from all ages hanging in frames lining the walls.

Turning into the first room, Mara saw a switch on the wall beside her. Slowly, she reached up and flipped it. There was a hum, and after a few seconds, the lightbulbs in the chandelier in the room flickered and came alive. Finn made a small, shrieking sound behind her, and there was a thud. She turned to see the sea elf on the floor.

"No fear, eh?" Kip asked, chuckling and helping Finn to stand.

Finn glared at the gnome, and Mara laughed and turned back to the newly-lit room. It was about what she'd expected. *At least none of them are touching the bulbs and asking how we trapped the sun,* she thought, remembering the scenario when a pioneer was zapped to modern times in a show she used to watch. She scanned around for a TV, but that was too far-fetched for a fantasy land. There were, however, two large armchairs and a couch set around the room with floor lamps and end tables between them. A large rug framed the room, and there were patterned curtains covering a large window and even more picture frames lining the walls.

Mara stepped into the room and slowly circulated it, scanning the walls. There were photos that were clearly from the Western era—tin types. A grumpy, mustached man glared back at her. She smiled and absently twisted Kara's bracelet. One thing that the girls had done grudgingly with their mother was watch old westerns. Her mother was infatuated with Tom Selleck, and, due to his—and other cowboy's—signature look, young Kara had dubbed westerns "mustache movies." Mara chuckled quietly and moved to the next photo.

A few mustaches later, the pictures morphed to something from the industrial age, complete with bowler hats and canes. As she made her way around the room, it was like a trip through American history. There was a pioneer family, a very proper man with an Abe Lincoln hat and Civil War soldiers in the frame beside him. As time passed there was a woman who looked like a suffragette, a flapper, a baseball player, a nuclear family, and World War soldiers. At the end, she saw colored pictures. The last was of a happy, young man with sandy brown hair and bright blue eyes holding a yellow Labrador like a baby.

Once she'd made it around the room, she stopped at one of the end tables. There was a newspaper from the late nineteen fifties from a town called Crawfordsville with the sandy-haired man pictured on the front spread. His name was Sam Sanderson, and the article was about the Sanderson family. All the pictures were various generations of the Sanderson family—parents who'd lost a child mysteriously. The man pictured was the last in a line of dozens over centuries. Since before the family came to settle in America from Europe, they'd had disappearances and strange appearances. Sam must have arrived with the newspaper when it was his turn.

She looked around. It was a family home. Maybe he'd met the other lost ones who'd come to Ambergrove when he'd come to this house. From what the paper explained, he may even have been the last. Mara marveled at the idea. *What history did the house hold? What stories could it tell?* Under the newspaper was a journal. That would tell them something for sure. She picked it up and clutched it to her chest as she continued through the house, oblivious to her companions' queries.

The kitchen was vast, and the first thing Mara saw was an old-fashioned refrigerator. Mara opened it and a light came on. There was a sink with a faucet. Murmuring to herself, Mara turned the knob. There was a spitting sound and a whine, then the faucet rumbled, and some dirty water choked its way out and splashed all over the sink. A little groaning later, and the water cleared. A working faucet. Indoor plumbing and electricity in Ambergrove. Who could believe it? She glanced around at the cabinets and opened one. It was full of jars. Jams and jellies, pickles, and beans.

A doorway off the back side of the kitchen led to an indoor stable, kind of like an attached garage. Except for some musty hay and straw scattered on the floor, it was empty. Returning to the kitchen, Mara peered around an open doorway to the hallway and saw stairs. As she continued exploring the house, she discovered that it was a traditional three bedroom, one-and-a-half-bathroom home. She did not envy the person who'd need to use the bathroom under the stairs.

Mara made her way back downstairs and found the men still in the living room. Kip and Finn were sitting in the armchairs. They'd split the newspaper and were reading it with the lamps on. Kip flipped his paper down to look up at her over it, as a chastising grandfather might. Teddy was laying on the couch with his arms folded, just as he'd lain under the tree when Mara was training her very first day with Cora.

Just as her dad had lain on the couch every time she'd come into the living room growing up and found him sleeping through another movie. She blinked and saw it. It wasn't Teddy laying on the couch; it was her dad. It wasn't the two boys in the chairs; it was her two sisters. They bickered back and forth about the movie while their dad snoozed. Mara saw herself walking into the living room, as if in a dream. She brought three bowls of popcorn in and handed two to her sisters before plopping down on the floor in front of the couch with the last one.

Just as soon as she chomped on a mouthful of her popcorn, a hand was thrust into her face, and from behind there was a mumble that sounded like "dad tax." She felt her dad pat her head as he took the offered popcorn. The pat became a shake. Someone was jostling her. Roughly. She felt light taps on her cheek and snapped into focus—almost. Her dad stood in front of her and was tapping her cheek to get her attention. A few more taps and the tanned skin turned green, but the russet beard held.

Teddy stood in front of her and gazed into her eyes. "Mara! Lass?" he shouted. "Hey! . . . You ok?"

"Y-y-yeah. Y-yeah, Teddy. I'm fine." Mara replied in a daze. She looked around. Kip and Finn stood behind him, eyes wide with worry.

"Maybe you need to rest," Teddy said quietly. Mara's lip trembled, and Teddy wrapped his arm around her and gave her a squeeze, whispering, "I know, lass. I know, I know. Shh." He kissed the top of her head.

She broke into sobs. After a moment, Kip's embrace replaced Teddy's. "Did you find beds in here when you took your little tour?" he asked. She nodded. "Okay then, let's get you laid down. Come on."

Kip walked with Mara up the stairs and through an open door into one of the bedrooms. He sat her gently down on the bed and wiped her face. After a moment of her continued sobbing, Kip pulled the covers of the blanket down and guided her under them, pulling the journal gently from her grasp and tucking the covers around her. "It'll be okay," he whispered. "I know something about this place upsets you, and it may be hard for you to get through it. But we're in this together. Don't forget about that. We all support you." He lightly kissed Mara on the forehead, this time as if she were a small child, smiled reassuringly, and turned to leave.

Wordlessly, Mara shot a hand out from under his swaddling and grabbed his wrist. He turned to look at her. Her face red, blotchy, tearstained, and covered in snot, she just gazed at him in earnest. "Okay," he replied quietly. Kip pulled the covers to one side and slid into bed in front of her. He pulled the covers back over them and wrapped his arms around her so her hands were pressed to his chest. "It's okay," he whispered. "Sleep, little Dragonwolf. Sleep now."

If Teddy had an opinion of the sleeping arrangements that night, he hadn't said anything to Kip when he poked his head in Mara's room on his way to find his own bed. However, when Mara woke the following morning, Kip had moved from the bed to a bedside rocker and had the journal laying open on his chest. She slowly slid out of the bed and went quietly to the upstairs bathroom. She tested some of the facilities, waiting for the water from the faucet to clear before splashing her face and washing off the dried snot from the night before.

She slid back into the bed and lie there for a little while, just looking at Kip's sleeping form before the gnome stirred. He stretched and yawned before meeting her gaze. "Ah, you're up!" he said. "Are you feeling any better this morning?"

"Yeah, a bit," she replied quietly. "I'm sorry about last night."

He groaned scratched his beard sleepily as he sat up. "Don't worry about it. It has to bring back memories, right?"

"Yeah, that's exactly what it did." She pulled the covers up to her chin. "There's so many things about this house, like the indoor plumbing and the electricity, that I haven't seen since I came here. And then—" She broke off, shook her head, and covered her face.

Kip knelt by the bed and pulled the blanket back from her face. "And then what?"

"And then . . . well, I saw you all in the living room and it reminded me of my dad and my sisters."

"Your sisters. Wow. Hopefully, I was the one you like, at least," he joked, reaching out and gently twisting her little, woven bracelet from Kara.

She laughed. "Maybe you were."

He chuckled and swept some loose hair behind her ear. "That's perfectly normal, Mara," he added seriously. "Really. It's going to be hard for you to be here in Chaosland. Dredging up good and bad. But we'll be there with you. And I'm sure since he's older and his Freya came from Earth, Teddy knows more about it and can help."

"Teddy knows what?" Teddy asked, appearing in the doorway.

"Teddy knows how to rattle a whole city with his snoring!" Kip replied, hollering over his shoulder before giving Mara one last pat and standing to face Teddy.

"Well, since I've roused the dead, I guess that means we're all ready to get started this morning. Doesn't it?" Teddy smirked and tapped the doorframe, then headed down the stairs, calling, "Come on, now," as he went.

As they had their breakfast at the dining room table, and Finn braved some of the jarred foods to prove he wasn't afraid, they discussed their plans for the morning. They weren't sure what they would encounter in the city, so they needed to be prepared, and they needed to stick together. Teddy had found a city map on one of the end tables the night before, and he hoped it was still current and would serve them well. They would need to simply follow the network of streets, checking for resources and signs of activity as they went. Once they'd explored New Switzerland, they would reassess to see where was best to try next.

"I'm hoping we find more of these here," Mara said, picking up the map. "Then, at least, we know some of what we're working with. Does that work?"

Her query was met with various agreements, so they finished their breakfast, gathered some extra supplies—Finn decided he really liked pickles—and prepared to head out. They'd been told Chaosland was dangerous and full of evil, but they'd been there for more than a day and met no one. After a long day trudging through the forest in full armor before reaching Fear, they decided the weight was better left behind as they explored the city. No warrior would ever go anywhere without weapons, though, so they gathered those, and Mara took an empty pack, and they headed out into the morning light.

Their trek through the city was surprisingly uneventful for a few hours. They moved building to building and found many homes like Sam Sanderson's. They searched for various supplies in each, and always left with something. The factories proved to be for items commonplace on Earth. Mara explained some of these to the men as they made their way through the city. The items in the general store and other food stores had mostly gone bad. There were a few jarred items that had been preserved, but the rest they left.

As they came out of the last building on the street, they heard the unmistakable buzz of voices. They silently drew their weapons, searching for the source of the newcomers, and then they heard a horrific sound only Mara could recognize. A gunshot.

Chapter Five

Firefight

Mara looked around wildly for the source of the sound. Behind her, Teddy groaned and patted a bloody shoulder. He'd been shot. How had he been shot? She heard another gunshot, and this time felt a pang of pain in her leg. She wobbled and when she looked down, she saw blood trickling.

"Cover! Take cover!" she shouted. "Get inside!" She ushered the startled men into the closest building and shut the door, hollering back to Kip, "Help me out with this!"

Kip and Mara took a heavy cabinet and barricaded the door. Then they covered the nearby windows and all backed into a windowless room. Once there, Mara looked at the wound on her leg. The bullet had only grazed her thigh, so she just needed to stem the blood flow. All these months after her bout with the gauntlet, Kip still carried pain-numbing poultice, so he slapped a generous portion on her leg. That would have to do.

She checked Teddy's shoulder and found he'd been just as lucky. The bullet had barely dug into the muscle above his shoulder. As Kip rubbed the poultice on the dwarf's wound, Teddy looked seriously at Mara. "What *was* that?"

"Evil magic of some kind," Finn grumbled.

"No," Mara began. "Not magic. Gunshots. They shot us with guns."

"What are guns?" Kip asked.

Wow. She'd never thought she'd have to explain that to anyone. She sighed. "Well, I didn't see them, so I don't know what kind they have, but guns are hollow metal weapons that are loaded with bullets. They're dangerous and lethal, because there's fire behind the force. More momentum than you can get with a bow by far. A bullet can break bones or go clean through you." Mara paused and rubbed her face before looking around to the men in disbelief. "I can't believe there's guns here," she finished quietly.

After a moment of silence, Teddy ventured, "Well, we knew that they brought bad things here, so why not these?"

"Well, guns aren't bad," she replied quickly. She'd always been taught that it wasn't the gun that killed, but the person using it. Just like with an axe or bow. But there were already weapons here. They could fend off against monsters with the weapons that were here. They could hunt with the weapons that were here. Bad people would always find a way to kill each other. Here, guns were brought only to kill other people. They were unnecessary. They *were* evil.

There was pounding at the door, shouting, and the sound of breaking glass. Whoever they were, they were making it in. "Get ready!" Teddy shouted, brandishing his sword.

These aren't going to do us much good, Mara thought, returning her axes to the rings at her hips and drawing her bow. She looked to her companions. Finn had his dirks, Teddy had a sword, and Kip had his hammer. All close-and-personal weapons. "Hey!" she called. "If they point metal sticks at you, get back. Get back quickly. Don't be at the end of those, okay?"

They each nodded to her, and she held her bow at the ready as light appeared in the room ahead of them, and the shooters came in the broken window. Mara just had the chance to see that the aggressors were people—humans—before she saw one raise a long barrel in her direction. She pulled her bow back and fired. The arrow drove deep into the human's chest. She didn't have time to agonize over the fact that she'd just killed her first human. More of them were coming, and the men had not heeded her directions.

They were avoiding being at the end of the gun, but just because they were charging the enemies and beating the barrels away. Teddy and Finn went straight for the guns as if they were swords. Kip just beat them back with his hammer. What they seemed to be using were lever action rifles. Mara didn't know how many shots they had before they had to reload, but they did at least have to pump the lever between shots.

Suddenly, while the men were locked into battle with their own assailants, a large man clambered through the window and boomed, "Enough of this." He drew two handguns, like a gunslinger in a western, and aimed each of them at the nearest of Mara's companions.

"Get back! Get back!" Mara shouted at Finn and Teddy.

No use—their reflexes were just a bit too slow. The giant fired, and the bullets hit their marks. Finn's shoulder. Teddy's shoulder right under the previous wound. Finn's stomach. Finn went down just as Kip brought his hammer down hard on the giant man's head, splitting it and hitting him again a few times for good measure. Kip turned and was shot in the side by one of the others with rifles. Mara shook her head to focus and fired her bow. She hit the man who'd just shot Kip, and he went down. She drew back and fired again, hitting a goblin who stood over Teddy. Kip finished the last.

They had won, but at what cost? Mara turned just as Teddy collapsed next to Finn.

Mara and Kip quickly made sure they were properly defended before attending to their wounds. They snuck out a back door to a nearby building they thought they could fortify—just in case more men came looking for the others. They prepared it as best they could, and then they returned to the battle scene to carry the others back to their new safe zone. They took Teddy first, while he was still a little awake, and settled him on a bed before going back for Finn.

When they got back to Finn, they found that he had dragged himself across the room to stab his dirk into the giant who'd shot him. Mara pulled the dirk out of the man, and she and Kip carried Finn to place him in the bed next to Teddy before more thoroughly barricading the building's exits.

When they returned to the others, Kip wiped some poultice on his side to stem the blood flow. Thankfully, like Mara, he had just been grazed. Teddy stood abruptly and insisted he was fine, so Kip turned to Finn, and Mara opened the medical bag to assess. They weren't equipped for one gunshot wound, let alone multiple. As she started to get the supplies out, Teddy collapsed to the ground.

Kip rushed to his side and checked him. "He's alright," he told Mara.

Big, tough warrior man doesn't remember that you don't jump up and do the hokey pokey when you have a bleeding wound, she thought, grumbling to herself before looking up at the gnome. "Kip, please go to one of the other rooms and get the sheet from the bed. Cut it into strips for bandages," she ordered. Kip nodded and disappeared.

Mara pulled her dad's dagger from her boot and cut Finn's shirt open. It was soaked with blood. The first thing she did was check for exit wounds. The shoulder had one, but the stomach shot did not. It could have been worse. She cleaned the shoulder as best she could, stitched it up, and wrapped it with one of the bandages Kip was making.

With a heavy sigh, she lowered to Finn's torso and pressed lightly on his stomach on either side of the wound. Blood seeped out but nothing more. Gently, she pressed various places on his stomach, and she couldn't feel the bullet. She groaned and swore before starting to bandage it up.

"What's wrong?" Kip asked.

"We're going to have to go back and see what kinds of bullets they used so we can figure out what we're looking for. Then Teddy and I are going to have to get that bullet out. But …"

"But what?" Kip asked, laying a bloodstained hand on her shoulder.

She sighed, returning to Teddy's wounds, cleaning them as she continued, "We can't stay here. We don't have what we need here. We don't know how many of them there are or where they are. We need to go somewhere safe, and it's going to take Finn a long time to recover. We have to get them out of here." She looked away and blinked back tears as she stitched and bandaged her uncle's shoulder.

"Okay then," Kip replied when she had finished. "I'll go back and see if I can get a bullet for you and then—"

"No!" Mara shouted. She pursed her lips and continued more calmly, "No. Kip, I grew up around people who used guns." When he gave her a disgusted look, she said, "No, not these kinds. They didn't kill people. They just shot at targets in the woods and had a few guns in the house for protection. Anyway, it's not safe to handle a gun unless you know what you're doing. I've handled guns before, but it isn't safe for you. Stay here with them. I'll go."

She stood and wiped the blood off her hands, nodded to Kip, grabbed her bow, and headed out the door. She kept an arrow nocked as she snuck back to the building they'd come from, but she didn't run into anyone. She went straight to the large man's body and gingerly picked up the gun beside him. What she'd told Kip was true, but she didn't know how these guns were made. It may not be any safer for her to handle this one. All she'd ever handled was a shotgun.

Thankfully, she recognized the overall structure from mustache movies. She didn't want to bring the gun itself back with her, so she tried to unload it. Remembering her gun safety, she kept it pointed at the ground as she inspected it. It was a simple revolver, and she figured out how to unload it after a few tries. Then she tipped it back and dumped the bullets back into her hand. She threw the empty weapon back onto the user's corpse, pocketed the bullets, and headed back to the safety of their new camp.

When she got back to the bedroom, she found Kip with the New Switzerland map spread out in front of him. "Mara!" he called. "Come look at this!" He pointed to a nearby spot on the map.

"Transportation?" Mara read, surprised.

"Yes!" Kip replied. "It's not too far from here. If we can get there and get something to use, then we can take these guys out of here immediately. What do you think?"

Mara nodded. "Let's go."

The building was only about a block over from their hideaway. Once they were there, they found that it was guarded by two men. Mara sighed, but Kip told her to wait for his signal. He snuck around the building to the guards, and, after a moment, they silently fell, and Kip beckoned her over to the building.

Expecting to see some sort of Ambergrovian abomination of a car, Mara was surprised to see horses and wagons. She and Kip quickly hitched up a horse and cart—smaller than a wagon, to better maneuver the forest—and led the horse back to their camp. They loaded up the injured men into the cart and led it away as quickly and quietly as they could, stopping at the Sanderson house for their foolishly discarded armor before leaving that dark city behind them.

With Mara and Kip walking slowly beside the cart, bracing each other as they led it, it took them about two days to make it back to the raft. Finn came to a couple times during the trip, but he quickly faded out. Teddy was awake and grumbling for most of it.

"Giants. I defy you to find anyone who could defeat a giant even if they didn't have one of those resolvers," he said bitterly.

"Revolvers," Mara replied.

As she walked alongside the cart, she'd been making friends with the horse. He was a dappled grey draft horse, and she'd been calling him Excalibur. Since she was a little girl, she'd always wanted to have a grey horse named Excalibur.

Mara rubbed the horse's neck and murmured to him as Teddy continued yammering on about how it wasn't an evenly-matched fight because of the giant's size alone and what sort of people have giant followers, when Kip interjected, "Uh, chaotic ones, I think."

Mara laughed and Teddy's grumbling silenced for a while. She spent much of the rest of the journey to the raft talking to Excalibur. "You're such a beautiful boy. Yes, you are. Do beautiful boys like pickles?" she asked.

"Best not give him too many of those," Teddy warned. "This one will be wanting a jar or two when we get him all patched up."

Mara's face fell. Excalibur nuzzled her and lipped at the pickle jar. She giggled. "Alright, one more, and then we'll save the rest of these for Finn," she told the horse.

When they made it to the raft, Mara was torn about leaving Excalibur. Teddy reasoned that they wouldn't be able to get the horse on the raft, and, seeing how distraught Mara was, Kip proposed a solution. They couldn't waste too much time with Finn in such a delicate condition, so they worked quickly. They found a natural pool surrounded by grass, miraculously also with an apple tree in the mix of trees surrounding it.

"The thing about horses is that they're gentle giants," Kip explained. "You learn that about other creatures when your whole race is small." Mara grinned at him as he continued, "Unless it has a very compelling reason to go somewhere, a horse will stay where you leave it indefinitely." He pulled a long, coiled rope out of his pack. "Now, we don't want to tie him up, because we want him to be able to get away if the need arises. But … if it doesn't, a thin rope stretched between all these trees will make a paddock he'll be happy to stay in until we get back."

They made sure the little paddock included plenty of grass, access to the apples, and water, and they made sure the ropes were secure before rolling the cart up under a tree and making their way back to the raft. Before leaving, Mara patted Excalibur's nose and told him to be a good boy, assuring him that they would be back for him. She procured one last pickle and fed it to him before turning to the raft.

They cast off on the raft, Kip and Mara intending to row back to Questhaven. However, as usual, Teddy had been right. Although it had taken them days to row to Chaosland against the current, they were now floating swiftly to their destination. Before nightfall, they had whipped around toward the island's cove, and Mara and Kip only had to row a little bit to get them up to the beach. As a courtesy to Ashroot, Teddy blew his horn to let her know they were nearby. So, as the raft neared the beach, they could see Fang's hulking figure standing guard, just in case.

Ashroot's form came into view soon after, beside a small, excited blur. It seemed Keena had learned a little in the time they had been gone. Once they made it into shallower waters, Keena glided poorly over the water a little, splashed down into it, and doggy paddled until she had made it all the way to the raft. She clambered up into Mara's arms and cried, *Mama, Mama!*

"Hello, Keena Keena! I missed you, pretty girl!" Mara cried, dropping her oar onto the raft and squeezing her pup.

When Mara looked up, she saw that they were moving very quickly toward the beach. While she had been reuniting with her own wolf, Fang had also paddled into the water and was guiding the raft up to the beach with his muzzle. As they banked, Mara gave Keena one last squeeze and jumped off the raft to hug her friend.

"I figured you would be gone much longer!" Ashroot exclaimed. "What's going on? Is everyone okay? What—"

"Ash, lass, I love you, and there will be time for us to hug and talk, but Finn is in a bad way. I need you to boil water so Mara and I can operate on him. Will you do that?" Teddy explained kindly.

"Y-yes, Teddy," Ashroot stammered, looking at the sea elf's still form.

The camp flew into a frenzy. Teddy gathered what supplies he had that he knew he needed, and he sent Kip out into the island to forage for some ingredients while Mara sterilized equipment and they prepared to care for Finn. The elf's shoulder wound was healing well, like Teddys. Mara had stuffed some cloth and poultice into Finn's stomach wound to keep it open until they could get to the right supplies to dig the bullet out, and that was their big task now.

On one of their walks in Nimeda, Mara's grandmother had explained to her how her wounds from the gauntlet had been tended. The wound had to be opened wide so the poisoned tissue could be removed. They would have to complete the same sickening process here with Finn. Mara hoped that nothing important had been damaged, but with a stomach wound that was unlikely. Teddy was still too weak from his own injuries to help hold him down, so they lay Finn in his bunk and tied him down to keep him still.

Mara shoved a hand in her pocket and pulled out one of the bullets. For a split second, she remembered a book she read in middle school where some boys digging in a dried-up lake found a lipstick tube and thought it was a bullet. It had the same look. About the length and width of her little finger, it was a brassy color, and it was round and unthreatening. *If only, if only,* she thought bitterly.

The plan was for Mara to work as Teddy's assistant, but Teddy's shoulder wound made his hand shaky with the scalpel, so he resorted to delegation. Mara delicately sliced open the bullet hole so it was large enough that she could get a few fingers into it. Finn snapped awake when she began cutting, so Ashroot ran to make a sedating tea before they continued. Once Finn was knocked out, Teddy instructed Mara to feel around with one finger to see if she could find the bullet.

As she felt around, Finn groaned a deep, painful groan. Blood oozed out. Too much blood. "Open it up some more," Teddy ordered. "Something is wrong."

Mara opened the incision a palm's width so she could see what she was working with. At least it helped her to clearly see the bullet. She removed it slowly, though without much effort, and it revealed the root of the problem. The bullet had gone into his intestine. Mara cleaned the wound and gently moved the intestine to the side so she could see the damage. The bullet had torn a hole in some of Finn's intestine and plugged it. The area around the now-vacant hole bore the signs of infection.

"Let me see," Teddy began, peering into the opening. "Hmm … mhmm."

"What is it?" Mara asked.

"This tissue is dying. It's been too long. You're going to need to take it out."

Mara looked at him wildly. "What do you mean, 'take it out?' I can't take it out!"

"You can and you must. Freya told me about this from that book she had. You can survive without chunks of intestine, as long as what you have is good. Just make sure you reconnect the right pieces." Teddy smiled at her and chuckled.

"Not funny, Teddy," Mara replied sternly.

"Okay, okay. Maybe not. Cut it about a pinkie digit's length on either side of the wound. Sew it back exactly as it lays. Be sure to stitch it tight. He'll be just fine, but you have to be precise. Got it?"

Mara nodded rapidly for a moment, then turned away, trying to slow her breathing. *You can do this; you can do this. What are you thinking? You* have *to or Finn is going to die. Get it together.* "Okay, Teddy," she said quietly, turning back to Finn.

"Just keep a steady hand, lass. You'll do just fine."

Mara nodded numbly and exhaled slowly as she brought the scalpel down again. She worked as delicately as possible, trying not to press too hard while still pressing hard enough to do the job. Agonizingly slowly, she removed the damaged tissue and stitched the new ends back together. When this was done, she filled much of the incision with a greenish ooze—an antibacterial concoction for any remaining infection—and then she stitched him up.

By this time Kip had returned, so Ashroot made a topical poultice for all their wounds. Mara applied this to Finn's incision before wrapping it well. Once Finn had been tended, she and Teddy left him to Ashroot's care. They settled in the main tent with Kip. Mara applied the poultice to Teddy's shoulder, as Kip applied it to her leg, and Teddy applied it to Kip's side. Then, hugging Ashroot and murmuring to her that they would all catch up in the morning, Teddy headed back to his own tent.

Kip followed suit, giving Mara a reassuring pat on the shoulder as he went. A few moments later, Mara settled into her bunk, speaking soothingly to Keena to get her calmed and prepared to sleep. Keena stretched out on Mara's stomach, lightly licking her chin as Mara scritched behind her ears and ran a hand along her fluffy body. As she fell asleep, she clutched her pup's fur, shedding tears for Sam Sanderson, for Excalibur alone in the forest, for the men she had killed in New Switzerland, for her companions who'd been shot, and for herself. She'd prepared for enemies that were servants of chaos, but how could they hope to beat monsters with guns?

Chapter Six

Into the Abyss

Mara woke early the next morning to Keena's kisses. She spent some time in her tent, petting her pup and talking to her soothingly. She told Keena things she didn't think she could talk about to the others. She told the dragonwolf about the city, about how the Sanderson family home had reminded her of her own home and her own family. About her dad and her sisters, how she loved them and missed them.

Then, she told Keena about how she heard a gunshot. The fear of looking down the barrel of a gun for the first time in her life. The fear of seeing her companions running at them, not realizing the danger they were in. Seeing Teddy drop and thinking that she'd lost her uncle forever. Seeing Finn gushing blood from a stomach wound, unable to get the bullet out, hoping he could hang on. She was terrified of going back there and so worried that she was going to fail.

Mama sad, Keena yipped.

"Yeah, just a little, Keena," Mara said quietly. She sighed and looked at her little dragonwolf's wagging tail and fiddled with her horn nubbies. "But I'm here with you now, aren't I?"

Stay?

"No, Keena, I can't stay," Mara whispered.

Keena's tail stopped wagging. She whimpered and left the tent as Mara sat up and called after her. With another sigh, she plopped back down onto the bed. Keena couldn't go far on the island. Mara could go talk to her later. She slowly reached her arm up in front of her and twisted the bracelet on her wrist. The pink and sky blue had faded to near white, and the purple had lightened to lavender. She did know how Keena felt. Kara probably did too. What was she doing? It was awful to leave Ashroot behind, but she was at least an adult. Mostly. Kara was so young, and there had been so many times growing up when they'd only really had each other.

Mara groaned and rolled out of her bed. She dressed and flung her tent flap open, following the smell of breakfast to the main tent where she found Ashroot plating up some eggs on toast.

"Come, sit, Mara!" her friend called.

As Mara sat, Ashroot worked on more breakfast beside her. Mara looked around, and none of the others were in sight. She figured she and Teddy would go check on Finn together and redress his injuries, so he probably wasn't up yet. "Ash?" she asked.

"Yes?"

"How are you doing with all of this? How were things with you while we were gone?"

Ashroot flipped eggs quietly for a moment before replying, "Well, Moon and I really got along. She brought her pups by a lot to take them on walks, and she came to visit me. She said sometimes you just need to talk to someone."

"That makes perfect sense," Mara agreed.

"It does, it does. And Keena went off and played with her pups a lot, so I had some time to myself. I've had a few little projects going on. I mean, I worried about you all—with good reason, it seems—but I'm happy to be here waiting for you. And I've been able to start a garden, forage for food, and make poultices, so I can still help," Ashroot finished quickly, plating a few more eggs on toast.

"You know, you don't always have to be useful, Ash," Mara replied as she chomped on a piece of toast. "You're a valued member of this family. We're leaving you here for your protection. You wouldn't want to have been there with us." Mara paused and sat quietly, eating her breakfast.

Ashroot brought her a jar of peach jam for her leftover toast and set it on the table before quietly asking, "It was really bad, wasn't it?"

Mara nodded.

"It was better with Mara's expertise," Kip replied.

They hadn't heard him approach, but now he entered the tent, sat next to Mara at the table, and took the offered breakfast. Mara slid the jar of jam over to him and muttered, "It wasn't that much."

Kip snorted. "What do you think us men would have done to the fire and metal spitting weapons they used if you hadn't told us differently? It would have been a lot worse, Mara. A *lot* worse."

"Each one of us would be worse off than Finn, if we were even here at all," came a gruff voice.

They all turned to see Teddy heading up to the table. He groaned and rubbed his shoulder as he sat. Ashroot brought him his breakfast and sat next to him to eat hers.

"What are we going to do about them?" Kip asked.

Teddy waved a hand as Mara opened her mouth. "Let's not worry about that now. We'll get Finn right and then we'll figure things out. First," he turned to Kip, "do you still happen to have that crutch you made for Mara after the gauntlet?"

"Y-yeah," Kip answered. "Well, I mean, it's on the ship."

"Best get someone to help you with it today. And see if you can't make some more—don't need to be fancy, though. Finn will need some help getting around for a bit, and I'm sure this won't be our last round of injuries," Teddy explained.

"I'm on it," Kip replied. He stuffed a last bite of toast into his mouth and gave Mara a gentle shoulder squeeze before heading out into the woods, calling, "Keena, Keena, Keena!"

Mara turned to Teddy. "What's the plan for Finn?" she asked.

"Well, I looked in on him a few times—and Ash here helped by giving him some herbal tea," Teddy motioned to the bearkin and took a bite of his toast before continuing, "We'll dress his wounds for at least a few days. Ash is giving him a sedative, so he won't try too much and hurt himself. Hopefully, he'll be in a right enough condition in a few days so we can get him up and moving. We'll have to get him right before we make any decisions about heading to Chaosland again."

"Him and you," Ashroot corrected sternly.

"Yes, me too," he replied. "I am very aware of my age and infirmity without being reminded."

Mara smiled a little bit into her final bite of toast. They sat in relative silence for a moment and let Teddy eat. After a few moments, Teddy mopped up his plate with his final piece of toast and beckoned to Mara to come with him to Finn's tent.

Kip and Keena collected branches for crutches in no time. While Teddy and Mara worked on cleaning and dressing Teddy and Finn's wounds, Kip took Keena with him on one final crutch mission.

"Now, this is very important," he told her. "I know you and I don't have the bond that you do with the others, because I can't understand what you say—if you can say much of anything right now—"

She defiantly yipped at him in response. He just raised a brow.

"Okay … well, we're going to the ship, and you need to go down below deck and get the really big stick that's by the boxes down there. Okay?"

They stopped at the edge of the banked ship, and she looked at him and tilted her head.

"I'll take that as a yes," he said quietly. He bent down and gave her a pat on the head and a scritch behind the ear, and then he grabbed her sides and threw her up in the air as hard as he could.

She squeaked as she was chucked into the sky, and she frantically flapped her wings. She held mostly in the air before crashing onto the deck. Then she ran back and looked over the bulwark at Kip, yipping a few times before disappearing with a clatter.

They kept Finn sedated for about a week so his stomach and intestines could heal without incident. Kip had just been nicked, really, so his side healed first, followed quickly by Mara's leg. Mara massaged pain-numbing poultice into her leg a few times a day and marveled at the luck that the gunshot was in her bad leg. Her leg had been sliced pretty deeply during her duel with Candiru, the champion of the sea elves, during the final stage of the Serpent's Gauntlet. At least she'd only have one bad leg, and not hobble around like some creature, but she did hope that she wouldn't end up with dozens of wounds in one spot. Her limp from her gauntlet wound had mostly gone away, but now it returned with a vengeance.

Teddy was feeling better, and he thought after a week that he'd made it to the point when he could handle Finn being awake. Mara passed Teddy the poultice, and he started massaging it into his shoulder as they sat and watched over Finn.

"We do need to figure something out soon, Teddy," Mara said suddenly.

He groaned as he massaged into some thick scar tissue. "Yeah—ah—I know. We need to discuss it all together once this one's up and running."

As if on cue, Finn stirred. He slowly raised a hand to touch his stomach, and his eyes fluttered open. Mara leaned forward and commanded, "Hey, now, settle. Don't get up too quickly." She placed a hand on his shoulder as he pressed to sit up anyway. "Hey!" she said more sharply. "You cannot get up. We cut you wide open to save your life, and if you want to keep it, you need to chill out, Finn."

"Listen to her, lad, or I'll be next to reach out and touch you," Teddy grumbled.

Finn lay back on his bunk and glared at Mara. "What happened?"

Mara explained how, when he'd been shot, one of the bullets was stuck in his gut and damaged his intestines. She gave him a short explanation of what they had done to remove the bullet and patch him up, and she had to make him lie back down again when she told him that she'd cut him open and taken out chunks of intestine. When he threw the blanket off to check his stomach, there was just a dark blue line across his midsection, held together with imperfect stitches.

"What did you expect to see? Your gut curled up like a pup on the bed next to you?" Teddy asked.

"Maybe," Finn grumbled. "Maybe I thought that you'd replaced them with some Earth magic pipes that are going to make me never have to eat again. Or that would allow me to shoot bullets out my navel. My very own gun," he said bitterly.

"Well, you definitely don't have to worry about that," Mara fumed, suddenly angry without knowing why. She stomped out of his tent without another word. A little while later, once Finn had recuperated enough to hobble to the main tent for meals and discussion, Mara found out what had made her so angry.

As they all sat around the table in the main tent, Teddy decided it was time to discuss what they might do to better prepare themselves to fight in Chaosland. As they ate, he asked Mara to explain what she knew.

"Well … I don't know a whole lot really. I didn't really grow up around them, because my family was from here. But I've seen some guns in movies, and I did learn how to use one when I was little. I think the ones we saw are from about the Wild West era. A lot of the pictures and other things I saw came from about that time, so that would make sense."

"It is the wild west, if you think about it," Kip said. Seeing the others' hard looks, he added, "Wha-a-at?"

Mara took a large bite of her dinner before continuing, "They'd need to have guns that shoot more than one round without reloading, so they couldn't be much earlier than that. The issue is that, from what Teddy said when I got here, when people come to Ambergrove from Earth, they only come with what they're wearing or holding." Teddy nodded, and Mara continued, "There would also need to be teenagers coming through with guns to have any idea of what they were or how to use them. In the old west, kids learned to shoot when they learned to walk. They probably brought some along with them, and then when they had models here, they decided to make more with what they had here."

"Makes sense," Teddy agreed. "Your da sent you with his dagger. He sent you with something to protect you. It's what I'd do too."

"So, they can be for protection," Finn added. He fished a pickle out of a jar and chomped on it. Mara glared at him.

"Sounds like they could be. Or at least the first ones were," Kip added quickly upon meeting Mara's gaze.

"Yes, sometimes they can be for protection, just like a bow or a sword, but not these. These guns were *made* to kill people. To kill *us*," she said.

"Well, if they *can* be used for protection, and they *are* used to kill, then what if . . ." Finn placed his pack on the table with a thud. "What if we used them?"

He pulled a bloodstained revolver out of his pack and laid it on the table. Teddy and Kip murmured in consideration. Ashroot gasped. She had been horrified at the thought of a weapon that could do such damage to Teddy and Finn with so little effort. Mara also gasped. The hammer was cocked back. She jumped to her feet and picked up the gun quickly, careful to keep her index finger straight out away from the trigger and the gun pointed to the ground. She released the hammer and opened the chamber. There were two bullets left.

Mara slammed a fist down on the table and tipped the gun so the bullets cascaded out onto the surface before rounding on Finn, shouting, "You could have killed any one of us with this! They're especially dangerous if you don't know what you're doing. This could have fired at a jostle when we were hauling your fool hide here in a cart or while we were in the middle of nowhere on a raft! *What were you thinking bringing that here?*"

"Calm down, Mara. We just have to learn how to use it," Finn protested.

"Yeah, Mara, you're overreacting a little, don't you think?" Kip asked quietly.

Mara turned to Teddy, the voice of reason. "It may be worth considering, Mara," he said slowly.

Mara looked to Ashroot, who was softly sobbing. She glared at the bullets on the table. Then she began in a dangerous whisper, "Worth considering?" She laid the gun down gently on the table and then shouted, *"Worth considering?* The whole reason Aeun sent me to Chaosland was to rid Ambergrove of the advancements of Earth that corrupt it."

"But if we used it—" Finn began.

"Then we'd be no better than they are!" she spat. "When we fight, we fight for each other, for our freedom from the poison that Chaosland holds, for those that have come before us who lost all they had ever known to a darkness they didn't understand, and for a bright future for all of Ambergrove. We are fighting for the good. If you gaze too long into the abyss, the abyss will gaze into you."

"What does that mean?" Kip asked.

"It means if we act like them, we'll become them," Teddy said quietly.

"We can't," Mara said fervently. "We have to find another way." She paused for a moment, resting her hands on the table, and then added quietly, "I know we're all working together, but when it comes down to it, this is my job and I have to do it right. We *cannot* use their weapons. We *cannot* get used to what they have when we go to Chaosland. If we hope to rid the world of the darkness, we will not become it. *You will not use guns.* That's an order. If you cannot abide that, you need to find your own way home, because you're no longer part of this company."

She picked up the gun and bullets from the table and chucked the bullets into the brush as she stormed off into the woods without a backward glance. She didn't slow down or notice how far she had walked until she was standing knee-deep in the water in the northernmost tip of the island. She looked down at the water and blinked. Then, with a guttural shout, she threw the gun with all her might out into the sea. It splashed in the distance and sank. Mara sank with it, sitting miserably in the water and letting the tears fall.

Mara sat in the shallow water until a rock splashed into the pool beside her and someone behind her spoke. "Well, that looks a little damp, Dragonwolf," Kip said.

"We can't use anything from the forbidden lands. There's a reason they're forbidden," Mara said bitterly.

"I thought we were calling it Chaosland?" Mara turned and glared up into Kip's amused face. He reached out a hand and she took it, allowing him to help her stand. He continued, "Anyway, surely not everything there is forbidden or chaotic. I mean, I brought something from a store there for you, and I think it seems harmless."

"What?" Mara gasped. "After everything that happened, you just took something that you knew nothing about? After Finn brought a loaded gun he didn't know how to use? How—"

"Easy, now. Easy. Do you think I would bring something here if I thought it might be dangerous?" Kip asked, grabbing Mara by the shoulders to settle her and keep her gaze.

"No, I guess not," she said quietly.

"No. This is something I saw in the general store, with description and examples of its use. It is safe, and I think you'll like it," he said with a smile.

Mara sighed. "Fine. Show it to me."

"Close your eyes," he ordered. She glared at him as he insisted, "Come on, humor me."

She obeyed, putting a hand in front of her eyes exaggeratedly. She heard a click and a mechanical sound, then flapping. "Are you almost done?" she asked, laughing.

"Okay, okay. Open them." Inches from her face was a photograph. Kip held it at arm's length, but she could see the self-satisfied grin behind it. It was a fresh picture of her that would still need a bit more flapping to fully develop. She looked ridiculous. As she went to grab the picture, Kip pulled it back and said, "Nah, I think I'll hold onto this. . . . but you can have this." He handed her a Polaroid instant camera with a shoulder strap.

"You found a camera?" Mara cried, swiping a hand out and grabbing the camera from Kip.

"Yes, you mentioned a Polar Oid before. This is not what I pictured, but—"

Mara burst into a fit of laughter. He asked her what was so funny, but she didn't try explaining to him what brands and trademarks were. She just shook her head and admired her new treasure. It looked to be used, like someone brought it with them from Earth and the general store was just reselling it. She looked it over. It may have been used, but it was still in good condition. Opening it, she saw that there was only a handful of instant film left. She would have to make the pictures count.

"We should head back. The others are probably worried about you. And we do still need to figure out what we're going to do to fight the darkness," Kip said after a moment.

"I think I actually have a plan for that," she replied. "Let's go."

By the time they made it back to camp, everyone had gone to bed. Mara found Keena curled up on her bed when she entered her own tent. Keena hadn't been mad at her for long, but Mara had lingered on what her pup had felt, so as she slid into bed—curling herself around the pup's sleeping form so as to not wake her—Mara thought about all her plans for the next sojourn into Chaosland.

The next morning, Mara rose early. She took Keena out for a walk in the woods and picked some berries for breakfast. They played fetch the whole way back, and Mara tried to teach Keena some more words. Keena had learned *hunt* from Fang, and she demonstrated this by catching a hare for them to bring back for breakfast. When they made it back to camp with their spoils, Ashroot was just emerging from her tent.

"Good morning, Ash!" Mara called. "Keena and I brought breakfast, if there's something you can make with these."

Ashroot gave Mara a look that plainly said, "Of course I can make something," and the bearkin silently went to work.

Mara threw a ball for Keena and scribbled on a piece of paper at the table in the main tent while Ashroot made their breakfast. The smell of seared hare made its way to the other tents and woke the men, and soon they were all sitting at the table eating Ashroot's breakfast in an uncomfortable silence. As Mara lowered her plate down to the ground for Keena to clean up, Finn was the first to finally speak.

"So, warden, what's your grand plan for us to complete our task and survive if we don't use the big, bad guns?" he grumbled.

"Well, my plan requires some wisdom, so you'd be best to pay attention and get some," she replied sharply.

Finn opened his mouth to retort, but Teddy spoke first. "Please tell us what you have in mind, Mara. We're all ears." He shot a warning glance at Finn, who settled.

Mara took a deep breath and began, "Well, foremost, we find a middle ground. When we made characters in DUNGEONS & DRAGONS, Jim always used to say that crossbows were outside our alignment. We were supposed to be lawful good, and crossbows were sneaky weapons that required little skill and did more damage than regular bows. We will not use weapons from Earth. We will not use anything that is meant to be forbidden. But crossbows are the middle ground."

She paused and surveyed the table, then added, "We can go back to Gylden Grotto and get crossbows. If none of us know how to use them, we can spend some time training here before we head back to Chaosland. We'll take only light, fast weapons and we'll plan for stealth and distance. Find a good way to take a knife to a gunfight."

"We're using knives?" Kip asked.

"No, sorry. It's an expression. 'Taking a knife to a gunfight' is going into a fight when the enemy has the advantage. We won't have weapons on the level of theirs, but we can work together to best them with cunning and teamwork. It'll just take some time and work. We'll have to fight like rogues."

Mara looked around at their faces—apprehensive, to say the least—and settled on Teddy's. Her uncle met her gaze and said slowly, "I do understand the need to blur the line without crossing it. However, crossbows are also used by farmers and grandmothers who never learned to fight. They're a weapon for the weaker man to fight an unfair fight. I think you've arrived at the perfect solution."

As Mara looked around the table again, the other men glanced at Teddy and nodded to Mara. "We're with you," Kip said.

"Good. Then, Mara, you and I will sail to Gylden Grotto for some crossbows," Teddy instructed. "It's better if just dwarves go, since we're asking them for weapons. Best head out today, since it will take us some time to get to them. We'll need to put *Harrgalti* back in the sea when the tide comes in, and head off. You and Kip come with me, and we'll get started."

As Mara stood to obey her uncle, Finn murmured, "Mara, could I just talk to you a moment first?"

Glancing back at them, Teddy bid Kip to head on to the ship with him, and Ashroot suggested to Keena that it might be good if they helped. After a few moments, Finn and Mara sat alone together, looking anywhere but across the table at the other. Finally, Mara asked, "Are we going to talk or are we going to sit?"

"Talk. We're going to talk," Finn said quickly. He sighed and continued, "Mara, I'm a sea elf."

"Wow, really? I thought with the blue skin that maybe you were—"

"I'm a sea elf, and sea elves are supposed to be fearless. We're supposed to be the best. Whatever the best weapon is, we're supposed to have it and to be able to use it well." Finn sighed and looked down at his hands before continuing quietly, "I-I'm afraid of those guns, Mara. They're a weapon unlike anything I've ever seen. I thought the only way to overcome this fear and to act like a true sea elf was to use them myself."

"It's natural to fear, Finn," she said softly. "Especially after the injuries you came back from. It may make you less of a sea elf to your *mother,* but it doesn't make you less to me. Besides … do you really want to be like her?" Mara asked.

Finn sat silently for a moment before whispering, "I guess not."

"No. You don't," Mara said firmly. "And we won't let you. You're part of this family, at least until our task is done and you decide what you want to do."

"I know that. And I'm grateful. I am. You've given me my life, Mara. I'll follow your lead from here on, I promise," he said. "I have no interest in going into the abyss," he added mischievously.

"Me neither!" Mara agreed, patting Finn's hand reassuringly. They sat awkwardly for a moment before Mara added, "Alright! Well, I'd best go help them if we're going to make any progress."

With one more pat, Mara stood and headed off toward *Harrgalti,* feeling more hopeful about their current predicament. As she walked away, Finn began to clear the table, noticing the paper Mara had tucked under her plate. Finn grinned. It was a list: *talk to everyone about crossbows; come up with a training schedule; get supplies; spend time with Keena; spend time with Ash; take a family photo; talk to Finn; try again.*

Chapter Seven

From the Ashes

Mara and Teddy set sail for Gylden Grotto as soon as they got *Harrgalti* back in the water. Before long, they discovered they had a stowaway. Keena was curled up in a cabinet in the galley when they headed below deck for a meal. She squeaked and burst out, bounding over to Teddy as he opened a container of cheese.

"Keena! What are you doing here with us?" Teddy scolded, holding the cheese up out of reach.

Stay, she whined. She tucked her tail between her legs. *Stay with Mama.*

Mara could feel her heart sink to her feet as she looked at her pup's sad eyes and distressed shivering. *Oh, Keena. I'm never going to leave you behind again,* she thought. "Come to Mama," she said, holding her arms out for an embrace. Keena rushed into them and licked Mara everywhere she could reach.

"Alright, then, girls," Teddy said sharply. They both turned to look as he continued, "Keena, if you're going to come around with us everywhere then *Mama,*" he gave Mara a significant look, "is going to have to teach you how to be around other people and to be safe in the wilderness. And you're going to have to listen," he finished, looming over the pup and leering at her.

In response, Keena wriggled out of Mara's hold and sat as properly as a puppy could—demonstrating to Teddy that she could be good. Mara laughed. "Well, that's a great start, Keena!"

"Yeah, a wonderful start!" Teddy agreed. He tossed Keena a piece of cheese, and she swallowed it in one gulp. He gave Mara a serious look. "Now you have to make sure she can do it on command." With that, he gathered a few more lunch items and headed back up to the deck.

Mara spent most of the sojourn to Gylden Grotto trying to teach Keena some basic commands. She'd told Keena that the only way she would be able to stay by Mama's side when she left Questhaven would be if she could learn all the commands and obey them, but Mara didn't think she had the heart to leave her pup behind—even if she didn't learn. Fortunately, Keena was growing fast. According to Ashroot's assessment, she was nearing a year old. It turned out she'd understood much for a while; she just didn't know how to communicate sooner because she wasn't around any of her own kind. Time spent with Fang and Moon had allowed her to understand more of her own language, so Mara decided she would spend as much time as she could sending Keena to see Moon so she could learn right.

"I don't want to mess anything up, Keena, so I want to make sure you don't learn bad habits from me. I'm your mama, but you're still a dragonwolf. You need to be able to talk like a wolf. I promise I'll still be able to understand you if you do," Mara explained. "So don't try to talk to me unless you know the words. If you know what I mean, just tell me 'Yes, Mama.' Okay?"

Keena's ears perked up and she yipped, *Yes, Mama!*

By the time *Harrgalti* once again docked at Gylden Grotto, Keena had mastered *sit, heel, stay,* and *quiet*—at least to Teddy's satisfaction.

"Now, little one, do we need to leave you on the ship or are you going to be very, very good while we're here?" Teddy asked Keena, steely eyed.

Good. Be good, Keena yipped. Her body vibrated with the effort of remaining still.

Teddy peered at her and squinted intently before sighing and rubbing his hands together. "Alright then! Let's do it. Come on, girls."

With empty packs, Mara and Teddy stepped onto the dock, and Keena heeled between them. This time, Hodd met them at the dock with a large grin and open arms. "Teddy! Dragonwolf! . . . Dragon*wolves!*" he exclaimed, eyes widening upon seeing Keena. He knelt beside Mara and reached out a hand to the pup, continuing, "Well, well! Aren't you a beaut?"

Keena whined softly and tucked her tail between her legs. It was the first time she'd seen anyone new in months, and the first time she'd seen anyone besides the crew of *Harrgalti*—not counting the goblins. She sniffed Hodd's outstretched hand and allowed him to pet her. Her horn nubbies had grown to the size of Bugle chips, and Hodd grinned as he poked them before scratching behind her ear. Her tail began thumping softly, and she licked his hand.

"Looks like I pass!" Hodd murmured.

Mara was relieved. Despite her promise not to leave Keena alone, she worried the pup would be in danger if she met other people—despite Teddy's assurances that the mining dwarves would hold the bond of brotherhood over any power they might gain from a dragonwolf.

Hodd stood and turned to Mara. "What's her name?"

"Keena," she replied.

"Well, Keena, you are welcome here in my grotto." Hodd turned to Teddy. "What is it you need?"

Teddy sighed. "Can we go somewhere and sit?"

Hodd made a beckoning motion and they followed him through the winding paths into the mountain and to the inn they'd stayed in their previous visit. They selected a table, and Mara commanded Keena to sit quietly while they talked. The barkeep passed out a warm, foaming liquid, and one sip sent the warmth through all extremities. Upon gingerly setting his mug on the table, Teddy asked Mara to begin.

"Have you heard of what they use in the forbidden lands?" she asked Hodd.

"What do you mean? Transportation? Tools? Weapons?" The dwarf took a sip of his drink and raised a brow.

"Weapons. The others I can handle well enough."

"Ah, yes, because you came from Earth and know its mysteries."

Mara laughed into her drink, blowing some foam up into her face. "Well maybe some mysteries, I guess. About those weapons?"

"Yes, I've heard about them. At least that they spit fire, and the bolt is too small and fast to evade. Why do you ask?"

"Well … we need to fight fire with something other than fire," she replied slowly.

Hodd turned to Teddy, who absently stroked his healing shoulder before replying, "It's true. We cannot use their weapons to complete our task, but we do have to face them to complete it."

"What's your idea?" Hodd asked Teddy.

Teddy gestured to Mara who explained, "We were hoping we could get some crossbows from you, and perhaps some other supplies that might help us better defend ourselves against them."

"That's a fine idea. Anyone I have heard of who's faced them has suggested chain or scale mail for defense and bows or crossbows to fight them. We can certainly arrange that for you," Hodd shared a look with Teddy and nodded into his mug. "We'll give you extras, too, so you have backups, but you are welcome to come back anytime you need. Also … since you will be coming back for supplies, you are welcome to take one of our dinghies. It may be of more use to you to make small trips without the need of a larger crew to sail—or the use of something primitive like a raft."

Mara gave Teddy a look, and her uncle disappeared behind his mug. She turned back to Hodd. "Thank you very much for your help and generosity. We'll be happy to repay you if—"

Hodd shook his head. "No need. As I said, we're kin. Your duty is not one I envy, though it is necessary, and I will do all I can to support it. We'll work together to get you whatever you need. You just rid us of the scourge in the forbidden lands."

Mara smiled. "Agreed."

Hodd instructed a few burly dwarves to haul a black dinghy onto the deck of *Harrgalti.* He'd chosen one with blackened wood and a plain black sail so it would blend in better to the surroundings. They would be able to sail back and forth to Chaosland with a lesser chance of being spotted—not as little as if the dinghy was sea elf made, but the best they would be able to do.

Teddy went off on his own to replenish some standard supplies while Hodd led Mara to the armory with Keena bounding at his heels. "Were you looking for anything particular?" he asked.

Mara scanned the weapons lining the back wall of the armory. Clearly, crossbows were not often used. "Speed, for one. We need to be able to fight them quickly, so not one of those things that need to be braced on the ground and cranked. But we also need something more lethal than a bow. They can kill us so easily, we need to even the odds."

Hodd scratched his beard. "Hmm … well there are some medium crossbows that might work well for what you need. You need to step on the stirrup at the front to prepare it to load. With practice, you can learn to do that quickly." Hodd took a crossbow from the wall and handed it to Mara. "These also pack a punch. And our best bolts for these are barbed." He opened a drawer, pulled out a bolt, and handed it to her.

It was like someone had taken a bunch of arrowheads and attached them all to one tip. Two levels of tips at different directions presented a deadly star. Mara poked the tips gently. "This'll work."

"See if you can draw it back and shoot one of these over here." Hodd handed Mara a training bolt and pointed to a bare wall behind the armory. "Set the head on the ground and put your foot in the stirrup here," he continued, demonstrating with another crossbow. "Pull back the string to the nock here. Keep your hand away from the lever, so you don't dry fire. When you've got it, tuck the butt here into the dip between your chest and shoulder to brace it, aim, and squeeze the lever. Don't pull. If you pull, it will change your aim." He fired the crossbow and the bolt shattered against the hard cave wall. "You try."

Mara stepped on the stirrup and pulled the string back. She could feel a muscle twitch with the effort, but she got the string set, placed the bolt, and rested the butt at her shoulder. She found the lever and squeezed. The bolt shattered against the wall. She expected a kick like when she shot a gun, but there was nothing. The crossbow was steady.

"Good for your first try," Hodd said, clapping Mara on the shoulder. "What do you think?"

Mara nodded. "I think these'll work."

"Good!" Hodd called over a couple dwarf women and instructed them to take the supplies to *Harrgalti*, also including a few small hip quivers and a wooden box of training bolts to accompany the large box of barbed bolts.

"There's one more thing. I still have to convince Teddy to wear something other than that worn, old jerkin, but do you have chainmail I can take—to at least try to convince him?" Mara asked.

Hodd crossed his arms and squinted into the middle distance for a moment before saying, "Well ... you wouldn't necessarily need to convince him not to wear the jerkin. It's actually probably better for the skin to be padded with leather if a bullet comes. One of these will help."

He held up a chainmail shirt with leather strips dangling from the sides. It had a neck hole and was meant to go over the wearer's head overtop of the clothes. The leather strips would be tied along the underside of the arm and down the wearer's sides. Teddy could wear it over his leather armor and hardly even know it was there. Mara grinned and nodded.

"Do you have something thicker for underneath your mail?" he asked.

"No."

"A quilted shirt will do you and allow you to also wear the mail you have."

"That'll work, then. Thank you. Could we get a few of them so we have spares? In different sizes? Just for padding, you know ..." she asked.

Hodd nodded, missing Mara's nervousness, and murmured something to another dwarf by the armory, and soon after, he and Mara headed out to *Harrgalti* with their spoils. When they made it back to the ship, the dinghy was settled on the deck and Teddy was emerging from below with some empty boxes and some laughing dwarves. They were done. Mara thanked Hodd and shook in closing, Teddy did the same, Hodd bid them good luck and gave Keena a pat and a treat, and they boarded the ship to return to Questhaven.

Do good? Keena asked when they were sailing away from Gylden Grotto.

"Yes! Yes, Keena, you did good! You're such a good girl! Hodd loved you and you behaved yourself so well!" Mara exclaimed, smooshing Keena's face and petting her. She grabbed one of Kip's wooden balls and threw it across the deck for her.

Teddy booted it when it came near to his foot at the helm. "Come here, Mara," he said.

Mara groaned and stood, making her way to the helm. "Yes, Uncle?" she asked brightly.

"Do you really think you're going to get me to wear that shiny shirt you brought?" he asked, eying her mischievously.

Mara inhaled sharply and winced. "Ooh," she mocked. "Yeah, I kind of think I can."

Teddy squinted at her. "Mhmm."

"Really, come on, Teddy. You put it on over your leather, and you won't even now it's there. Honest. It'll help you."

"Yeah, sure."

"Oh, so you'd rather have some more holes in you?"

"Could always do with one more hole," he muttered.

"Yeah, we'll see about that. Also, the chainmail ..." She patted him on the shoulder. "I'll get you into it, don't worry."

"Why am I wearing this?" Kip asked.

Mara and Teddy had returned late in the evening with their spoils. They unloaded the supplies and hauled *Hárrgalti* onto the bank as before, made much easier with Fang's help, and then they fell into bed. The following morning, Ashroot made breakfast for everyone, and Teddy rebandaged Finn's wounds—and gave his approval for Finn to begin training with the rest of them—while Mara snuck off with Kip to her tent.

Kip held up the chainmail shirt and raised a brow.

"I want Teddy to realize there's nothing wrong with wearing a little chainmail. Even overtop of something else, it won't be too encumbering," Mara explained.

"Mhmm." Kip laid the chainmail on Mara's bed and picked up a quilted shirt. As he slipped the shirt on, he asked, "Why are you so adamant about the chainmail?" When he looked back to Mara, her eyes were filled with tears. Kip steered her to sit on the bed and sat next to her, a hand in hers. "Hey, hey! What is it?" he asked her softly.

"H-he could have died," she said miserably.

"When? When we were in that city?"

Mara pressed her face into Kip's chest and nodded.

"Hey. It'll be okay. We're preparing. He'll be fine this time," he murmured. "How do you know chainmail will help so much?"

Mara told him about a movie—and explained to him what movies were. Her favorite actor had been in it as a crackpot inventor. One of his inventions was chainmail as a bullet resistant vest. That was the only merge she had seen between modern and medieval that would help them in their situation. She knew that it wouldn't work as well as in the movie, but Hodd said they did it here, too, and she thought it was the only way she might be able to help them with what she knew.

"The only way?" Kip burst. "You don't think you've helped us already?"

Mara shrugged. Not a noncommittal gesture, but rather the gesture of one helpless. She had done helpful things, but she didn't see them in that moment. Fear, insecurity, doubt—they were all she could think of then.

Kip wrapped his arms around Mara and squeezed, keeping his hold tight as he spoke into her hair, "You know, you don't have to be strong all the time. We know that Teddy cried when we first arrived here. We just don't talk about it. It doesn't change who he is. There's no shame in being afraid or being sad. This is new for all of us, and it's more new for you than you think. You've never shot anyone or been shot before—until now. You've never been expected to be the expert on all things in your world. You know what Polar Oids are, but that doesn't mean you're expected to know how they work."

Mara laughed softly and sniffled. "No, I guess not."

"You are our leader. You are the one of us who knows something about Earth. But just because Earth inspired Chaosland doesn't mean they are one and the same. You're not expected to know everything, and you can't plan for every future. You know?" Kip put a hand gently under Mara's chin and raised it.

After a moment, she nodded, and Kip kissed her forehead and hugged her again. They sat that way for a few moments before Mara sighed and told Kip they needed to get going. When they stood, Kip turned away from her to slip the chainmail over his head, just so he could cover the snot smear across the quilted shirt before she could see it there. He turned back to her and held his arms up so she could tie the leather strips.

When she was done, Kip sighed and said, "I'll wait outside for you until you're ready to head back."

As he opened the tent flap, Kip saw Keena at the edge of the clearing chasing a butterfly. He whistled sharply, and her ears perked up. She snapped her head around to look at Kip, and then she barreled across the clearing to where he stood. Kip put a hand to his lips as he knelt to receive her. "Your mama needs you to give her kisses and show her you love her. Can you do that?" he whispered.

Keena gave Kip a few rapid licks and entered Mara's tent.

While Mara and Teddy had been away, Kip had been building targets for crossbow practice. Ashroot and Finn helped as they could—Ashroot sewed person-like bags to attach to the stands Kip was making, and Finn sat and weaved classic targets that could be hung. Increased blood flow from even minor exertion had been causing him to bleed through his bandages, his own stubbornness extending the healing process, but he was determined to be of use as the crossbow practice area was constructed.

So, when Mara left her tent, following a contented Keena who was bounding with pride after helping her mama, she headed over to the new crossbow training area. Tucked up against the cliff face on the western edge of camp were five person-like targets. Staked in various places along the cliff face were Finn's round targets.

The table from the main tent had been carried out to shooting distance, and Finn sat in one of the chairs. Teddy stood at the table, inspecting the crossbows that lay upon it, and Ashroot skittered around the table and over to the targets, where Kip passed from one to the next, working on his own inspection.

Mara met Teddy at the table and saw the crossbows and bolt quivers lining the surface. Drawing one bolt from the quiver, she nodded. They were full of the blunted practice bolts, as she suspected. She slid the bolt back into the quiver and turned to Teddy, but he spoke first.

"Are you going to teach here with me today?" he asked.

"Me?" she squeaked.

He turned to her and raised a russet brow, before replying, "Yeah, you. I know Hodd taught you how to use one of these when we were at the grotto. No, you aren't an expert, but you do know what to do from what I've taught you, and you can show one of them the moves and practice together."

Mara nodded slowly, and the gears began turning in her brain. "Yeah, that sounds like a plan."

"Alrighty then. Which do you want? Finn … or Kip?" Teddy asked, peering at her.

She grinned. "I'll work with Finn. We need to have a one-to-one chat before we head back to Chaosland anyway. You could always use some more bonding time with Kip anyway, right?" She nudged her uncle playfully.

"Okay." Teddy raised his head toward the targets and sharply hollered, "Kip! You're with me!"

Mara picked up a crossbow and quiver for Finn and walked over to him, grinning when Kip winked at her when he passed on his way to Teddy. She handed Finn his crossbow and quiver, and then went back to retrieve her own. When she'd returned to Finn, he'd stood.

"I taught you to sail, and now you're teaching me to use a crossbow," he said, strapping his bolt quiver to his hip.

Mara propped her crossbow against his chair and did the same, looping the lower strap around her thigh and buckling it before replying, "Well, the greatest commonality, really, is that when you taught me, I only knew the basics, and now I'm teaching you … and I only know the basics."

"Then we'll just have to figure it out together!" he said.

As he stepped to pick his crossbow back up, Mara could hear the catch in his breath. She exhaled slowly and shook off the unease that had begun to set in. They were working on it right now. It would be okay—she'd make sure of it. She and Finn went to the left side of the targets and Kip and Teddy went to the right. Ashroot settled in Finn's chair to watch.

Mara explained what Hodd had said about loading and aiming—and about squeezing the lever rather than pulling—and then asked him to follow her movements as she demonstrated. His arm shook briefly with the effort of pulling the string back into place, and he groaned as his stomach tightened, but he prepared the weapon.

"Now comes the hard part," Mara said. "Actually hitting the mark." She aimed her crossbow at the torso of the nearest dummy, deciding to begin with the broadest target. She took a deep breath, eyed the target, and squeezed. The bolt clipped the very edge of the dummy, just under where the ribs would have been. She sighed. "Well, that's why we're practicing, isn't it?" She beckoned to Finn. "You try."

Finn squared himself before the target and brought the crossbow up as Mara had done. He winced softly as he brought his arm up, and Mara could see a small bloodstain flowering in his shirt from the exertion of increased movement. Taking a deep breath, he fired. The bolt grazed past the head of the dummy and splintered against the cliff face.

Finn groaned, but Mara said, "It's pretty good for your first shot, though. No one expected us to get it first try."

He made a face, clearly indicating *he* had expected to, and drew another bolt from his hip, resting the head of the crossbow on the ground and loading it. His hand shook slightly more as he drew the string back, no doubt quickly fatiguing. His second shot clipped the shoulder. After the second shot, he and Mara took turns, and Mara insisted that he let her help him load the crossbow to prevent him from injuring himself.

She couldn't coddle him. With the state he was in, that would only make things worse. So, she helped him as much as she could, and allowed him to practice longer than she would have wished. As he practiced, each shot was closer and closer to the mark. After a dozen shots, Finn's muscle fatigue became too much, and Mara ordered him to stop and rest. They left Kip and Teddy to continue their practice, unloading their crossbows and quivers on the table before Mara took Finn back to his tent.

"Take off your shirt," she said, opening his bedside trunk and pulling out poultice, ointment, and a small bandage.

Finn obeyed, groaning as he pulled his shirt up over his head. "Yes, Ma."

Mara surveyed his wounds, cleaning and redressing the one that had begun to bleed, before sitting down next to him and beginning to rub the poultice on his scars and spent muscles. He winced.

"Sorry."

"It's alright. I know it's necessary—ah."

"You know," she ventured, "it would probably be best to ease into fighting again. It'll take some time. It's like relearning how to do everything."

Finn sighed sharply. "Well, it's a good thing you're the one mothering me and not my actual mother."

Mara sat silently for a moment. When her fingers glided across the incision from his stomach wound, the one that had nearly killed him, she stopped massaging and looked at him. She couldn't put it off any longer. It was time for the tough love, and she just hoped that he would be responsive.

"Finn, I'm not trying to mother you. Neither one of us really had mothers who would have set a good example in that area. But you know what? You're going to sit here and listen to me for a minute," she said forcefully. "You have to listen to me when it comes to this. Not because I'm the leader of this group. Not because I know more about Earth than the rest of you. But because sometimes you're going to face a fighter that's better than you, who has better weapons than you have, or who knows devious tricks that you don't."

Finn opened his mouth to speak.

"No. Shut up and listen." Mara snapped. "You've been taught your entire life that you have to be the best warrior, and now you've found out that gunslinging makes for a far more deadly warrior, so you want to be like them. You cannot be like them. You will not be like them. You are going to have to come to terms with that and learn how to deal with the fear of a weapon you cannot use." She shoved the poultice jar into his hands and glared deeply into his eyes. "If you succumb to this fear and take a gun again, or you otherwise endanger the rest of us because you can't get it together, you will become the darkness yourself. … And I will kill you if I have to." She stood and opened the tent flap before turning back to look at him. Before she walked away, she added dangerously, "Don't make me."

"Center of the head." Kip squeezed the trigger and whooped when the bolt hit its mark.

Teddy clapped him on the shoulder and grinned. "Okay, now right shoulder," he said, aiming with his own crossbow and firing. The bolt hit its mark.

"Yeah, well, it's not as big of a feat for someone who already knows what they're doing, is it?" Kip joked, placing his foot in the stirrup to ready his crossbow.

Teddy turned around to Kip and drew a bolt, pointing it at Kip. "That's fair, I guess. Now, tell me what your plan is, lad, since Mara is out of earshot."

Kip straightened and loaded his crossbow. "Watch. Far left target." He fired and turned to look at Teddy after the bolt lodged in its mark. "See what movement and control I have, even with a chainmail shirt on?"

Teddy groaned and set his crossbow on the table. "I figured that was it. I told her she isn't going to get me to wear one of those clunky things."

Kip set his crossbow next to Teddy's and sighed. "Look, this is a new experience for you. I get that. I do. But it isn't for me."

Teddy began unstrapping his quiver. "Meaning?"

"Meaning you're a big guy. Forest dwarves are some of the biggest people in Ambergrove. You've been able to live your life using only your leather jerkin for armor, because most of the enemies you face are smaller than you. But," he leaned down and unstrapped his own quiver, "you didn't question Mara wearing chainmail during the gauntlet. So, you know it can be helpful for others. The sea elves use it, and they're among the fiercest. Me—you know my people are defensive by nature because of our size. We all wear scale mail because we know it's what we need to keep us safe. It's a small thing for you to adapt to wearing the chainmail to humor her. Even if you are an old dog," he finished, placing his quiver on the table.

Teddy slowly placed his quiver next to Kip's. "I don't like chainmail. And she worries too much," he muttered.

"Yes, she worries," Kip replied exasperatedly. "But that's why we—" He stopped.

"That's why we love her," Teddy finished.

Kip looked at him and nodded gently.

"Mmm … well … you'll have your time." Teddy smiled softly and turned back toward the main tent.

"And you?" Kip asked. "Are you going to wear the chainmail? It won't hurt you to do it. For her."

Teddy sighed. "I'll think about it."

If things were tense between Finn and Mara for the next few weeks, both of them took great pains not to let it show. Mara was testy in general, because she had sent Keena away to work on talking with Fang and Moon before they went away again. However, before too long, there was too much to do for them to worry much about anything.

They had all gone back to the basics of their training, mainly to humor Finn so he wouldn't feel bad about having to work back up to a hundred percent. Teddy said they'd all gone far too long without structure anyway, and Mara found that she was getting worn out quickly too. After a few weeks, Finn's stomach had healed well enough, and they had all become decently adept with the crossbow. Enough, at least, that Mara was satisfied in their ability to hold their own from a distance. They would still be relying heavily on stealth in order to survive.

One thing that caused some uproar was their selection of melee weapons. Mara had explained that for this part they would need to travel light. They would need to be using small, fast weapons. Her battle axe and Kip's hammer would have to stay behind. They would take crossbows and throwing knives, Finn would use his dirks, Teddy and Mara would use their swords—and Mara still would not go without her small axes—and Kip would have to select a weapon from the ones Teddy had brought from Gylden Grotto.

Finally, after much grumbling, he selected a spear. Mara had marveled at this, but he'd argued that the range of the spear would allow him to swipe with it and hit the enemy weapons from a distance. Unlike the javelins he'd previously fought with, this spear was entirely made of steel and would handle being used as a blunt weapon as well as a piercing one. Plus, it would be quicker and less encumbering than the hammer—and could double as a walking stick.

After a month of vigorous retraining, they loaded up the dinghy—which Finn had decided to name *Earthbiter*—and said goodbye to Ashroot before setting sail back to Chaosland. Before casting off, Mara had everyone gather in the main tent so she could take a group photo, and she handed it to Ashroot with one last hug before returning the camera to her tent and boarding *Earthbiter.*

Despite everything that had happened the last time they went there, Mara felt like a phoenix reborn. They knew what they would be facing, they had a plan to face it, dear Keena was scrambling around in their tiny boat with them this time, chasing after one of Kip's toys, and steering the dinghy into open waters, bearing a look of utmost grumpiness, was Teddy … clad in a chainmail shirt.

Chapter Eight

A Crossbow to a Gunfight

Although it was more spacious than the raft, the dinghy didn't offer much privacy. Thankfully, the many months together had allowed everyone to get at least somewhat used to their companions' sleeping habits, if at a further distance. Teddy snored loudly, but to Mara this had become a soothing sound. Familiar. She slept soundly next to him with Keena curled up in her arms, and Kip lay next to her.

Finn volunteered to take command of the dinghy to allow the rest of them to get some sleep. The anticipation of heading back to Chaosland had left him too tense to get any rest of his own. After reaching up gingerly to redirect the sail, Finn surveyed the ship and met Kip's steely gaze.

"I thought you were asleep," Finn whispered.

Kip shook his head slowly.

Finn exhaled sharply and tiptoed over to where Kip lay before speaking. "You need to get some rest before we get there, you know."

"So do you," Kip replied, "Especially since you aren't going to rest again until we head back to Questhaven."

"Why is that?" Finn snapped, coming to a stop looming over Kip.

Sighing, Kip sat up. With Finn still looming simply due to being head and shoulders taller than him, Kip replied, "Come on, Finn. You and I both know that going back there is a trial in itself for you."

"Wh—" Finn began loudly.

"Shh! Do you want to wake the dwarves?" Kip hissed. "Sit here." The gnome gestured to the bench beside him. Finn plopped down next to Kip, and the ship rocked slightly. "I know that look in your eye. I've seen it my entire life," the gnome said fiercely.

Finn glared at him. "What do you see?"

"Well … you're like Teddy," Kip began. "You're used to being the biggest and the scariest. The deadliest. But sometimes being, big, scary, and deadly means being evil too. It's not something to aspire to … or to be ashamed of fearing."

Finn glared at the deck for a moment, but when he opened his mouth to retort, Keena had stirred. She whimpered and woofed and wagged her tail, trampling all over the formerly sleeping forms of the forest dwarves, clearly trying to explain something very important. Mara groaned and sat up, and Finn asked, "What is she saying now?"

Mara yawned. "She says there's a friend nearby. Someone she wants to be her friend." She listened to the pup's excited yips and continued, "It smells like another animal."

Teddy peered out over the water. "I wonder if it's—"

"Excalibur!" Mara cried. She jumped up as the horse came into view on the bank of Chaosland, and his whinny met her ears. Unceremoniously, Keena tumbled out of her mama's lap and onto the deck as Mara jumped up to wave at the horse. Keena, startled at the sudden turn of events, thumped her tail excitedly when she saw what Mara was looking at, and both dragonwolves impatiently waited for the ship to near the shore.

Mara met the silver horse in the shallow water, and he huffed with pleasure as she wrapped her arms around his neck.

Nice lady, she heard in a booming voice.

"Wait, I can understand you?" Mara whipped around to see the dinghy make it to the bank right after her. She turned to her uncle. "Teddy, why didn't you tell me we could talk to horses?"

"We usually can't," Teddy called, grunting as he and the men hauled the dinghy up on the bank. He dusted off his hands and walked over to stand beside Mara, giving the horse a rub on the nose. "What do you think of Mara?" Teddy asked him.

Nice lady, Mara heard again.

"See?" she exclaimed, rubbing Excalibur's neck.

"Yes, I do," Teddy replied slowly. "You've made an impression on this fellow."

"What do you mean?"

"I didn't understand what he said, Mara."

She stopped petting Excalibur and peered at him for a moment before turning to Teddy. "I don't get it."

"Horses are usually worker friends," Teddy explained. "We train them and care for them, but they have to really trust us to talk to us. This boy doesn't trust me, but he trusts you."

Nice lady, Excalibur repeated, huffing into Mara's hair.

"And you're a good boy!" she replied, hugging his neck.

The horse looked at her, and she could see the recognition in his amber eyes. She quickly explained to him why he could understand her and what Teddy had said about her understanding him. *What is 'Excalibur?'* he asked.

"Oh! Umm . . ." Mara scratched her neck awkwardly. "It's—uh—it's what I named you. I'm called Mara. I didn't know what to call you."

He huffed. *My mother called me Swish.*

"Swish it is then!" Mara replied. "So, what—"

"What?"

Mara turned. She'd forgotten about her companions until Finn had spoken. Finn frowned, confusion and frustration showing in his deeply furrowed brow. Teddy stood next to him, arms crossed, grinning. Kip sat on the ground with Keena, scratching her belly and laughing softly.

"He says his name is Swish," she explained.

Swish? Swish to be Keena's friend? Keena wrenched out of Kip's grip and barreled over toward Swish and Mara.

Feeling the slightest twitch of alarm from Swish, Mara grabbed Keena mid-run and hefted her up into her arms. Before long, the pup would be too big for Mara to hold. For now, this snatch and minor control settled the silver horse. His nostrils flared as he sniffed Keena's face and gently nipped her ear. She licked his nose.

Yes, small friend, Swish said.

"Great!" Mara exclaimed. She turned around and translated for the others, "They're going to be friends."

Teddy chuckled. "Yeah, I can see that."

"Should we maybe hide the dinghy and go somewhere sheltered to rest and prepare?" Kip asked, raising a brow and rolling his eyes pointedly toward Finn.

Mara glanced over at Finn. "Uh, yes!" She released Keena and turned back to Swish. "Where have you been living since we left? Can you take us there?"

Swish bowed his head, what Mara suspected was a horse nod, and said, *Follow me.*

Swish had stayed around the pen they had made, waiting for them to come back for him. They hefted the dinghy into the bushes they'd hidden the raft in before, and they set up a temporary camp in the now-ruined pen they'd made for Swish. Kip and Finn went off to forage for supper and gather firewood, with Keena grudgingly dogging behind, leaving Mara to talk with Swish and Teddy to observe. The dwarves sat on the ground in the pasture—Teddy with the Chaosland map and some spare paper—and Swish lay down next to them.

"So," Mara began, "what have you been doing here since we left? Did you have enough food and water?"

Yes, you left me safe and taken care of here, Swish replied. *After so long, I just left to see if I could find you.*

"I'm so sorry we were gone so long," she said miserably. "We didn't want to leave you here, but we knew we couldn't take you with us."

Swish bowed his head as if to say he understood.

"Well … would you tell me about this place? What did you do here before we found you? What was it like?" Mara crossed her legs and settled in for his reply.

"Why don't you begin at the beginning? Life story type deal?" Teddy added, gesturing to Mara to convey this to him. Swish bowed his head again.

I was born in a city. Not the one you found me in. A different one. Further from here. They had all the mothers in a big building together. They took me away one day when

I was very young, and I never saw her again. They didn't call me Swish either. They called me Gunpowder. Swish whinnied sadly, and Mara frowned and translated for Teddy as Swish continued, *They started training us early on. We pulled their wagons, and they used their angry weapons around us to make sure that we could keep pulling them no matter what.* His eyes glistened, and he twitched slightly. *If we were scared, they would punish us and keep the loud noises and fire up close until we didn't move.*

"That's barbaric," Mara whispered, shaking her head. She tenderly rubbed Swish's neck.

After she'd translated for him, Teddy replied, "Desensitization is an important part of training a horse, but there's a fine line between training and trauma." He shook his head in disgust.

Mara turned back to the horse. "What did they have you do?" she asked quietly.

We just pulled the wagons. Every few days, they would take us out to another city with a wagonload of supplies. We'd rest in that city for a few days, and they'd take us to the next city with another load, he explained.

"Wait, so all they had you do was transport supplies?" Mara asked.

Swish bowed his horse nod. *I've been on every route to every city.*

"Well … there's an idea," Teddy murmured, understanding that the bow was a nod, even if he didn't understand the words.

"What is?" Mara asked.

"Once the lads get back, we can all get together and talk about it," he explained. Grinning, he added, "I do believe I have a plan."

Kip and Finn returned shortly after with their spoils. Before long, the rabbits were skinned, gutted, and roasting on a spit. Kip had also brought back a few apples he'd found, mainly for Swish—which the horse gratefully gobbled up before running out to the waterfall at the other end of the pasture with Keena at his heels. The rest of them all gathered around the fire as Teddy began.

"Alright, lads and lass, Swish has given us a unique opportunity. We need to figure out how things work around here. We need to be able to blend in so we can go all over this land and find this leader. Swish can help with that."

"How?" Kip asked, rotating the rabbits on the spit.

"It's perfect!" Mara interjected. "If we go back to Fear, I know there were dusters in the general store we could get. If we wear dusters over our clothes, and we travel from city to city with Swish and the cart—or get a wagon—it will help us to infiltrate the cities and maybe get information from one of the baddies we find."

Teddy grinned and nodded.

The next morning, they hitched Swish up to the cart, loaded up enough supplies to make it convincing, and began their journey north toward Fear. After a few hours, Swish warmed up to Keena, realizing perhaps that she was just an excited baby, and he allowed her to ride on his back for the remainder of the trip. Mara grudgingly permitted this, telling Keena that if they heard anything suspicious, she was immediately to hide in the cart. No matter how convincing their ruse, any of these agents of chaos would surely realize a dragonwolf was out of place—or at least they would kill each other for the opportunity to take their leader such a weapon.

For now, Keena yipped and squeaked as she stood on Swish's back, flapping her wings and pretending to fly. Mara turned to her uncle. "Teddy?" she asked.

"Yes, lass?"

"When is Keena supposed to start flying?"

Teddy rubbed his beard and said thoughtfully, "See the tricky thing here is that no one has seen a dragonwolf for centuries. That's not the sort of thing people typically know."

"Oh."

"Well, now, hang on. We can still make a guess. Most flying creatures begin to test their wings when they're still very small—around what we would say is toddler age. This is helpful for us with Keena, because it would also be when she's able to talk to us properly and begin to think for herself."

"We're about there now," Kip said.

"Yes, it seems we are. Look!" Finn added, pointing at Swish's back.

Every few flaps, Keena was able to hold herself up for just a moment before falling back onto Swish's back. There wasn't a dragon around to teach her how to fly like the wolves had been teaching her to speak, but at least if what Mara had heard of birds were true, birds just booted their young out of the nest one day and expected them to figure it out.

"I suppose using a horse for training wheels is better than the alternative," Mara offered, smiling at Keena's efforts. The smile turned into a cackle when the men all asked, "What are training wheels?"

They made it to Fear around suppertime. Not wanting to dally too long out in the open, they headed to the Sanderson house again. They stored the cart in the attached stable, though Mara insisted that Swish come into the house with them to keep him safe. After their meal, Keena curled up with the horse on the living room floor and the others headed to the bedrooms they'd slept in the previous time—apart from Kip, who bunked with Finn this time.

Kip lay in bed with his back to Finn's. As he suspected, the darker the day became, the more frantic was Finn's breathing. He'd waited for this chance, hoping that when it came he would have the clarity to help Finn the right way.

Kip's fellow soldier, Hamek, had faced an enemy so foul he had lost a leg and nearly died. For years, he'd woken up in the night with fear sweats. He lived in terror, his mind always bringing him back to the day he'd lost his leg. He'd lost his battle with the fear and the pain of the harshest memory, as many other good people did, and Kip would not let the same happen to the sea elf. Not again.

He reached out into his pack and procured a candle. Wordlessly, he lit the candle and placed it on the bedside table.

"What are you doing?" Finn asked quietly.

"Ah, I just think this room is a little musty. It could do with a bit of light. Not as pleasant being here with you as it was to be with Mara," Kip replied with a gentle nudge. He rolled onto his back and interlaced his fingers on his stomach, adding, "A little light in the dark is always good, isn't it?"

"Yeah."

The reply was barely a whisper, but with his arm against Finn's back, Kip could feel the beat slowing. "Sometimes a story helps too," Kip ventured. "Do you like to fall asleep to a story?"

"Dunno. I never have."

"You've never heard a story? At all? Was the one for Mara's birthday your first one?" Kip asked.

"It was."

"Well, we'll definitely need to fix that! Settle in and let me tell you a story."

Kip waited for a retort of some kind, but none came. "I used to tell Loli stories all the time," he said, leaning over again and this time retrieving a small piece of wood and small knife from his pack. "I used to carve something while I told the story, so that's the only way I know how. Anyway, here we go."

He sat up and began to make delicate little cuts as he told his tale. "Long ago, there was a little boy named Rueh. Rueh was the fiercest boy in his village. He used to defend his little sister from any pests that came into his home, and one time, he even faced a fox. After facing the fox, he decided he was a man and was ready to join the village soldiers.

"He did. He wanted to make his family proud, and he wanted to help others. To be a protector. So, when he was old enough, he joined the soldiers. But the young boy wasn't ready for the fight ahead. In his first fight, they tangled with a hill lion. The other men wanted to see if he could make it on his own, so they let him fight by himself, and he lost.

"The boy was so badly injured, and he went home to his family afraid of what he had seen. What had happened to him had scarred him. He was afraid to run into another hill lion. He was afraid of being afraid. He lived in fear for years, but eventually, he felt that his end was near if he did not learn to live with this experience.

"So, he went to the wise woman in town. She told him that to face his fear he needed to get used to it. Don't try to hide the experience or the loss. Embrace what had happened to him and what could happen again. Realize that fear is natural, and learn to use that fear to drive him to do his best in all things. She gave him a hill lion necklace and told him to carry his fear with him. When he realized that it was just an object and not a monster, when he realized that his fear was quellable, if not conquerable, he would be able to fight again, and live again without being imprisoned by his fear.

"He wore the wise woman's necklace every day, and he looked at it often. Seeing the fear as a harmless object allowed him to lessen its hold on him. That fear cannot and will not ever go away, but he was able to face it and to learn better ways to keep it at bay when it really mattered. Over the years, he became a devoted soldier and had many successful missions and many more scars and scrapes, but he never forgot what the wise woman had said, and he always wore the token she'd gifted to him."

The room was silent for a moment, but for the sound of Kip's carving. Finally, Finn rolled to lay on his back and looked at Kip. "What was that all for, eh?" he asked.

Kip carved one last groove in the wood and blew on it before turning to the sea elf. He held out his hand. "It was for you. You are not the first soldier to be injured severely or to be taken in by fear after near-death. Fear takes hold at night, because in the dark, your brain imagines the awful things in the space you cannot see and tricks you into thinking that they're there. Fear takes hold often, but if you carry your pain with you, you will learn how to live despite it."

Kip handed Finn his carving. It was a small, wooden bullet. Finn's eyes widened as Kip dropped the bullet into his hand. Before Finn could speak, Kip reached a hand under the neckline of his own shirt and pulled out a small metal necklace. A hill lion.

"W-what? You?" Finn asked quietly.

Kip shook his head. "These are given to the soldiers in the Big Hill before their first mission—to remind us all that we will face dangers and overcome them. We will be in fear, but we must not let it overcome us," he explained.

"But you don't know, though. You don't know what it feels like," Finn said harshly.

"I do and I do not. I have not faced a horror so dark as what you have faced, but I have few areas of my body that are not covered in scars from battle. And I have known men who have fought the battle with the darkest enemy and lost … and men who have won," Kip said. He stuffed the necklace back into his shirt. It was a token he kept, but not one that he wore. He just hoped that wearing it would help him reach the sea elf. Kip sighed. "Fear is a part of you now, whether you like it or not. It is an undefeatable enemy. Only you can find out how to best live despite your fear, but you are never alone."

Finn's hand closed around the wooden bullet, and he rolled back over. "What if I cannot live despite it?" he asked.

"Then you must live *to* spite it," Kip replied. "Figure out what fills your heart to the brim. What you cannot breathe without. Live for that. Live to show your fear that it may weaken you, but it will never defeat you."

Finn sniffled, and Kip would not acknowledge what he knew the elf to be ashamed of, so he hummed softly until the sea elf's breathing slowed to sleep. Then Kip fell into a dream and saw that which he could not live without.

The next morning, after a quick breakfast, they headed to the general store. Careful not to draw attention to themselves, they left Swish and Keena behind in the house when they went. In the back of the store, they sorted through the racks of leather dusters, each selecting one that was slightly too large to make sure they could still move to fight when necessary. The trouble was that the ones that were large enough to fit over their armor were too large in other places.

They each slipped their dusters on and buttoned them. Thankfully, the dusters all sported two inner pockets and two outer pockets at the hips. Mara stuffed her hands deep into hers before buttoning it up. All modern women knew that pockets were a luxury, and although there was less need for pockets in Ambergrove, Mara was still elated to find them. Once the dusters were buttoned up, and they put on wide-brimmed hats for good measure, they could easily pass for locals—from a distance, anyway.

Teddy hunted for basic sewing materials next and slipped them into his pocket. When Finn raised a brow, he said, "Well, it won't be nice stitching like Ashroot's, but at least I can trim these down so we don't trip over these silly things in battle."

"Death by coat. Not a good way to go," Mara joked.

Finn smirked, and Kip laughed, but Teddy scowled. "You laugh, but you'd be surprised what ill can befall a man in ill-fitting clothing."

Finn laid a hand on Teddy's shoulder. "It's okay, big man. If you perish on this journey due to tripping over your petticoat, we'll be sure to tell everyone a grand tale."

"A big fish story!" Mara added.

"What's a big fish story?" Finn asked.

"Well, basically, whenever a fisherman tells a story about a great fish they caught, the fish gets bigger every time," she replied.

"Yeah, that sounds like fish people," Kip jeered, nudging Finn gently before adding in a theatrical and self-important voice, "The legend of Tederen and the great, brown coat will be told for generations to come!"

"Yeah, alright, alright. You can sew your own coats then. The stuff's over there," Teddy grunted. He turned and went to the grocery section and grinned when the others all grabbed small sewing kits and tucked them in their pockets.

Mara went next to shelves of folded clothes, rifling through to see if she could find anything else useful. Picking up the ugliest sweater she'd ever seen, she threw her head back and laughed.

Keena whined and whimpered, chewing and pawing at the strange, new obstacle. She growled the sound of a puppy frustrated at a new thing that doesn't work as it should—and this thing had her trapped.

"Keena Keena, don't fuss about it so much," Mara said soothingly. "You'll get used to it."

Why, mama, why *get used to it?* Keena whined. She flopped down on the floor in the living room, rolled around like a toddler having a tantrum, and let out a prolonged, pitiful howl.

Mara sat down on the floor next to her. "Come on, sit up and listen," she said.

Keena groaned and obeyed, snorting a little puff of smoke in frustration as she sat and glowered at Mara. Ignoring the muffled laughing coming from behind her, Mara smiled at Keena and adjusted the sweater. It was a dirty-brown knitted thing, made dirtier by its obvious use, and it was riddled with small holes, likely from another unsuspecting wearer demonstrating frustration. Sporting simple leg holes and a buttoned strap across the bottom, a solid brown mass covered Keena's wings entirely, keeping them neatly tucked at her sides. Mara clasped the hood and pulled it up over the dragonwolf's ears, covering her small horns.

Keena huffed again, and Mara gave her a scritch under her chin and sighed. "I know you don't like it, Keena. I know. It holds your wings, and it's just weird and different. But sometimes you have to deal with uncomfortable things so you can stay safe. You see, this sweater will disguise who you are, just like these big coats and hats do for the rest of us. That way, you can walk around out here, and you don't have to worry about anyone getting you. You see," she paused a moment and rubbed her nape awkwardly, "dragonwolves like you haven't been out in the world in a really long time, because there's bad people who'd want to make you do bad things. It's just to help keep you safe."

"And it's cute too!" Kip called.

Kip and Finn sat on the couch in the living room. Teddy had taken Swish out for a walk and some grass, and they were taking the opportunity of his absence to rehem their dusters. Finn nudged Kip at his remark, causing Kip to prick himself with his needle. Kip swore and sucked on his finger.

Finn turned to Keena. "Think about me," he said. "I always wear bright colors—purples, blues, and greens. My people always have. But I'm wearing this," he held up the poorly-hemmed duster for her to see, "because I know this is the best way for us to go through this place. Your mama just wants what's best for you."

"It's true!" Kip added. "It's just a bonus that it's cute—on you, not on him." He gestured to Finn before continuing to work on his hemming.

Keena snorted and laid on the floor, grumbling, *Fine.*

"Good, good!" Mara said, pushing Keena to her side and rubbing her belly until her grumbles turned into playful growls. She booped her pup's nose lightly, and Keena bared her teeth in a puppy grin. Mara grinned back, then stood and grabbed her own duster from the arm of the couch and plopped into the adjacent armchair to begin her own hemming.

The following morning, once they'd traded the cart for a wagon and loaded it with supplies, and Teddy had done his own hemming, they all donned their new dusters—sure to wear their chainmail underneath this time—hitched Swish to the wagon, and continued through the streets of Fear. Finn marked certain locations on the city map as they passed and investigated—a few more general stores and a few stables mainly. Mara wanted to release all the horses, but Swish explained that they would just train more, and new foals would have to suffer for nothing. Grudgingly, they continued through the town until a sight at the outskirts gave them pause.

It was a similar sight to theirs. A horse pulled a wagonload of supplies. Four figures in dusters walked alongside the wagon while a fifth drove. As the mirror group approached, Mara could pick out two goblins, one walking and one driving the wagon, two humans, and one—

"Giant," Teddy grumbled. "That big one there is a giant. She'll be tough if we have to fight."

As if she heard, the giant woman stepped ahead of her group and raised a hand for them to wait. She wore a black duster that flapped open to reveal blue jeans and a white shirt poking out from under a red waistcoat. Her jet-black hair was cropped short and spiked in all directions. She stepped toward them and whipped her duster back to rest a hand on the revolver at her hip.

"State your business," she ordered. Her amber eyes narrowed, and she scowled.

Before Mara could figure out what to do, Teddy stepped forward. "I could ask the same to you," he said haughtily, crossing his arms and leering at her.

"You're a forest dwarf!" she gasped, tightening her grip on her revolver. "What are you doing here?"

"Half forest dwarf," he lied, maintaining his gruff demeanor. "It's not unheard of for us to turn on the ridiculous notions of tree-loving fools. One day they will taste the ichor of chaos. Now, if you don't take that paw off your revolver, I'll have to show you just how devoted to Haeyla we are," he finished loudly.

At the mention of the goddess of suffering, the giant relaxed somewhat. "Apologies, brother," she said. "Can't be too careful around Fear nowadays, after what happened here a few months ago." Mara shifted uneasily, but the giant continued, "Barbarians came here and killed all our men on a routine supply run. Jumped them, the savages. Left their bodies to rot in one of the houses."

"Despicable! Haeyla will come for them," Teddy replied. "Now, what's your business here?"

"Supply run."

"Well, it seems someone must have gotten their schedules mixed up," Teddy replied, tapping the wagon.

"If we keep double-dipping in the supplies here, we won't have enough supplies to last for our settlements. That shows you what the sergeants know," she joked.

"The higher up the command you are, the less you know about the actual workings of things, right?" Teddy chuckled. "Speaking of, we'd best be on our way. I don't want to deal with his wrath today."

"Today? Where are you headed? What city?" the giant asked.

Teddy paused. He twitched slightly, just enough for Mara to tell he was uneasy. What could they say? They didn't know any other cities. He cleared his throat, taking a wild shot, "We're headed to the next city up, along the coastline."

"Darkness?" one of the humans piped up excitedly. His partner gave him a thump and he quieted.

"Yes, that's it precisely," Teddy replied quickly.

The giant turned to look at her companions, whose faces tightened. The driver hopped down from the wagon and reached back into it for something. The giant turned her amber eyes back toward Teddy, and when she turned, her hand was back on her gun. "You see ..." she began slowly, "the sergeant in charge of supply in Darkness is a woman. If you were from Darkness, you would know that. And seeing as we're the first group to come to Fear since the massacre—because of the ridiculousness that others were afraid to come here—she can't have sent you. So … again, who are you and why are you here?"

"It's not happening with them," Kip whispered, his hat tipped low enough they couldn't see his mouth moving. "We're going to have to fight."

"Get ready," Mara whispered. "Keena, you hide in the wagon and stay out of the fighting. Get ready, boys. Count of three. One, two …" Mara screamed in mock horror and pointed out into the distance. As their enemy turned to see the danger, Mara and her companions drew their crossbows.

Chapter Nine

Quelling Fear

Finn squeezed the lever of his crossbow, and his bolt whizzed past the giant's ear.

"To arms!" the giant shouted.

Finn saw the flash of the barrel as the nearest person drew a revolver, and something strange came over him. Without realizing what he was doing, his feet had carried him away from the danger to hunker behind the wagon. He shivered. He moved mechanically to reload his crossbow, hearing shouts echoing in his ears. Eyes widening, he dropped the crossbow and smashed his hands to either side of his head.

As bullets flew around him, Finn was no longer in the street hiding behind the wagon. He was back in the ruined building their first trip to Fear, being shot over and over again and wondering if that was the last, wondering when he would die. He pressed his head as hard as he could, trying to force the pictures out, trying to drown out the banging of gunfire.

"Finn! Finn, we need your help! Finn, there's a goblin coming! *Finn!*"

He heard the screams, but he couldn't move. All the training, all the experience, and he couldn't move. A gunshot rang in his ears, too loud to drown out this time, and he felt the impact. His hands jerked down to the bullet in his chest. He looked down frantically. No blood. The bullet was lodged into the links of the chainmail and hadn't made it through even to graze the quilted shirt. Finn looked up at the goblin and grinned. Then he grabbed his crossbow and fired.

Mara made it to Finn right as the goblin dropped, and she stepped over the fallen form to place a hand on her friend's shoulder. "Are you good? You have to tell me right now if you're not," she commanded. Looking into Finn's eyes, Mara saw a spark. He nodded. She clasped his arm and helped him to his feet, and they both crouched behind the wagon to reload. Teddy was standing just inside one of the near buildings, shooting from the window like someone from a mustache movie, and Kip crouched behind a bush.

Mara peeked out from behind the wagon, and a bullet whizzed past her to lodge into the wood right next to her face. She ducked back. Both goblins and one of the humans were down. Mara and Teddy both had put a bolt in the giant, and she was still coming at them with her second revolver.

Mara turned to Finn. "Count of three," she said. "We both jump out from different sides of the wagon. Aim for the head."

Finn nodded. Mara counted down, and they burst out from behind the wagon. The giant fired at her and hit Mara in the shoulder right as Mara's shot hit her in the throat. The giant fell. Seeing all his companions down, the final human ran toward their wagon, so Finn changed his aim and managed to clip the human in the leg—just enough to slow him down—and charged. When the human got to the wagon, Swish let out a shrill whinny and the horse bolted, taking the wagon with it. As the human turned, betrayed, back to the sound of the whinny that lost him his only hope, Finn caught up to him and rammed the butt of his crossbow into the human's face. The sea elf staggered and dropped the crossbow just as Mara slammed into him and gave him a fierce hug.

"Great job!" Teddy exclaimed. He came out of the building he'd been camped in and gestured over to Kip, calling, "Grab some rope from the wagon and tie him up."

Kip obeyed, pausing to give Swish some praise and a good neck rub for the assist, and then he and Mara tied the human up while Teddy gave Finn a hard clap on the shoulder, and they began to clean up the scene. The patrol's horse hadn't gone far, so Mara went to calm him and bring him back. Once the wagon was back to the downed patrol, they set the horse free and piled all the bodies in the back of the enemy wagon. After pulling it into a nearby alley, Kip and Mara carried the human back to their own wagon and led Swish back to a large building across from the alley.

Teddy tied the human to a dining chair so they could first assess the damage to their companions. Finn probably had a cracked rib from the bullet to his chest, but he was otherwise unscathed. Kip had only been grazed in the leg, so it just required a little patching up. He did this himself. Mara's final shot to the shoulder had pierced a rusty spot in her chainmail, and the bullet had sunk about half an inch into the meat of her shoulder. Teddy worked to patch this up, cleaning out the rust—tightlipped when Mara pointed out that, unlike her chainmail, his had protected him entirely. He had been hit three times, and the worst he would have would be a deep bruise.

So, once Mara and Kip were patched, they sat down along a wall, within view of the human but at a fair enough distance to go unheard, and waited for the human to wake. As she inspected her chainmail, Mara was the first to speak. "We'll need to get chainmail repair supplies the next time someone goes to Gylden Grotto."

"So much for your plan, I guess," Teddy grumbled.

Mara opened her mouth to retort, but Finn replied first. "Actually, she was right. I was shot in the chest. I should have died instantly, but the chainmail blocked it. You were shot three times and you have barely a scratch. I'm alive because of this, and so are you. A few repairs are a small price to pay for our lives." He glared at his bullet necklace and the others sat quietly for a moment, watching. Finn continued, "Anyway, what are we going to do about him?" He gestured to the human.

"I don't know about you, but I want to know about Darkness," Kip said. "What is it? Where is it? Why was he so interested in the idea we were there? … And how many others are there?"

"I bet there's a lot we can learn about Chaosland from him. If someone knows how to get him to tell us?" Mara added, turning to Teddy.

Teddy sat on the end of their little line, and he glanced down to see everyone looking expectantly at him. He sighed and rubbed his bald head. "Yes, I think I can manage," he said finally.

"But we're not going to torture him, right?" Mara asked quietly, suddenly concerned

The men all said no—fervently—in unison.

"There's no honor in torture," Teddy said in earnest, shaking his head. "Never—nor will anyone else do it under my watch." The others nodded in agreement.

"Good," she replied.

"Though there are other ways to get him to talk," Kip added, smiling at Mara.

It was so easy for Mara to forget that Kip was a soldier. Although he was perhaps only a few years older than she was, this world was different. He'd probably been training to be a guard since his early teens. He'd have at least five years of experience under his belt. He and Teddy could figure it out. Surely, they knew what to do. There was a groan as the human stirred.

Kip slapped Mara's thigh and said, "Well, time to get to work!"

The human's brown duster had been removed to ensure he couldn't conceal a weapon. He wore blue jeans and lace-up work boots underneath, as the giant had done, and his white shirt and blue waistcoat were stained with blood. Finn's blow had busted his nose. As he stirred, strapped to the chair, his blue eyes snapped wildly open, and his mass of straw-colored hair only served to make him look wilder. When he spoke, however, his voice was soft and small.

"W-who are you?" he asked.

Kip sat backwards in another dining chair, just a few feet away from the man, and Teddy loomed from a decidedly dark corner. It was Kip who spoke first. "Neither of us are the one who rang your bell, not to worry." The gnome tapped his own head as if in reference and smiled.

Mara sat at the back of the room next to Finn with Keena laying in her lap, listening but out of view. She smiled. *So, he's good cop.*

"G-good, I guess," the human replied.

"My name's Gaetan," Kip lied, using the name of a gnome from the popular story Salali had told for Mara's last birthday. The human had apparently not heard the story before. "What's your name, human?" Kip pressed.

"Frank," the human answered quietly. There was no way to know if he spoke true.

"Well, Frank, why don't you and I have a little chat about this place, and we'll see about getting our lady to bring you some water? How does that sound?" Kip asked, smiling at the human and making his voice gentle.

Frank's eyes hardened and he straightened as much as he could while bound to the chair. "Betray my people? No, thank you, *little man*. I'm loyal." He spat at Kip's face and missed.

Kip just stared at him, maintaining his smile as Teddy slowly emerged from the shadows. His face and hands bore bloody smears that had not been there before, and he glowered wickedly as he silently moved toward Frank. Teddy wiped a bloodied hand on the human's shirt before settling to stand behind him with a hand resting on either shoulder. He leaned forward so he could hiss terribly in the man's ear.

"Loyal?" he asked. "Do you think the others were loyal to you, *Frank*? Do you think anyone cares if you come back? Do you think anyone will come to save you?" Teddy chuckled evilly. "You're the *little man* here, Frank. Loyalty? Loyalty is for big men." Teddy squeezed the human's shoulders.

Frank shivered.

"Everyone in this room is a big man—or woman—except you, Frank." Kip said softly. "But that's not your fault. We're all a team. Isn't that how things are supposed to be?" Teddy clapped the human on the shoulder, making him jump. Frank nodded miserably.

It seems as though the fear of torture is *torture*, Mara thought. Keena yawned and crawled out of Mara's lap to lay in Finn's. Mara leaned forward and crossed her legs, watching as Teddy leaned back down to hiss in the man's ear. "Now—if you aren't the big man, why don't you tell us who is?"

Too far too soon. Frank jerked his head to the side in a poorly-placed headbutt. Teddy remained eerily silent, but he stood and turned away, standing behind Frank where the human couldn't see the effort it took to remain silent. When Teddy turned toward Mara, she saw that he now sported a bloodied nose like Frank's. Frank thrashed in his chair, trying poorly to free himself. With a growl, he thrashed a little too much and tipped the chair. He squeaked as it fell, and his head bounced off the floor. He let out a string of curses. Teddy threw back his head and laughed a deep, throaty laugh. Mara stifled a giggle.

Kip slowly stood and settled himself cross-legged on the floor in front of Frank, who peered angrily up at him. When Kip spoke, there was a heavily-inserted kindness. "Now, Frank, why would you do this to yourself? We're just having a conversation. Don't you want to be comfortable and just chat with us for a bit?" Frank glared. Kip continued, "Now, we can fix this situation you put yourself in, but you'll need to answer just one question for me first. I promise it's not about your boss. Just answer one question, and we'll right this chair."

Frank glared at Kip for a moment, and then nodded curtly. Mara's eyes darted to Teddy, who slowly grinned and winked back at her.

"What do you want to know, gnome?" Frank asked, hatred spilling out into every syllable.

"How do you *live* in a place like this? I mean, I wouldn't want to live here, especially with so many half-ruined buildings and all the food coming out of a jar! How do you do it?" Kip asked.

"I *don't* live in a place like this. This is the lost city. We just come here for supplies. My city is beautiful and alive. Savages like you wouldn't fit in there,"

"Darkness?"

"Yeah," Frank snapped. "It's a thriving city. Imagine this city in its prime. Bustling with people of all kinds, all with the same glorious idea for the world." Frank's eyes glistened, and he looked almost manic. "Skyscrapers tall as the eye can see, elegant mansions, and uses for electricity Earthers have hardly dreamed of. And within? Not just general stores with old junk. Gunsmiths, tanners, power shops. War horses are trained in special arenas and working factories send darkness in a cloud throughout the city. We. Are. Everywhere." He laughed.

He's seriously bragging about smog? Mara thought incredulously.

"Hmm, that certainly sounds like a wonderful place. If only there were more places like that around here," Kip said, standing and righting Frank's chair.

Frank laughed drily as the chair thudded back into place. "Oh, oh, you don't know the half of it. There's a half a dozen cities just like

Darkness—and some are even bigger! All are filled with people like me who follow the Great Harbinger."

"The Great Harbinger? Sounds impressive. Who's he?" Kip asked, smiling at Frank.

Frank froze. "H-how did you do that?" His voice cracked, panicked. "Nothing. Nobody." He fell silent and looked at the ground.

"No, no, that's okay, Frank. We can take a break for now." Kip raised his head and nodded to Mara. "Dear lady, could I trouble you to come with me to get some refreshment for Frank?" He turned his back slightly so Frank couldn't see, and then he made a flapping gesture to indicate she should bring Keena along. Teddy moved to block Frank's view so he couldn't see Keena trot past. Mara walked with Kip until they were out of earshot and turned on the kitchen sink to further drown their voices as he spoke.

"Okay, so there's seven fully-functioning cities around here. That's much more than we thought we'd be dealing with. We need to figure out where they are. There has to be something in their supplies that will point us in the right direction," Kip explained. "Take your horn with you in case someone else comes and you need to call for us, and you and Keena go search the bodies and the wagon. See what you can see." Mara nodded, and Kip touched her arm lightly and added, "Be careful out there."

Mara nodded again and smiled. "Well, I would tell you to be careful in here, but everything you're doing is careful and calculated. It's peak film noir watching you and Teddy work off each other." Kip raised a brow, so she added quickly, "Never mind. Don't worry about that. It's *amazing* what you're doing in there. That's all you need to know."

"And Teddy is so scary, right?"

"Yes! Oh, man. Where did he get that blood to wipe all over himself?"

As if he heard, Teddy whistled loudly, clearly beckoning for Kip to return. Kip quickly got a cup of water from the sink, winked at Mara, and headed back into their little interrogation room.

As soon as they stepped outside, Keena began talking a mile a minute. Mara listened to her yammer on about how it had felt to be in a fight again—her first time since the goblins, even if she wasn't really *fighting* this time—and how Teddy was trying to act all scary, but she could smell that it wasn't blood he had on his face, and wow, Kip was so scared, but somehow, he made the other guy feel more scared. Mara laughed at this. She would never have been able to tell that Kip was just projecting confidence. It made the whole situation more impressive.

They reached the secluded wagon, and Mara hopped up into it. When Keena whined, she said, "No, no, Keena. I want you to be here with me, but I don't want you this close to them, okay?"

Keena snorted and sat. *Fine.*

Mara turned and looked at the wagons. *Mistake.* Her stomach gurgled. She was thankful it had been a while since she'd eaten. She'd been in Ambergrove for nearly a year and a half, she'd fought, and she'd killed, but this was the first time she'd really seen the aftermath. The stench was immense, and flies had begun to settle around the wagon. It was something out of a horror movie.

Keena scratched at the wagon. *Mama, what's wrong? Are you okay, Mama?* she whined.

Mara turned to her pup and smiled. "Yes, I'm just fine, Keena. Don't worry," she said, watching, relieved, as Keena's tail slowly came untucked from between her legs. "Why don't you sit there and keep a lookout? Let me know if I need to call for help. Okay?"

Keena bobbed her head in her little wolf nod and trotted over to sit at the end of the alley to keep a lookout. Mara turned back to the wagon and sighed. First, she pushed the bodies around so they weren't overlapping each other. Looking down at the glassy eyes of the final person—the giant—Mara reached out and closed the lids before looking up into the now-darkened sky.

"I don't know if there's a god who watches over giants like Aeun watches over forest dwarves," she whispered. "But if there is one, please take her to some sort of peace. The goddess she served surely isn't looking after her now. … Thank you," she finished awkwardly.

Mara did the same for each—closing their eyes and calling to the sky for someone to watch over them. Finishing at the other human, she apologized quietly before beginning to rifle through possessions. The human had many. Strapped to a hip was a revolver. Mara unloaded this and slid it up to the front of the wagon. Later she would insist that they destroy all guns they found. He had a dagger in his boot, which Mara set at the back of the wagon. His jeans pockets were full of ammunition for both revolver and rifle, and his duster pockets were full of snacks. In his waistcoat, Mara found an old, silver pocket watch. She pocketed it herself before unbuttoning the waistcoat and checking the inner lining. She found nothing else except a necklace with a bindrune pendant, which she slipped off the human and pocketed.

The goblins had similar possessions, though what Mara assumed was their food was certainly nothing humans could eat. Both goblins wore the same bindrune necklace, and Mara took theirs as well. The second goblin, the one who'd been driving the wagon, also had a photo in his pocket. In it, he sat, grinning a gnarl-toothed grin, next to another goblin and held a small goblin baby. As Mara looked at the goblin baby, a tear dripped down onto the photo. She wiped it, sniffling.

Sure, they tried to kill us. Sure, they serve someone who's evil. Yes, they have to be stopped. . . . But this child is going to grow up without a parent—and grow up hating us for taking that parent away. She stared at the picture for a few moments, and back at the goblin, then she slid the picture into one of her large duster pockets.

Moving to the giant woman, the leader, Mara hoped to find something more. To begin with, she found a lot of the same. The bindrune necklace, which she collected and placed with the others, ammunition and food, which she piled next to the body as she rooted for more in the pockets, guns and two daggers, which she placed at the front and back of the wagon with the others. Exasperated, Mara searched through the waistcoat—nothing. Peering at the woman's stony face, Mara raised a brow. "Sorry about this," she said quietly, unbuttoning the woman's shirt. There, inside her bra, was a folded-up piece of paper. Mara grinned and took it, sliding it into her duster pocket with the goblin's picture.

As she was rebuttoning the giant's shirt, Mara heard a rustle from the end of the alley. She turned. Keena was bounding toward her. "What is it? Reinforcements? Do I need to call for help?" she whispered to her pup and grasped for her horn.

Finn's coming, Keena replied, wagging her tail.

Keena made it to the edge of the wagon just as Finn made it to the end of the alley. He'd been running, and he skidded to a stop at the entrance. "We think we've found something," he panted.

"I've found something too," Mara replied. "Let's go."

This time, Mara told Keena to stay with Swish while they went to talk to Frank, but they still lay inside the house—Mara didn't want to leave Swish outside unless absolutely necessary. When Mara and Finn made it to the doorway, Teddy came out to meet them. As he laughed harshly for Frank's benefit once more and turned to Mara, the change in his face was staggering. It reminded Mara of a teacher she'd had—he'd always tried to be stern to get his classes to cooperate, but she found out he was actually a huge dork and had simply perfected the ability to throw up a stern façade, just as Teddy did.

Teddy grinned at Mara and pulled her and Finn out of earshot. "What did you find?" he asked.

Mara first pulled out the now-tangled wad of bindrune necklaces. Teddy and Finn both pulled a piece from the wad to examine it. "Is that …" Finn began.

"Yes, it is." Teddy's face tightened. He held up the bindrune to show Mara as he explained. "Bindrunes, like the one Kip made for you, are comprised of a combination of symbols meant to mean various things. These are dark. These are the symbols of Toren and Haeyla—chaos and suffering."

"If they all wear them, perhaps this is the symbol of the soldiers of chaos," Finn offered.

"We should hold onto these," Mara added, looking disgustedly at them. "If these are worn by all the people here, they should help us to blend in the next time we run into a group of them."

"Aye," Teddy said quietly. "Though I hate the idea of wearing something so evil."

"Me too, but it does beat the alternative," she replied. They handed the bindrunes back to her, and she stuffed them back in a pocket.

"What else did you find, Mara?" Finn asked.

Mara pulled out the folded piece of paper. She explained to them where she'd found it and why she'd looked there. "I didn't have the chance to see what it is yet, because Finn arrived just then, but to be the one thing stored there it has to be important."

"Too right," Teddy murmured, taking the paper and folding it open. He raised his brows and made a small noise in surprise before quickly walking into the kitchen to a table, spreading it out, and dragging over a nearby floor lamp. Finn and Mara followed him over and peered over his shoulder as he craned over the table.

A map. A near-complete map. It showed all the cities Frank had mentioned, with a web of dashed lines connecting them to each other, and depicted the other sorts of things they'd seen on their Ambergrove map. Along the bottom was a legend—only, it was just a box with the word *legend* written in it and no symbols or labels to speak of.

"What does this mean?" Mara asked.

Teddy sank into one of the dining chairs and scratched his beard before replying. "When we sent you to check the bodies, he knew. He had a hand to play. He said it didn't matter if we were able to find anything. We would never be able to read their secrets because they could only be deciphered by something from Earth. That's when we sent Finn to get you."

"He thinks we're all Ambergrovian," Mara mused, grinning. "He doesn't think we'll know what he's talking about."

"But you will," Teddy pressed.

Mara grinned once more, then lightly slapped her cheeks and breathed slowly, working to straighten her face. With one more sharp exhale, she turned and walked into the room, deciding on the way what character she would try to play.

When she made it to the entrance, Mara leaned on the doorframe and glowered at Frank. Kip still sat in the chair in front of him, so he stood and backed toward the door. Frank bristled. "What, now the angry dwarf's daughter is going to come in and rough me up?"

Mara shook her head slowly. "No, I just want to know about Polar Oids."

"Polar Oids?" Frank repeated. He laughed. "Polaroids, you mean? Man, you all are apes!" He spoke slowly, as if talking to a small child. "Polaroids are pictures. You know like the ones you draw? Except they're *magic* pictures that look just like the thing you wanted to draw."

"What are they for?" Mara asked, maintaining gruffness.

"For? They're not *for* anything. They're just pictures, you silly girl!" Frank dipped his head to gesture toward Kip. "And this one would have me believe that you apes could figure out our secrets!" He threw his head back and laughed wildly before turning back to Mara. "Do you know what a kaleidoscope is? Hmm? Ever heard of one of those?"

Quickly breaking up the syllables and assuming what another of Kip's misconceptions would have been, Mara scrunched up her face and replied, "Kaleye? Who is Kaleye, and why would we care if he copes?" She looked at Frank in mock confusion.

Frank laughed again, more loudly this time. He turned to Kip. "See? *See?* You need a kaleidoscope to read any sort of intelligence here. You dull apes will never figure out what that is, so it doesn't matter that they're available in every general store. You've doomed yourself with your small minds!"

He laughed and kept laughing. Mara slowly walked toward him and sat. As his eyes met hers, she grinned, and his laughing choked to a halt. "Oh, Frankie," she began. "For someone who swore he'd never betray his people, you've divulged a lot of secrets just now. You see, this," she pulled the goblin picture out of her pocket, "this is a polaroid. It's referred to simply as a polaroid because it comes from the common Polaroid instant camera. They're unique in that you just have to take the picture, and it comes out a slot and just needs to be flapped to develop. No negatives. No uploading. Instant. Kind of like your instant assumption that none of us would know what you were talking about." Her face snapped into a pleasant smile.

Frank blanched. Sweat beads formed on his forehead and upper lip. "B-but h-how ..." he stammered.

"How do I know?" she asked. "Well, Frank, I came from Earth. Not too long ago, actually. It's my *job* to correct the corruption our people brought to Ambergrove. Fate and all that. So, you see, Frank, you've spilled your secret to the one person who'd try to fight you and would understand the things you know. The person who is going to destroy the realm of chaos forever. Because it's right. Because it's part of a prophecy that was set before I was born. Because I *want* to." She paused for a moment and stood, heading toward the door before adding, "It's been a while since I've used a kaleidoscope—and that was just a silly, little one I won at an arcade—but I don't expect I'll have a problem finding one in the general store."

Mara tipped her head to gesture for Kip to follow her, and they left Frank screaming and thrashing in their wake.

Chapter Ten

Honor in Chaos

It only took a few minutes for Mara to get to the general store, find a kaleidoscope, and return. She decided to grab a handful, just in case they found more maps or one of the kaleidoscopes was broken. When Mara returned, all was silent. As she made her way to the dining table, she peered into the room where Frank had been interrogated. His chair had fallen over again, and he'd been gagged, but he glared at her all the same.

Her companions sat around the dining table eating dinner—a stew quickly thrown together by Finn. Teddy pushed a plate in front of Mara as she came to sit beside him. Setting the kaleidoscopes on the table, she began to wolf down her stew. Thankfully, Finn's time cooking with Ashroot had paid off—at least to the point that his stew was edible.

"That's it?" Finn asked incredulously, nodding at the kaleidoscopes.

Kip picked one up. "They don't look too special," he added.

Mara set down her spoon and reached for one, but before she could speak, Teddy lightly slapped her outstretched hand and said, "No, no, lass. You eat."

Mara obeyed, taking a few bites before quickly saying, "You put it up to your eye like a telescope."

Teddy glared at her disapprovingly, but Kip picked up a kaleidoscope and peered through it. "What the—" he began. Finn had already done the same and began muttering as well. Teddy dropped his spoon and sighed before picking up a third kaleidoscope and following suit.

Mara took the opportunity to explain, "I don't know how they work, but kaleidoscopes have these colorful lenses in them, so when you look through them you can see all sorts of colorful patterns, and you get a different pattern when you turn it around. I'm guessing they modified these to reflect light from some ink that's on the map, so the kaleidoscope will show us different items on the map depending on how it's turned."

Halfway through her explanation, as if by command, all three men shot their kaleidoscopes down to look at the map and swore. Grinning, Mara finished her stew while the men looked at the map and talked over each other excitedly. Teddy suddenly fell silent, set the kaleidoscope down, and turned to Mara.

"We'll need to go to Questhaven for a while before we do anything else. It'll take some time to figure out this map, and we need to come up with a plan to get the most use out of it," he said. His eyes darted to the room where Frank lay.

"We can't just let him go," Kip said quietly. "He knows too much about us, and we can't risk him telling his people what we know, or they might change everything or come for us."

Mara choked on a bit of stew, and spat and sputtered for a moment before managing, "So now we're just going to *kill* him?"

"Well, not exactly," Teddy replied awkwardly. "What my people and Kip's have done in this situation is a duel to the death. We give the prisoner a fair, fighting chance. You see, it wouldn't have been fair if we'd tortured him first."

Mara turned to Finn, who was still looking through the kaleidoscope. He turned, and no doubt saw a distorted version of her, before lowering the kaleidoscope and saying, "Hey, don't look at me. You know my people would just kill him."

She turned to Teddy and sighed, pushing her bowl of stew away. "Well, what will we do then?"

"I've been thinking about that," Kip began. "It's not fair to him to have a swordfight, because he doesn't have a sword and may not know how to use it if we gave him one. We cannot have a gunfight because none of us know how to—or will," he added quickly, as Mara glared, "or will—use them. What we're left with is the thing we used to level ourselves to begin with."

"Crossbow." Teddy nodded and added, "But crossbow to what?"

Kip continued slowly, "Well, if we have a crossbow loaded and ready with one bolt, and he has a gun loaded and ready with just one, uh, bullet, then both dueling would have one shot and about the same amount of time to fire."

"Like an Old West gunfight in the streets," Mara murmured, more to herself than them. Seeing their confusion, she explained, "A lot of things here seem to be based on—or at least stemmed from—Old West customs. In the old west, if two gunslingers had issues with one another, they would have a duel. Stereotypically at high noon. They'd stand some ways away from each other in the middle of the street, and they'd draw and fire once as quickly as they could. That settled it."

"Well, let's do that," Kip said, looking around to each of them.

Teddy nodded. "Which of us will be dueling him then?" He peered around the table.

Mara opened her mouth to reply that it clearly needed to be her, but Finn spoke first. "I will." He spoke with such conviction, and when he looked up, there was fire in his eyes.

Mara understood. When they had to fight Frank and his companions, Finn had been afraid. He froze on the battlefield, unable to fight for fear of the guns. The determination in his eyes wasn't to represent the group or their cause, wasn't to step in so someone else didn't get hurt. It was for him to face his fear head-on. He wouldn't be able to hide behind a wagon until he was ready to fight this time. He would have to fight or die. *He needs this,* Mara thought. Turning to each of her companions, she could see they knew it too.

"Alright, then," Teddy said finally. "We'll get some rest, and Finn and Frank will duel when the sun is up tomorrow."

No matter how he tossed and turned, Finn couldn't sleep. Why had he volunteered to face someone with a gun by himself? His mother would have just had Candiru execute Frank. Volunteering to face a weapon much greater than her own? Never. No sea elf would. If they were to fight a duel to the death, they wouldn't be as terrified as he was the night before their duel. They would be proud to fight. Confident. Ready. Even when Mara had been about to face the gauntlet, she'd surely been scared, but her sense of purpose had won over her fear. He wasn't sure his would.

Finn sighed. He lay alone in one of the bedrooms. Teddy had insisted he skip a watch shift because he would need his rest, but he didn't feel like resting. He felt the scar on his stomach from the first fight and traced his hands from one darkened blue scar to another. He'd been gutted. Literally. He'd been unable to stop them, and he barely survived. He felt a hand on his shoulder, and he jumped.

"Shh, shh, shh." Mara knelt in front of him. "Hey, Finn, it's okay. Shh."

He hadn't realized just how much he'd been sweating. The bed he lay in was drenched with it. Mara knelt on the floor beside the bed and patted his damp arm. "What are you doing in here, Mara?" he managed.

"It's nearly dawn, but . . . also I could hear you moaning," she said softly.

Finn smashed his face into the pillow. *Of course, she did. Big, fierce sea elf I am.*

"No, it's okay, Finn. It is. I know you don't think it is, but it is. You need this. You need to face Frank in order to work through your feelings about guns, but just volunteering to face someone who has a gun makes you stronger than you were the day before."

"I don't feel stronger."

"You will. You will when you win. You don't have to believe in yourself, because we all believe in you." She patted his arm gently, and added, "Breakfast is ready whenever you want to come down for it," and she was gone.

Teddy explained to Frank what would happen while Mara took a revolver and loaded it with a single bullet. Frank was not on board. "How am I supposed to trust that you'll just let me go if I win? Especially after I've killed your friend? I don't want to let any of *you* go," he spat.

"Are you telling us that you'll kill us all rather than take your freedom if you win?" Teddy replied.

"Winning is not freedom. Going back and telling my people that there were filthy apes here, and I let you live? And I told you our secrets?"

"What, does that loyalty not go both ways, little man?" Teddy mused.

"Whatever!" Frank shouted. "Let's just do this."

They kept Frank bound as Teddy led him outside into the street. Mara marveled at the sight. The way the fog rolled in surely set the mood for what they were about to do. Finn stood in the street, waiting with his crossbow resting on his boot. His blue and purple chainmail glistened in the morning light.

"You said this would be fair," Frank demanded. "I saw already that our bullets didn't go through your chainmail. How am I supposed to be able to kill him if most of his body is protected?"

Mara and Teddy glanced at each other, and then Mara made a face as if to say, "he has a point." She delicately handed the revolver off to Kip and went to Finn. "Finn, he—"

"I heard," Finn choked. "Hold this so I can take my chainmail off." He handed her his crossbow.

"Finn, are you sure you want to do this?" she asked quietly.

"It's only fair, Mara. It's not a fair fight if his bullet can't harm me." He'd surely meant to sound confident, but his voice broke as he spoke. She didn't press the matter.

A few moments later, Mara draped Finn's chainmail over a horse hitching rail and stood next to Kip at the edge of the road. Finn held his crossbow at his side, ready. Teddy untied Frank's bonds and handed him his revolver—reminding him that he just had one shot and he needed to use it wisely. Then Teddy joined Mara and Kip on the sidelines.

Finn and Frank just stared down the road at each other. They couldn't see it from the side of the road, but Finn's shirt had been drenched with sweat when he'd given Mara his chainmail. Frank seemed at ease by comparison. Kip slid his hand into Mara's and gave it a comforting squeeze.

"You both have one shot," she called to the men in the street. She tried to keep her voice strong. "One shot to fire at the count of three. This is an honorable duel. Do not fire before three. Ready?" Both men nodded curtly without taking their eyes off each other. Mara cleared her throat. "Okay. One … two … three!"

It all happened so fast. In the time it took Mara to fully say three, both men had raised their weapons and fired, and they now both lay motionless on the ground. She bolted across the street to Finn, not hearing her garbled wail until she made it to his body. Keena had been left sleeping in the house, but she'd run out to Mara at the sound of the gunshot and slid to a stop at Finn's body to lay on his leg.

Mara searched frantically for the bullet wound, unable to speak or focus. He wasn't moving. He was dead. She hadn't even prepared for the loss, and he was gone. She should have been the one to duel. She should never—wait. There it was. The bullet was lodged in his clavicle. He stirred, and Mara realized there was blood at the back of his head from a rock he'd hit when he fell. He was alive.

She turned as Kip's footsteps met her ears. "Finn?" he asked.

"He's alright," Mara managed, realizing then that she had been crying. She sniffled and swallowed. "What about—"

Kip shook his head. "He's gone. Straight to the heart. Teddy finished it for him quickly." He gestured over to where Teddy knelt beside Frank's now-still form.

Kip knelt on Finn's other side, and he and Mara helped their friend sit up. When she looked into his eyes again, she saw a different kind of determination—one laced with pride. He'd done it. They'd done it. They had the information they needed, and once Finn was patched up and able to travel, they'd be headed back to Questhaven.

Teddy patched Finn up while Mara and Kip dealt with another matter—those they'd beaten. They hitched Swish up to the enemy wagon and loaded Frank into it, and Mara shortly found a good place for it. There was a dried-up inground pool in what appeared to be a community park, so Kip found two planks to use for a ramp, and they lowered the wagon into the pool. When it was a safe distance from all surroundings, they set the wagon ablaze and left it to burn. Kip bowed his head for a moment before following Mara back to their companions, and she could only guess that he had also cast up a word for them to be looked after in their next journey.

When they entered the house, Teddy sat at the table with Finn, stitching up the entry wound. The bullet had come out cleanly, and Finn was shortly bandaged up. Despite his protests, they insisted he ride in the wagon, at least for the first leg of their journey, so they could get started while he began to recover. In the end, he ended up in the wagon—not due to his giving in, but because Teddy had put a sedative in the healing tea he'd given Finn to drink, so the sea elf wasn't awake to protest further. Within the hour, Finn lay in the back of the wagon with Keena laying on his stomach, and they journeyed past the roaring flame of the other wagon, away from Fear, and toward their dinghy.

This time, when they left Swish on the island, they left him happy. They didn't bother with a pen like they had before, but they made sure to leave vegetables for him, and Mara instructed him to stay by the waterfall for their return, as he did before.

Miss you, nice lady, Swish whinnied sadly.

"I know, Swish. I'll miss you, too, and so will Keena." She gestured to her pup, who whined. "We'll be back soon, though. I promise."

She gave Swish one last neck rub and called for Keena, and they boarded the dinghy to head back to Questhaven—and Keena immediately shook off her sweater and spread her wings. She didn't stop stretching them until Questhaven was coming into view, and the healing Finn blew his horn to signal to Ashroot that they were on their way. They could smell the aroma of cooking meats when they met her on the beach.

Over dinner—savory grilled turkey with vegetables—they took turns explaining what all had happened since they last saw the bearkin. Mara told her about Swish and how she was the only one who could talk to the horse, Teddy told her about the firefight, Kip told her about the interrogation, Finn told her about the duel, and then Mara pulled out the map and a kaleidoscope to tell her what they'd found.

"It sure sounds like a lot has happened since you've been gone," Ashroot said quietly, as she was clearing up the table.

"I just figured you'd be more interested to hear how we've been, but I want to know how you are. What have you been doing? And how are the wolves?" Mara asked, helping her friend clear the table.

Ashroot looked out toward the forest, where Keena now bounded toward the amber eyes that gleamed from the darkness of the canopy. "Things have been good here," she said quietly. "To tell you the truth, I'm glad I wasn't with you on this adventure. I don't know what I would have done in that situation." She placed the plates in a wash bin and continued, "Things have been peaceful here. Fang and Moon have been keeping me company. One of their pups, Claw, has actually been staying here at the camp with me most nights. Bears, you know, are more often solitary creatures, but wolves just have a pack. It's part of who they are. They can't imagine me being away from my pack—from you—and they seem to be accepting me into theirs."

"That's good though, isn't it?" Mara asked. "I hate the thought of leaving you alone while we go to Chaosland, but I couldn't imagine bringing you along."

"Oh, and I couldn't imagine going," she said quickly. "Remember, the only fighting I've ever really done was when we were going through the Ice Mountains last year, and I don't even know how I survived that."

Mara took the wash bin from Ashroot, and they walked together to the beach to wash the dishes in the water. Mara enjoyed the water, so she just sat in the shallows and let it rise to her waist. She grabbed a plate to begin cleaning before speaking again, and when she did, her voice was quiet.

"Ash, do you … regret coming along with me?" she asked.

She expected a quick answer, but Ashroot was silent. They washed a few dishes in silence before Ashroot growled, "I wouldn't trade this experience, no. It is not what I expected it to be, but I have been useful on this journey—less so now, I guess, while you are getting many of your supplies from the forbidden lands and Gylden Grotto—but I have been able to help, and I'm sure I will again. You're a dear friend, Mara, and friendship isn't something that's measured by time spent together. I'm here for you, for whenever you need me, and I was already able to complete my personal quest."

Ashroot fell silent again. It was the first time she'd been away from her family, and Mara knew what that felt like. She knew better than to venture into that topic, at least not then. "So, what about Fang and Moon?" she asked. "Our friends didn't come out to see us."

"They just wanted us all to have time to talk. They'll be around tomorrow morning."

Mara stretched and sighed. "Speaking of, we should probably be getting ready for bed. What say we leave the rest of these to soak until morning?"

Ashroot laughed her bearkin laugh. "Yes, we might as well. I wouldn't want the lads to get up before us and get themselves into trouble."

They laughed together as they sank the wash bin into the water to fill it and carried it back to the main tent.

Keena had stayed the night with the wolves, so the next morning, Mara woke alone in her tent. She took the goblin's picture out and traced the features of his baby. She'd really expected a goblin baby to be grotesque—sort of like the adult ones—but she thought this fire-haired ball of rolls was quite cute. Because her mouth was closed and her teeth hidden, the mother's features were soft and almost kind. Mara sighed, wondering if they knew yet that he wasn't coming back. She slowly stood and dressed before placing the picture in her trunk.

Mara took the opportunity of an early morning alone to go back out to the beach. She wore the pants and shirt she'd cut short for swimming, and she put her hair in the tightest braid she could before wading out into the water. She took her time to enjoy it, knowing that she was in a place that was safe. She felt the sand between her toes, and she plucked out a few vacant shells. Using a wayward log as a floatie, she relaxed in the cool water.

Just when she had fully relaxed, she heard a rustling near the beach, and the rising sun was darkened. She opened her eyes just in time to see a gliding Keena crash into her. She spat and sputtered up the salt water before noticing Kip's cackle from the beach. He cheered.

"Yeah, go Keena! You did such a good job!"

Mara wiped her face and looked back toward the beach. It was at least a full ship's length away. "Did she fly that whole way?" Mara called back, shocked.

"Yep, she sure did!" Kip hooted and clapped.

Mara grabbed Keena and squeezed. "You did such a good job, my girl! Even after being all wrapped up when we went to Fear, you're a natural!" Keena just licked Mara's face and yipped. "Well then, why don't we see what we can rustle up for breakfast? I'm sure Ashroot has a treat for you!"

Keena flung herself out of Mara's arms and paddled back toward the shore, muttering, *Treat, treat, treat,* as she went.

When Mara made it back to the shore, Moon and some of her pups were there to meet her. She greeted the wolves with a grin. "How has your family been, Moon?" she asked.

We have been well, she replied, *thanks to you and your kin. The bearkin has gotten along well with my pups. She is teaching them how to act around people and how to fight when the enemy has a weapon. They have become good friends.*

"That's great!" Mara replied, throwing her hands up in excitement. "And how about you? Are your wounds all finally healed?"

Yes. I cannot run like I used to, but I am here, and I am well and caring for my pups. I cannot ask for more.

Star, one of Moon's pups, skidded to a sandy stop at her mama's feet and announced that Ashroot was ready with breakfast, so they all headed back to the main tent.

Ashroot had treats for all the wolves, though for nature's sake they did still hunt their own food. When Mara caught up at the table, she saw Teddy and Finn sitting there, with plates of eggs going cold, looking over the map with kaleidoscopes. Kip was taking notes beside them on a small piece of paper.

"What's all this?" Mara asked Kip as she sank into the seat beside him.

Kip, who was actually eating his breakfast, swallowed quickly. "Finn and Teddy are finding important places in each big city, and I'm making a list, so we have an idea of what we're working with without all having to look through those thingamajigs at the map."

"Kaleidoscopes."

"Yeah, those."

Mara sat and listened, eating her breakfast as the men went about their work. Each of the cities was fully stocked with various supplies and citizens—far different from the abandoned Fear. Each city held two or three garrisons and a half dozen each of stables, gunsmiths, grocers, and general stores, among other places.

Teddy lay his kaleidoscope on the table and took a bite of his cold eggs. "Based on this, there's at least a few thousand citizens in every city, maybe more. Likely most of them know how to fight, even if they aren't trained at the garrison. A formidable enemy."

"It will definitely be a job to take them down," Finn added, setting down his own kaleidoscope and taking a bite of his eggs, grimacing at the rubbery texture from their sitting out so long. He produced a pickle jar from under the table and chomped on one of those instead.

Mara stared at the map for a moment. She could see slightly through one of the abandoned kaleidoscopes to a greenish hue. "Robin Hood," she murmured.

"Who's Hood?" Finn asked.

"No, *Robin* Hood. He's a folk hero from Earth. He would rob from the rich to give to the poor, and he was able to do substantial damage in his efforts not by attacking at the source but by attacking supply wagons when they came through his forest," she explained.

"So, he picked them off in smaller numbers," Kip said.

"Exactly." Mara stood over the map and pointed. "If we stay along these supply routes, we can take their supplies while they're on the road. Food we can keep, and guns and ammunition we'll destroy. Sure, they can always make more, but they can only make more for so long. And if we work quickly, they won't be able to replenish their stores before we hit again."

Teddy leaned forward and grinned. "If we weaken their supply lines, we can force the leader—this 'Great Harbinger'—out from wherever they are, and we can defeat them all."

"Good plan, Dragonwolf," Kip added.

"We'll just need some things before we get started," she said. "We need to have supplies to repair the chainmail when we get shot, and we need to have an easy way to destroy the supplies in case things get rough."

Teddy stood. "I'll head for Gylden Grotto now and get what we need."

Mara sat alone in the main tent poring over the Chaosland map with the kaleidoscope. When Frank had mentioned Darkness, Mara wondered if it was the new name for an old city, like Fear. It turned out it was. Each of the cities on the map had two names. First was a name from Earth, like New Switzerland. The others were mainly large or important cities—New London, New Philly.

Each city had a new name, which Mara discovered after some thinking was always something to do with chaos. Fear incites chaos, and so does darkness. Some of them were puzzling, however. Freedom causes chaos in that there is a lack of order, but Plague? Yes, plagues cause chaos in that such a pestilence turns worlds upside down. Dealing with a major sickness that spreads through the people like rumors in a school could definitely make society fall into chaos. But whereas Freedom could be seen as positive, Plague was most certainly only negative. How could followers of chaos think they're doing good works with names like that? They were just dark, twisted, and evil.

Mara shook her head and brought her attention back to the task at hand, making a list of everything she knew from the map that would need to be translated for her friends.

It took Teddy a few days to get to Gylden Grotto and back. When he returned, he had ample supplies for repairing their chainmail—he'd even gotten one of the blacksmiths to scorch some to match Finn and Mara's mail. For destroying supplies, he brought bladders of combustible liquid. In a pinch, all they would need to do would be to throw one of those at a supply wagon—or at an enemy for that matter—and the spark of gunfire would be all it would take to ignite the liquid. If that failed, a torch or flaming arrow would do the job just fine.

They spent a couple weeks at Questhaven. Mara and Teddy both hated the idea of coming to see Ashroot only to leave immediately, so they spent some time with her on the island while they prepared to head back. Kip was the handiest of them when it came to armor, so he patched up their chainmail for them. Keena disappeared into the woods with the wolves to learn while she could, and Finn spent all his time at the crossbow range, practicing his aim. Although he'd shot true in his duel with Frank, his skills had otherwise not been tested, and though his fear of guns had been somewhat dampened, it was still very much alive.

When they could put it off no longer, they loaded their new supplies in the dinghy once more and said a tearful goodbye to Ashroot. The beach was lined with wolf pups as they sailed off into the distance, ready now to make some trouble.

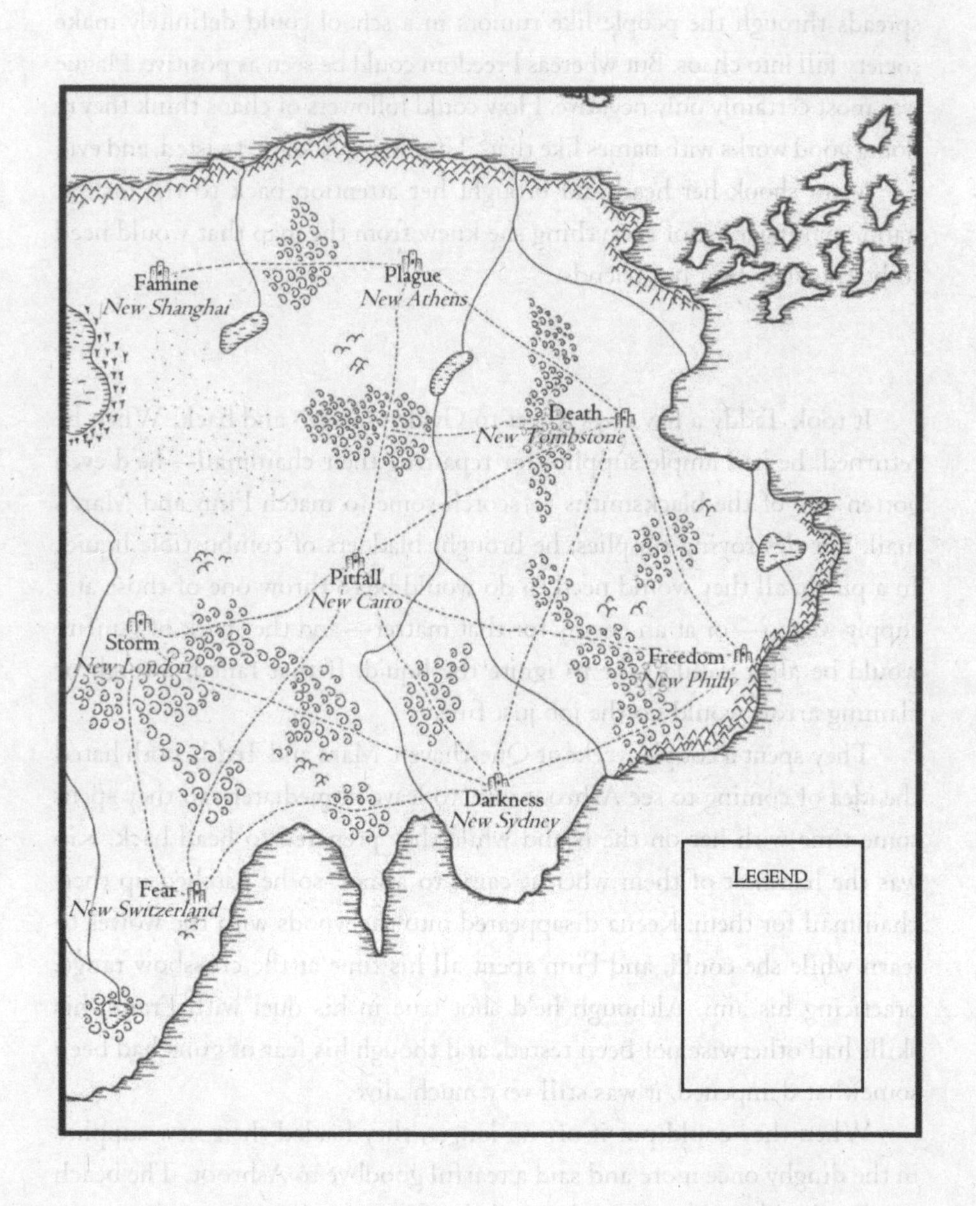
Famine
New Shanghai
Plague
New Athens
Death
New Tombstone
Pitfall
New Cairo
Storm
New London
Freedom
New Philly
Darkness
New Sydney
Fear
New Switzerland
LEGEND

Chapter Eleven

Goods and Services

Mara stood by the waterfall and whistled sharply. Nothing. She whistled again. Nothing. Again. With a harsh whinny, Swish crashed out of the forest by the waterfall, charging toward Mara and nearly knocking her over in his excitement.

"Swish! How've you been, buddy?" she asked, rubbing his neck.

Keena ran up behind Mara and launched herself in the air, just barely gliding enough to make it onto Swish's back. *Hey there, big friend!* the dragonwolf cried.

Nice lady! Little friend! Swish replied. *Missed you!*

"Aww, we missed you too." Mara gave him a little hug around the neck and added, "Are you ready to show these meanies what for?" Swish blustered happily, and Mara chuckled. "I'll take that as a yes."

As the men unloaded the supplies from the dinghy into the wagon, Mara explained their plans to Swish. They would take the supply roads and ambush wagons, destroying the materials. With any luck, they'd find something that would help guide them to the leader. With a little luck, they would disrupt operations just enough they could draw the leader out. Swish liked the plan—though he probably would have liked any plan that involved being with Mara and hurting those who hurt him.

They had a quick meal, caught up with Swish, and then they made their way to their first supply road. To avoid running into avengers in Fear, they bypassed the city altogether, making their way through the forest and along the coast. Their first test would be the road between Darkness and the city to the north of Fear called Storm—previously New Sydney and

New London, respectively. It proved to be the best place to test Mara's first comparison to Robin Hood and the men of Sherwood, because the whole road was shrouded in trees and brush.

When they made it to where they thought was about halfway, they hid the wagon in the woods and prepared. They would remain out of sight of the road. From the nearby bushes, they would be able to toss the combustible bladders into the passing wagon. As long as the wagon didn't pass through at night, one of them could be ready with a torch to set it ablaze then and there. The trouble was that they didn't really know when the next supply run would be. However, since a few convoys from Darkness had already gone missing without completing their mission, they suspected the patrols would try another route soon.

Teddy set up a simple camp for them. A tarp attached to the wagon and propped with sticks would create a shelter big enough for them to lie under, because there would only need to be two there at a time. They couldn't use their horns to warn of an approaching wagon, because that would alert their enemy to their presence, so instead, one would take watch along the road, out of sight, and would signal to someone at the camp. The one at camp would wake the others.

"How are we going to signal each other without alerting the patrol?" Mara asked the first day as they were having their supper.

Teddy grinned into his sandwich. "Well, that'll be up to you and me," he said.

"How so?" Kip asked.

"Mara and I can talk to the woodland creatures around here, so we just need to find some animals who will help us. Then, the sounds they'll hear will be actual animal sounds, and they'll be none the wiser."

Finn chuckled. "That's a nice plan."

Kip's brows furrowed, and he scratched his beard. "There's a flaw in that plan. How will we know that the signal is the signal and not just animal sounds?"

"Simple," Teddy replied. "They will be distress sounds. We'll have our helper make a sound of ultimate distress, as if they're being slaughtered. Either it's the signal for a wagon or there's a predator out here we'll need to all get up to fight anyway. Whichever it may be, we'll all be ready."

As the sky darkened the first day, Teddy and Mara went out together to look for an animal to help them. They met with quite a few who understood them well enough, but most were unwilling to work with people—even people who could talk to them. Others were just afraid. Just as they were about to give up and regroup at the camp to see if they could come up with another plan, Mara saw amber eyes coming from the shadows. She swung her arm out to tap Teddy's chest to get his attention and ended up swatting him in the mouth. He turned.

"Hello there, forest friend," he said gently.

Friend? the creature growled. *How do you know I'm a friend? How do I know you are a friend?*

"Forest dwarves have always been friends to animals," Teddy replied.

The creature stepped out into the light, and Mara gasped. Scarred and twisted, with one eye sealed shut, was a coyote. Teddy groaned softly. Mara understood why. Although she'd always loved every animal she saw—even to the point of approaching a rabid dog like it was a harmless puppy—her dad had explained to her that coyotes weren't to be messed with. They were shifty and dangerous, and they took what they wanted from others. Fitting that a coyote was the only creature in this cursed land willing to speak with them.

Mara cleared her throat politely. "Friend, what is your name?" she asked.

The coyote bared his teeth and peered at her. *Shadow,* he growled.

"Shadow. Shadow, I'm Mara, and I'm here to help this land and everyone in it."

Shadow growled. *And what makes you think I need your help, human?*

"I'm not a human," she said, stepping forward and pulling her collar down to show him her token from the Great Silver Bear. "You may not know what this means, but I've proven myself to be a forest dwarf. Chosen, not born. And I will one day be their leader. I care in a way others probably never would." She crouched in front of the coyote, pointed at his scarred body, and finished quietly, "And I know bullet wounds when I see them."

"We don't have to trust each other to help each other," Teddy added. "But ridding this land of the agents of chaos and their weapons will help you too."

The coyote glared at Teddy, and then he slowly stepped toward Mara, growling and staring into her eyes. It took all her willpower to remain still. Inches from her face, the coyote snapped his teeth, looked her over, and snorted. He sat. *Mara, chosen dwarf, I will help you until it serves me better to leave you to die.*

"I wouldn't expect anything less," she replied steadily.

For the following weeks, Mara took shifts with Kip and Teddy with Finn. Kip or Finn stayed at the camp, and Keena stuck with one of the dwarves in the daytime and Shadow took her place at night. Although Shadow had thought that crying in distress was undignified, he demonstrated for Kip and Finn to hear, and he sat with Teddy or Mara during their watch. To Teddy he didn't have much to say. To Mara—

Your friend doesn't like me much, he said a few nights into their watch.

"Oh, so you will talk to me!" Mara replied. "Here I thought I was getting the silent treatment."

You were.

"Oh. Well then. It's not Teddy's fault any more than it's your fault for not liking us. It's the way he was raised."

So, being raised to hate another creature is a good reason to do so?

"No, it isn't," she replied quickly. "It's just—it'll take him more time to get used to different things than it would me. He's more set in his ways at his age, and I have the benefit of not being biased a certain way. Well, at least it didn't take."

Shadow tipped his head in question.

"My dad was one of them. A forest dwarf born in Ambergrove. The first time I saw a coyote on Earth, he told me all sorts of terrible things about coyotes. But that stuff always went in one ear and out the other. Teddy is different."

So how can I trust him if he was born and raised to hate me?

"I thought there would be no trusting here?" Mara joked. Shadow leered at her. She cleared her throat and continued, "In all seriousness, I could tell you that Teddy is different or give you a million other excuses. At the end of the day, he's following me so I can complete my quest. If I say we're working together, he can grump about it all he wants, but he'll do it. And maybe, if you are trustworthy, it can convince him to change his views as well."

Shadow whined softly and licked a scar on his foreleg. *I think you underestimate the power of hate,* he said.

Mara looked at his wretched form and shook her head. "No," she replied. "I think hate underestimates the power of *me*."

A few weeks into their vigil, while Teddy stood watch, a wagon finally came down the road. To their luck, it came through during the night, and the wagon and escorts all bore torches. "Now's the time," he told Shadow.

The coyote nodded and yowled a heartbreaking, painful sound. The driver of the wagon hooted. "Yeah! Some scavenger out there getting what was coming to him."

At the camp, Finn roused Mara and Kip, and they prepared themselves by the road. They each took their crossbows in addition to two bladders of the combustible liquid. Finn and Kip crouched to one side of the road and Mara to the other, joined soon after by Teddy and Shadow.

"Shadow! I didn't know you were coming," Mara whispered sharply.

"Oh, he's going to kill the driver," Teddy replied casually.

Mara raised a brow, shook her head, then added, "Remember, we're not going to kill them unless we have to. Robin Hood didn't kill."

That's nice, Shadow huffed, *but you will have to kill. These people are trained never to turn away from the fight, even if they should.*

Mara thought about Frank. Although she would never tell Finn of her suspicions, she was sure that Frank had thrown the duel. He couldn't have gone back to his people empty-handed, with even one of them left alive. Was death really the better choice for them? "How many are there?" she asked.

"It seems like they have similar parties in each patrol. There's a giant leader, a goblin driver and a goblin behind, and a human and a mining dwarf on either side," Teddy explained.

The lights from the wagon came into view, and they went silent, waiting. The patrol silently marched right into their window as Teddy and Finn readied their bladders. Teddy threw, and his bladder hit and ruptured right in the back of the wagon. Finn's followed suit, nicking—by sheer luck—one of the wagon's torches, knocking it down into the wagon, and setting the whole thing ablaze. The force of the blast blew the goblin off the wagon and caused the horse to bolt. There was a commotion and then the giant hollered for order.

"Ready!" the giant shouted. "Fire!"

They all began shooting wildly in all directions around the road. Mara ducked to grab her crossbow, and when she looked up again, Shadow had bolted into the fray, straight for the goblin driver. He barreled right into the goblin, knocking him down, and then he went for the throat. As the goblin thrashed and screamed for his companions to help, the giant turned and shot Shadow. Once. Twice. A third time for good measure. Shadow collapsed.

Mara yelled in fury at the giant, but Teddy fired first … and the battle began.

Before long, it was all over. They had the advantage of being in the bushes, shrouded in darkness. As before, the giant was the last to fall, but Finn was able to fight the whole battle and it was he who made the final shot. When the giant fell to the ground, Teddy bolted to Shadow, but he was gone.

Because their enemy had just fired blindly into the forest, only one shot had hit any of the rest of them, and it was just a graze. They were victorious. Before they rested that night, Teddy insisted that Shadow be buried, and they waited until the following morning to assess the other bodies. On each, they found similar items to those they found on the group in Fear. They found the wagon down the road. The harness straps had burned through, freeing the horse, so they pulled the wagon back to the bodies, piled them and their guns into it, and set it ablaze again.

"Now what?" Finn asked.

"We're just getting started," Mara replied.

So began a four-month excursion. Not wanting to go too far away from Questhaven, they stuck to the lower routes, marring all supply travel between Storm, Darkness, and the nearby Pitfall and Freedom—formerly New Cairo and New Philly. They discovered a pack of coyotes ran between a few of the cities, and they were able to get the kin of Shadow to assist them. As the months wore on, the patrols grew larger and their weapons fiercer.

Mara, Finn, and Teddy perfected their chainmail repair techniques, finding that the chainmail needed to be repaired at least every other skirmish—and they were lucky to go through one skirmish without a close call. Keena stayed out of the fighting as much as Mara could enforce. There was no good way to protect her, so she just ran to hide whenever enemies appeared. Despite the restriction of her silly sweater, Keena grew from the size of a small dog to the size of a Saint Bernard. Her wings remained contained, but it became harder and harder to conceal her growing horns—they'd already begun to grow steadily and curl backward like raptor claws.

Charred wagons were all that were left to be found by later patrols, and they were able to perfect the same collection of processes for each. Partly because they ran out of fluid and had to do it the old-fashioned way, and partly because they were running low on their own supplies, they began to only set fire to guns and ammunition wagons. Unfortunately, even after four months and nearly a dozen battles and supply capture, they were still no closer to finding the leader. After a while, everything became rather monotonous. However, they were definitely causing a stir. Each time, more soldiers were sent. Each time, the supplies were burned or taken. Finally, when they decided to venture further north to the road between Freedom and Death, something changed.

The more they raided supplies, the less supply wagons came through at night. However, as Kip took the early morning watch, they had their first patrol arrive just before sunrise, and they weren't ready.

"What supplies do they have?" Finn hissed as they all rushed to put on their chainmail and prepare.

"I-I can't tell," Kip replied. "It's a wagon unlike any I've ever seen. It ... looks more like a barrel."

"What?" Mara asked incredulously.

"I know it sounds silly, but—"

"No, Kip, it doesn't," she replied, barely containing her excitement. "It's a carriage. They're special wagons that are meant to transport people who are too important to walk or ride in the open."

"Someone important, like—" Finn began.

"Now, now. Let's not get our hopes up," Teddy interjected. "Someone important, yes. Someone who may be able to give us information, certainly. Let's leave it at that. We need to capture whoever is in there."

Mara nodded, the others nodded, and they headed out to their positions by the road. The more soldiers were added to the patrols, the more often they had actual injuries. Their chainmail had been repaired in so many places it was practically brand new again—though Mara refused to do more than repair the holes in hers because it was a treasured gift she wanted to keep the same as long as she could. They'd come to expect to be outnumbered, so this patrol was a complete surprise.

The carriage was headed north on the road, toward Death, and it was led by one rider on horseback and followed by another—both giants—and the carriage itself was driven and shotgunned by two goblins. That was it. Fortunately, they had a system for dealing with giants. Two headshots by Kip and Teddy to the leading giant, and two by Finn and Mara to the rear one, and the giants were down. Before they could process what had happened to their companions, the goblins were down too.

Finn and Kip calmed the giants' horses and tied them to nearby trees, then grabbed the carriage's reins as Mara and Teddy approached the carriage door. "I'm opening this door!" Mara shouted. "If you attack, the same thing that happened to this patrol will happen to you. Clear?"

"Y-yes," came a man's voice.

Mara flung the door open, but the occupant was not what she expected. A short, stout man in a brightly-colored suit stared wild-eyed back at her. She checked the corners. He was the only occupant. She climbed up into the carriage and sat opposite the man, pointing her crossbow at this chest. Teddy stepped forward and blocked the doorway.

"Who are you?" Mara asked sternly.

"My name is Ralph," the man said quietly.

"And what are you doing here, Ralph?" she asked. Ralph shook his head and averted his gaze. Mara continued, "Ralph, if you tell us what's going on here, we may be able to work something out. You're not a fighter, see. Don't you want to go back home?"

Ralph's face changed, contorted into a vicious mask. He looked up at Mara, his eyes filled with hate. "Four months plaguing our lands and you still don't know how we are?" he spat. "There's a reason there have never been any survivors … and we're not about to start now."

Before Mara could move, he slapped a hand to his mouth and swallowed. His eyes bulged and reddened, his skin blued, and his mouth foamed. In just a few moments, he slumped to the side in his seat, dead. Teddy sighed and bonked his head frustratedly on the doorframe of the carriage, then said, "Search him, and this carriage."

She nodded, amazed. Baffled that he would rather die a horrible death than answer a simple question or have a fighting chance. She searched him thoroughly and found nothing on his person but more poison and one of the bindrune necklaces. Mara peered around the carriage, and then had a thought, *Of course!* Remembering one of her favorite renditions of the musketeers' story, she tested the seats to see if they lifted. Nope. She felt around the wall and floor. In the center of the floor, she felt a small hole.

Mara drew a crossbow bolt from her hip quiver, stabbed it in the hole, and pulled. A section of the floor popped up to reveal a secret compartment. "Aha! The sacred snack chamber," she said.

"What? What's that?" Teddy asked.

"Never mind. It's from a movie. And I thought no one on Earth caught it when I quoted a movie," she muttered. Inside the compartment was a collection of letters, sealed with the bindrune symbol everyone wore. She took them all out and stuffed them in the pockets of her duster.

"That it?" Teddy asked.

Mara nodded. "Let's go. Kip, Finn, release the horses, please."

Kip and Finn did as they were bidden, and, as had become their standard, they piled the bodies in the carriage and burned everything before heading back to Swish and Keena. Once back at their wagon, Mara took all the letters out and began tearing them open. One after the other, they were all the same. Mara beckoned to her companions and then read out loud: "From the humble city of Darkness to the Great Harbinger. Great Harbinger, we have emptied our stores as directed, taking all supplies through the wilderness to the abandoned city of Fear. The cursed raiders have not been there in many months, so the supplies will be safe ..." She picked up another, and Kip and Teddy did the same. She scanned the letter and added, "From Freedom to the Great Harbinger, all supplies to Fear."

"Same here, from Pitfall," said Teddy.

"And Storm," said Kip.

Finn scratched his head. "Every city has emptied their stores and sent them to the abandoned city to keep them safe. Safe from us."

"If we were to go there, surely it wouldn't be too heavily guarded. They need soldiers to protect the cities and they don't know we're coming. We could take out all their supplies in one fell swoop," Mara replied.

Kip rubbed his beard absently for a moment. "I don't know about you, but to me this seems like a trap," he said.

"Aye," Teddy agreed. "We've been raiding the roads for months and there's always more soldiers. Always more. Never less. Now we come across the first group in months we can defeat unscathed, and they were carrying vital information for the whole realm. It just doesn't make sense."

Mara groaned and chucked the letters into the back of the wagon and began to pace, thinking. Finally, she said, "What if it *is* a trap?"

"Yes, thank you, we've already established that," Finn said dryly.

"No, no, I mean *so what*?" she said emphatically.

"So what?" Teddy replied. "So we go into a trap, and we all get chopped to bits. That's it. Quest over."

"Well, what's the alternative?" Kip asked Teddy. "Either we go to Fear and hope that we can destroy all the supplies, we go into the cities to see if we can destroy their supplies, or we tuck tail and run."

"We can't run," Finn hissed.

Mara shook her head. "No, we can't. But which is the lesser of the evils? There's no way to know the truth without trying one of them. Teddy?"

Teddy put up his hands in a defensive gesture. "Oh, no. Don't put it on me. I have no way of knowing the right way."

"Well, none of us do!" Kip shouted. "How can any of us bear the brunt of the consequences of a wrong choice here?"

"We can't," Mara whispered. "We'll just have to pick one and deal with the consequences together."

"Aye," Teddy murmured.

"Yes," Finn added.

"Agreed," said Kip. "But how will we decide?"

"Majority rules," Mara said. "We put it to a vote. Each of us picks what we think we should try—Fear or another city—and we'll go with the majority choice." She strode back to the wagon, ripped up four pieces of paper, and handed a piece to each of the men. "Write on these. One for Fear and two for another option. Fold it up and give it to me when you've voted."

Mara stared at her piece of paper for a moment before sighing deeply and quickly writing a one. The others also seemed to struggle with their choice before finally making it and handing Mara their papers before they could change their minds. She shuffled the papers and took a deep breath, looking to each of her companions in turn. They nodded. She opened the first paper.

"One," she whispered. She set the paper on the wagon and opened another. "One." Another, this time more slowly. "One." That was it. It was decided. She opened the final paper anyway. "One," she said.

They stood in silence for a moment. Finally, Teddy clapped his hands. "Well, it's decided. We'd best get ready and head out. There's a long journey from here to Fear."

A fog blanketed the city when Fear finally came into view. Thankfully, all was quiet. Not really sure where to start looking or how to find the supply stores without being caught, they decided that it was finally time for disguises in full. Donning bindrune necklaces and buttoning up their dusters, they planned their excuses. If they were stopped, they would say that they were a straggling supply wagon that had gotten lost in the woods.

Keena's sweater had long since stopped fitting her. Now the size of a full-size Great Dane, with a four-foot wingspan and six-inch curled horns, there was no way to disguise her fully, so Mara improvised, covering Keena with their tarp and tying it around her neck like a cloak.

"Now you listen here, Keena Keena," Mara said. "I know you're big and strong now, but I still don't want you fighting. If things go bad, you have to promise me you'll run. Okay? Promise."

Keena hung her head and whined. *Y-yes, Mama. I promise I will.*

"Okay, good. Just remember, I always love you, my Keena Keena," Mara whispered.

They were ready. It was time. Keena climbed up into the wagon and hid, Kip drove, Teddy led, and Mara and Finn walked on either side of the wagon. Swish whinnied to Mara, and she stepped over to walk beside him, petting his neck.

They slowly entered the city, listening for signs of movement. There were none. Building to building they went, checking for signs of recent visitors or stores. Nothing. Down the streets they went. Nothing. Eventually they made it to the road where Finn had dueled Frank. His blood still stained the dirt. A door slammed. They all snapped to look toward the sound but saw nothing.

Hooting, whooping, and jeering rose up from all around them, and enemies appeared all at once. They were surrounded. In every building in every window stood agents of chaos. They seemed to fade in out of the fog. There would be no escape. There would be no fight. There were just too many of them.

A giant stepped forward out of the crowd and cackled, drawing his revolver. "Caught," he jeered. "Caught like flies in a web. You're mine now, and not even your traitor can help you."

Before Mara could figure out what he meant by traitor, he fired his revolver. Swish let out a harsh whinny and fell, tipping the wagon over as he did. Kip shouted, trapped under the edge of the wagon. "RUN, Keena!" Mara screamed.

Keena bolted out from the edge of the wagon, tarp flapping as she raced, looking for an escape. Finally, with a yelp, she jumped and spread her wings. With the tarp to cover her, she looked like some sort of giant, demon bat. The crowd fell over each other to get away from her. As Mara watched her dragonwolf fly away, the giant stormed toward her, and Keena's flight to freedom faded into darkness.

Chapter Twelve

Bearkin's Adventure

Ashroot sat on the beach outside the Questhaven camp, with Claw curled up in her lap, and gazed out across the sea. It had become an everyday ritual for them to watch the horizon to see if they could spot *Earthbiter* coming back. They spotted dolphins jumping in the distance, whales poking up to take a breath, and all manner of small creatures—mostly turtles and fish—but no dinghy. No friends.

Ashroot sighed and looked down at the pup, scratching his head. "Are you ready to start the day, Claw?" she asked.

The giant wolf pup—now much bigger than her—raised his head and yipped, *Ready. Ready. What today?*

"Today, we're going to make something!" Ashroot replied, in a tone meant to excite him. It worked. Claw sprang up and wagged his tail. Ashroot chuckled. "Alright, big boy, let's go."

She beckoned the wolf pup back to the main tent of the Questhaven camp. After so many months together, they had a system. Fang and Moon's pups adored Ashroot, and they always wanted to keep her safe and keep her company. So, after a while, she gave them jobs so they could feel like they were truly helping her. Whenever she gathered supplies for anything, she had cargo bags hanging over a pup's back like saddle bags. That way, she could gather everything she needed and keep her hands free.

She flipped the bags onto the excited Claw and grabbed her signal drum. The island had been peaceful, but there was always a chance of more goblins returning—or someone just as foul—so Fang had told her to take her drum with her at all times. If she needed him, he would come.

She strapped the drum to her back and picked up her small foraging blade, and then she headed out into the forest with Claw.

What making today? the wolf asked as they walked.

"Today, we're going to get the ingredients to make a special thing the green man's Moon made," Ashroot explained. She knew the wolf wouldn't understand terms like "poultice" or "lifemate."

The wolf asked her what special thing she meant, so Ashroot began, "Well, I've never been good at telling stories, but here we go."

Claw's ears perked up as they headed into the forest and she began her tale.

"Freya came to Ambergrove from a magical land. There, the people were really good at patching up wounds. They had things they called hospitals with experts in them who could perform complicated surgeries—even take someone's heart out of them and put it in you!" Ashroot raised her voice to add some spookiness to her tone.

The pup squeaked, and she grinned as she continued, "Well, Freya's mother was Ambergrovian, but her father was a big doctor—what they call the healers on Earth. He taught her a lot about what they call medicine as she was growing up. By the time she was sixteen and came to Ambergrove, she had already gone to a special place to learn about medicine and helping people."

Ashroot paused as they reached a cluster of purplish, spiky plants. Gingerly, she harvested its bulbs, severing the bulb at the base but leaving the plant intact and alive, wrapped the bulbs in some cloth, and added them to Claw's bag before moving on.

"When she arrived in Darbut, a human town, she was excited and happy to be in Ambergrove, but sad to be away from her pack," Ashroot continued. "When she saw how the healing man worked and what he worked with, she was very upset. Many people died before they even made it to the healer's hut after an injury. After all that she'd been used to, what Ambergrove had for medicine was not good enough."

Ashroot stopped again, this time at a yellow flower with blue stripes. She carefully removed the leaves from the flower stems and added them to Claw's supplies. When she stretched and turned to continue walking, Claw excitedly yipped, *What next? What next?*

She smiled and went on, "Freya spent a lot of her time traveling through the forests looking for ingredients for a special medicine. She gathered many plants—the same ones we're getting now. The last thing she was looking for led her into the forest of Aeunna—where the green man lived. She didn't find the thing in Aeunna, but she did find the green man, and all the people. After some time, they welcomed her into their pack. In return, she helped their healing man. She also made her new thing for them. It was a special thing meant to help the wounded warrior until they could get to a healer who could help them. There were plants to stop poison from moving and plants to help slow the blood flow. Some helped to keep the wound from getting infected, and there were many other properties—much more than I know."

Her helped? Claw asked when Ashroot paused again for a blue vine climbing up a tree.

"Yes, Claw, she helped," Ashroot replied, smiling. "Everyone in Aeunna, and many other forest dwarves and good humans, carry some of the special thing everywhere they go. But it takes someone trained to make it who knows how to make things."

Not green man?

"No, not the green man."

Though not for lack of trying, she thought. For as long as she could remember, any time Teddy went on a long journey, Freya would try again to teach him to make the poultice. He would grumble and do his best, but it never turned out right, and Freya always ended up just sending him off with a giant bag full. When he'd officially confirmed that he would be helping Mara complete her trial, Freya had gathered Ashroot and Teddy to try to teach them both to make it. Teddy couldn't figure it out, but Ashroot did. They made sure to keep well-stocked, but every so often she'd need to go into a forest to gather ingredients to make more. Thankfully, the last time her stores needed replenishing had been in Nimeda, and supplies were plentiful.

As they went deeper into the forest, Ashroot talked to the animals they passed, explaining to them that Claw wouldn't hurt them—at least not right then—because he had a job to do and wasn't hunting. The animals who understood this enjoyed these gathering times, because they would take the opportunity to antagonize the pups when there was nothing they could do about it. Ashroot had ordered that there would be no ruckus while they were gathering supplies unless a real danger came for them. But none did on this trip, so Claw walked for much of the rest of the trip grumbling because a fox curled up to nap on his back as he walked.

When Ashroot had everything she needed and returned to the camp, Claw bolted as soon as the bag was lifted from his shoulders, darting through the woods in search of the pesky fox.

Once the poultice was made and her lunch eaten, Ashroot sat at the table in the main tent with a book propped open in front of her while she absently sewed, patching one of Kip's shirts. After the first terrible trip to Chaosland, Mara had brought a book back with her. A journal. The writer, a woman named Maggie Sanderson, had been brought to Ambergrove right before New Switzerland fell into chaos. Her story made Ashroot feel like she was connected to her friends so far away.

Each day, Maggie wrote about her own life and how the place they called Lesser Earth was changing. How nothing was what she thought it would be. According to her earlier entries, she'd stubbornly decided to stick to Earth's special calendar, and journaling helped her to keep the days straight—even if it wasn't actually November or whatever other silly name they used. Ashroot enjoyed pretending she knew what the woman was talking about, fitting herself into that world, and she hoped that one entry would eventually contain something helpful for Mara. The Sandersons kept to themselves, so this would never happen. The stories ended up much the same. Today, Ashroot read:

May 17, 1889 (?)

Margaret,

6:00AM: It's a warm day today. It will be a perfect day for the New Switzerland Festival. I've got my pie baked and ready. Peach and crimsonberry. I really hope the Sandersons can beat the Davissons this year. It's really time someone taught them a lesson. Grandmother is knocking. Time to head out. Check back later.

9:00AM: The festival is going well! I snuck the journal with me. There's games this year, like the festival games I used to play when I was little. I can't wait to play them when the judging is over. Now, we're waiting for the judging to be complete. John Davisson made a basic apple pie, so I should win this year. Oh—the judges are coming back. Standby.

12:00PM: I WON! I won this year! The judges loved my pie! I pinned my ribbon to my chest when it was over, I had the rest of the morning to explore. I played the tossing game with Annabelle Morrisson. In case I forget when I'm old, you take a wooden ball, and you throw it at bottles to win prizes. I won a beautiful scarf. It's now lunchtime here. The baker made some very nice cheesy bread for the occasion, and we had a potluck with tasty bread bowls. The stew was amazing, and I can only hope that it continues to get better every year. Next, I'm going to—

7:00PM: Today was ruined, Margaret. Men came to the city from New London. On horseback. With torches. And clubs. They destroyed the game carts. They set fire to all our festival decorations and threw torches through many windows. They dumped our stew in the dirt, and they hurt us. They hurt me. A man beat me with a club and laughed. They told us that we'd gotten away for too long being backward, and the other cities could no longer stand by and allow New Switzerland to be different. This festival would be our last, and a grisly end would come for all who didn't follow their new plan for us. The mayor stood up to them and was shot by a big man on a horse.

This is not what we dreamed of, Margaret. We dreamed of dragons and fairies. We dreamed of magic and daring swordfights. Nothing here is as it should be. Knowing what I know now, knowing what happened here today, if I had the chance to go back home, I would. This isn't a better place. It's just more of the same. Men on horses coming to take what isn't theirs, not leaving the people in peace. It's a terrible place full of poison and poisonous people.

It's time to go now, Margaret. Grandmother says that the fires in the city have all been put out, and all the bad men are gone. The sheriff brought out much of the city's ice stores for the injured, and we must go

> *that way if I am to get any relief for his wound on my head. Today was awful, Margaret, but we're still here working together. We still care about each other, and we won't let their poison overtake us.*
>
> *Tomorrow will be better.*

Ashroot closed the journal. Horrible. Absolutely horrible. So many people came to Ambergrove with dreams of magic and adventure, but their hate and their treachery came with them. This is what Mara and her friends were trying to protect. The innocence of a young girl who thought she'd realized a dream, only to have it destroyed by the greed of others. She was tempted to turn the page, to see what the next day held for Maggie, but that was for tomorrow. It was time for her to move on to the next task.

Later in the evening, when Ashroot had her supper, Moon came to sit with her so she wouldn't be alone. It was a curtesy at least one of the wolves took for her every meal. As Ashroot ate—a grilled fish and some fresh vegetables and berries—Moon stretched out by the dying fire outside the tent.

Did you have an eventful day today, strange bear? Moon asked.

"Same as usual, I guess, Moon," Ashroot replied, popping a strawberry into her mouth. "I just feel so unhelpful. So useless tottering about here. I just feel like I should be *more.*"

The wolf cackled and sat up, peering at Ashroot with a large, twinkling eye. *Don't we all! Don't we all wish to be more? To do more? Don't you think I wished I could have done more for my pups when your pack saved us?* the wolf asked.

"Well, yes, I mean—"

Of course, I did. Of course, you do. We can't be helpful at every point in time. We just have to do what we can when the opportunity arises, Moon explained.

"I suppose," Ashroot replied quietly, taking a last bite of her fish.

Had you still been in your home, what would you have been doing?

Ashroot stared out at the water for a moment before replying, "Do you mean if I hadn't come with Mara or if we'd all been there?"

Moon cocked her head to one side, thinking. *Either.*

Ashroot twisted the remaining fishtail absently. What *would* she be doing? She reached out and opened the back of the Sanderson journal, sliding out a worn picture. Five faces stared back at her—Keena's bright, Finn's stern, Kip's merry, Teddy's mischievous, and Mara's … warm. "I don't," she mumbled.

You what? Moon asked.

"Uh—um," Ashroot stammered. She looked down at the picture. "I don't want to be there. I know that I'm not doing much now, really, but I've made good friends on this journey. There is so much I wouldn't have done without this journey—without them and you …" she quieted the longer she spoke and then went silent.

Hmm, Moon growled, *Even the smallest voice, when paired with the greatest heart, can and will make a difference. You have a good heart, strange bear, and your pack loves you for it.*

Ashroot smiled. "Thank you, dear friend," she said quietly, turning and looking at the darkening sky over the horizon.

Ah, it is time now, isn't it? Moon asked, standing and stretching.

Ashroot looked back at the wolf and nodded.

I will leave you then, strange bear, Moon said, bowing her head and turning to pad back into the forest toward her den.

Ashroot gathered her things, washing her plate, dousing the fire, and cleaning up. Then, she grabbed her signal drum, walked to the edge of the forest, and looped around to the southwestern tip of the island. She sat on the edge of the cliff overlooking the camp to give herself a further view of the sea beyond.

For the past five months, since *Earthbiter* had vanished into the horizon, Ashroot had ended her days the same way. She would tell the water about her day, dreaming she was telling her friends instead. As she regaled her small adventures, she would watch the horizon, hoping that a black sail would appear in the distance. Hoping her friends had finally returned. Finally, when she did see something on the horizon, it was not the dinghy. It was something that crushed all her hopes and left her standing at the edge of the beach, pounding on her signal drum and holding back tears, her eyes wide with fear.

Chapter Thirteen

Harsh Lessons

The first time Mara stirred, she woke in a pile of jumbled limbs in the back of a wagon. Her head ached, and her heart was heavy. Swish dead, Keena lost. It was unthinkable. Unbearable. She groaned and tried to sit up.

"One of them is moving, boss!" came a gruff voice.

"Well, hit them again," was the reply.

Mara whipped her head around to see the butt of a rifle coming toward her face, and then she saw no more.

The next time Mara stirred, she was tied to a tree in the middle of a dark forest. Her eyes fluttered open, and she panicked, struggling against her bonds.

"Hey, hey, calm yourself, lass," Teddy whispered.

Mara froze and looked around. Teddy was tied to a tree opposite her, Finn was tied to a tree to Teddy's left, and Kip was tied to a tree to Mara's right. In the faint moonlight she could see blood staining each of their faces. From the pounding in her head, she assumed hers matched each of theirs.

"W-where are we, Teddy?" she asked quietly.

He shook his head. "No idea. They kept knocking us out when we woke. Best I can figure, they brought us to a secluded forest so they can get information from us without worrying about reinforcements."

Mara cocked her head, about to ask Teddy what reinforcements he was talking about, when Finn coughed theatrically, spat, and replied, "Yeah, I wouldn't want to deal with a whole regiment either when I could deal with four."

"Hey, quiet about the regiment!" Kip whispered harshly. "You never know who may be listening."

"Or watching," came a decidedly evil voice.

Mara peered in the direction of the sound. Where before she had seen only darkness, vague figures and glowing, amber eyes came into focus. She shivered.

"Now then." The giant commander who'd captured them stepped out of the full darkness into their little hostage clearing. He looked at each of them in turn, continuing, "My men and I are going to have a chat with each of you. By the time we're done, you're going to tell us everything we want to know about your operation—how you know our supply routes, why you've been stealing our supplies and destroying our weapons, who you serve, and why you're here. Then, you're going to tell me things I just feel like knowing. By sunrise, I'll know things about you that don't matter at all, because you'll tell me anything to stop what I'm about to do to you." He grinned and cackled.

A buzz of evil laughter resonated from the depths of the forest. *Torture. These are people who torture,* Mara thought. The fear seeped into her like a sponge. She'd never been taught to withstand torture. It had never been on the table. When she got hurt in battle, she'd always been so full of adrenaline she didn't notice much until it was over. But torture was different.

"Now, who shall we start with on this fine evening?" the giant said.

"Let's start with the little one," someone growled.

"No, the sea elf! I've always wanted to sink a knife into one of them," said another.

"How about the *woman*?" another asked. Mara turned to the voice. A human stepped into the moonlight and looked her over. "I'm sure we could have lots of fun with her." She felt the color drain from her face, and she heard Kip next to her, struggling against his bonds.

The giant threw his head back and laughed, looking into Kip's fiery eyes, and then Teddy's and Finn's to match. "Oh, I think her little friends would put up quite a fight if we started with her. Besides," he turned to Mara, "we should save the best for last." He grinned wolfishly at Mara before scanning the group in mock speculation. "No, no …" he continued. "No, why don't we start with the leader of this band of thorns? … I'm betting, that's …you." He turned his back to Mara and pointed.

Teddy stared back at him defiantly and spat.

"Ah, yes! Definitely you!" the giant boomed delightedly. He turned to the men in the darkness. "Get him up and take him to the campfire," he ordered.

Mara watched helplessly as Teddy was dragged through the clearing and out of sight, unable to force herself to move or utter a single sound.

Although Teddy was a seasoned warrior, he'd lived a cushy life for many years, and he expected those years were about to catch up with him in one go. Two things he vowed. First, if he ever made it back to Aeunna, he would take an active hand in the warrior training once more. No more napping under trees while Cora trained the students or they trained themselves. He needed to stay sharp, and he needed to make sure they did too. Second, most important, and flooding him with a rush of anger that heated his whole body, he would die a terrible death before he let a single one of their captors lay a finger on Mara.

Teddy was thrown to the ground by a small campfire. The giant man sat on a stump in front of him, and various captors surrounded him. Teddy looked the giant over. The man oozed confidence, and with it darkness, evil, and a twinkle of joy. He would enjoy torturing Teddy—every moment of it. Teddy righted himself to sit on the ground and stare into the giant's hard, dark eyes.

The giant leaned forward and smiled. "Forest dwarf," he began, "you're a long way from home, aren't you? Let's say, leader-to-leader, you tell me what it is you're doing here."

Teddy glared back at the giant. "If you think I'm going to just *tell you* anything, you're new to the interrogation business," he replied.

"Oh, no, you've got it all wrong," the giant said in mock assurance. "This isn't an interrogation. No, not really. I mean, I'd like you to tell me what you know, yes, and I'm sure my men and I would get commendations from the Great Harbinger if you did, but no. No …" The giant reached out and grabbed Teddy by the beard, jerking his head slowly from side to side. "No, I'm here to see how much pain you can take before you break—give up your people, faint, die, it makes no difference to me. But you will stay here with me until I break you. Now what do you think about that?"

Teddy chopped at the giant's arm and shoved him as roughly as he could manage, freeing his beard. He spat at the ground. "Get on with it, then! Your yammering certainly isn't going to get you anywhere," he shouted.

Teddy was clubbed on the head from behind—not enough to knock him out again, but enough for him to see stars. The giant sat back up on the stump and raised a hand. "Now, now, no need for that. He'll learn soon enough, and I want to be the one to teach him," he said.

Teddy watched as the giant reached around for a stick and jabbed it into the campfire. The giant cast a hand over the flames and allowed them to lick his palm before slowly drawing the stick from the fire and blowing out the flames that came with it. He ordered his men to remove Teddy's chainmail and hold him down, and Teddy struggled against their grip until they cast the chainmail shirt into the fire and locked his arms behind him, forcing him to kneel and look at the giant.

"First lesson," the giant said calmly. "What happens to green skin when met with hot embers?" He smiled at Teddy for a moment before slowly lowering the stick to rest against Teddy's bare arm.

The skin sizzled. Teddy groaned softly and clenched his teeth to bear the pain. The smell of burning flesh was not unknown to him, but it had been a long time since it had been his own. Teddy closed his eyes and tried to slow his breathing. *Mara,* he thought. *This is just the beginning. You have to take it until your body gives out or this is what they'll do to Mara. Or worse.* Teddy's eyes snapped open, and he glared defiantly into the giant's eyes.

The giant removed the stick and looked down. "Hmm, dark green burns and pink underneath. How disappointing," he said.

The giant continued in this way for a long time, calmly and slowly applying one painful practice or another, determined when Teddy sat still and silent, and delighted when Teddy reacted to the pain. After burning his arms and neck, cutting into his legs and face, and touching him with something identified as a "cattle prod," the giant began to get frustrated at Teddy's resolve. He instructed his men to tie Teddy down, and they brought a log to lash his hands to before the giant knelt in front of Teddy and drew a small, boot dagger.

"Fourth lesson," the giant murmured, licking his lips. "How many fingers can someone lose before he cries like a newborn babe and begs me to let him keep them?" Teddy's eyes widened and the giant grinned, satisfied. He continued, "Let's see, shall we?"

As the giant brought the knife down, Teddy's face twisted in horror.

Finn listened to the echoing screams and clenched his fists. He never thought he'd hear Teddy make such sounds. Unlike Teddy, Finn had very recently been trained to withstand torture, so he was feeling at least a little confident in his ability to outlast them, but he'd never been tortured outside of training, and he didn't know what to expect in such an awful place. He heard a sniffle and looked up.

Tears streamed down Mara's face as she whispered, "Oh, Teddy. Teddy. I'm so sorry, Teddy. Oh, no. Oh, Teddy."

Kip shifted his position, and Finn turned to look at him. Kip's determined eyes mirrored his own thoughts. *Curse these people. What they're doing to Teddy, what they're going to do to us, what that's going to do to Mara. Curse them, torture or no. They're going to pay for this.*

He jumped when he heard a rustling from the darkness in the direction of the campfire. He hadn't noticed the screams finally stopped; they still echoed in his ears. An unconscious Teddy was dragged unceremoniously through the clearing and back to the tree where he'd been tied. Both hands were covered in bloody bandages—the left slightly bloodier than the right. Teddy groaned softly as they dropped him to the ground and tied him back up to the tree.

The giant strode into the clearing and scanned each of their faces before landing on Finn's. "Why don't we take you next?" he said. "I'll take the Doberman before the chew toy." He jerked his head to indicate he meant Kip and then he turned back to his men. "Take the sea elf."

Finn met Kip's hard gaze as he was untied and dragged away, but Mara only sobbed and stared blankly at Teddy's bloodied and maimed body.

Sitting on the ground by the campfire, the grass glistening with Teddy's fresh blood, Finn glared at the giant with all his might. The giant sat once more on the stump by the campfire, leaning forward and smiling. "You see," he'd said, "I'm not going to hurt you until you spill your secrets. I'm going to teach you some lessons, and I won't be done until you've learned—and until you can't take any more."

"I'm ready," Finn spat.

The giant leaned forward and smiled. "You see, that's what the forest dwarf said too. And then I took a few of his fingers to teach him a lesson." Finn growled and lurched forward, but hands pulled him back and down to the ground. The giant continued, "But you know what? By the time I was finished, he did tell me something. About why you're here. I could have guessed, of course, but it was nice to be told all the same."

The giant leaned back on the stump and reached a hand out expectantly behind him. A goblin handed him a charred piece of fabric, and the giant held it up to Finn. "Do you recognize this?" he asked. He glanced at the cloth for a moment before looking back to Finn. "No, I suppose not. I have heard that sea elves know their ships like a first-born child, but a dinghy isn't really a ship, is it?"

The giant tossed the fabric at Finn's face. The sea elf looked down at the charred remains. They really were in a bind. Even if they did somehow manage to survive all of this, Swish was dead. They would have to find their own way walking across Chaosland. But to where? Their transportation had been destroyed. They didn't have a way out. They were trapped in Ambergrove's darkest land.

"Mmm," the giant breathed, closing his eyes. "That there. The realization of hopelessness. Like mother's milk."

He gestured to the goblin to retrieve the material from Finn, and as the goblin bent down in front of him, Finn jerked to the side with all his might, knocking the goblin into the campfire. The creature shrieked as his companions rushed to get him out quickly, but it was no use. Once they'd patted out the flames, another goblin leaned over his charred friend and put him out of his misery.

The giant's eyes flashed briefly before he returned to impossible calm. He grabbed Finn by the shoulders and pressed his face near the smoldering embers of the partially doused fire. "First lesson," he whispered into Finn's ear. "What happens to you when you kill one of our own?"

He pressed Finn's body close to the fire, and the links of his chainmail began to sizzle into his blue arms. Finn winced but remained silent. His first lesson in torture had been that his belongings would always be used against him. This was something he was ready for. Finn held his breath and endured. After a few moments of light roasting, they threw him back to the ground and the giant stood and began to slowly pace.

Finn sat up and panted. "If that's … just for killing … one guy …" He gulped. "What about … all the other guys?" he asked.

"Oh, all our men on the road?" the giant asked, not turning. "You'll all pay for them."

"No, no," Finn replied, struggling to right himself and to add some gravity to his tone. "No, I mean at the beginning. So many months ago, when we just arrived here. You may have captured us in Fear, but we killed plenty of your men there too. And not just filthy goblins," he spat.

The goblin who mercifully killed his dying friend lurched forward, but the giant held up a hand and leered at Finn. "Oh, I know," he said. "You killed giants too. One was a woman I've known since childhood, out for her first patrol as the leader and out for a routine supply run to Fear. We found her charred body with the others. Is it her blood that stains the street even now?"

Finn shook his head and grinned. "No, no. That was a human. We questioned him about your land, only we didn't need to resort to torture to get what we wanted. He spilled your secrets for us without that. Told us how you lived. Showed us how to find you. He was *weak*," he taunted.

"Ah, yes, we did find a map and kaleidoscopes among your belongings," the giant replied. "But I assume your big man executed him, soft as he is."

Finn threw his head back and laughed, trying to continue the charade of confidence as long as he could. "No, no, that was me. Took him out to the street and just let him bleed. What was his name? Oh, yeah, *Frank,*" Finn said. "Frank was sad. Sad as a warrior, sad as a man, sad in death," he finished, emphasizing each word.

From behind the giant, a woman, a human with greying hair, charged forward, wailing in pain and fury. She flung her duster flap to one side and drew her revolver, pointing it at Finn. As she fired, the goblin, pushed her arm and shouted, "No, Wendy!" The bullet missed its mark.

But the giant wasn't looking at the bullet. He wasn't looking at the goblin or at Wendy. He was looking at Finn, whose skin had turned a pale bluish white when the gun was drawn, and who had flinched when the shot was fired. The giant walked slowly toward Finn, his eyes searching. "Do my eyes deceive me?" he said incredulously. "A sea elf . . . *afraid*?"

The giant threw back his head and laughed before striding forward and plopping down on the stump in front of Finn. He watched Finn's face as he slowly slid his duster to the side to reveal his own revolver, slid the gun out of the holster, and raised it to Finn's face. He ran the barrel down Finn's cheek once and poked him in the chest with it.

Finn began to sweat uncontrollably, flinching at every movement of the gun before whimpering softly when the giant dry fired it right next to his cheek. He was terrified. Terrified. Yes, he could try to hold his own against a torturer, and he could last against cuts and burns like Teddy had, but not guns. He thought he had been doing so well, but now, surrounded by them, all alone, all he could think of was lying on the floor that first trip to Fear, his gut wrenching from the pain of multiple bullet wounds, sure he was going to die. Here he was again, sure that he was going to die. Sure that death for him came at the wrong end of a gun.

"You *are* afraid!" the giant shouted. Laughing reverberated through the forest as the captors all came to the same realization. "You! A sea elf! Afraid!" The giant stood and paced around the campfire, laughing and waving his arms around, gun still in hand. "I mean, really! A sea elf. Have you ever heard of a sea elf to be afraid?" There were scattered chuckles in response. "No, no. Me neither. Man, did they get it wrong with you. No wonder you're out with a soft forest dwarf, a puny gnome, and a *woman*. Why, you're practically a woman yourself!"

The giant crossed his arms and looked up at the sky, disbelieving, still going on about the impossibility of the situation. How unlucky were they to finally find a sea elf—probably the worthiest opponent in Ambergrove—only to find out that he was nothing but a frightened boy? The injustice! Finally, with a sigh, the giant wiped the gleeful tears from his face and returned his revolver to his holster. When he turned back around to face Finn, his face had flattened.

"Second lesson," the giant murmured, walking toward Finn. "What kind of sea elf is afraid of something—anything—much less a tiny piece of metal?" He drew a tiny blade from his boot and nodded to his men, who grabbed Finn by the shoulders and shoved him roughly to the ground so his head rested on a bloody log. Finn struggled against their grip. The giant kicked Finn in the jaw to quieten him before adding terribly, "Answer? … There isn't one." Kneeling in front of Finn, his eyes glistened as he met Finn's gaze. When he continued, his voice was a dark whisper, "But you know what? We can fix that."

The giant pressed one massive hand on Finn's head to hold it still against the log before reaching the blade out to rest against the pointed tip of Finn's ear.

As Finn's screams were drowned out by echoing laughter, Kip could only wonder what they could be doing to him. Teddy remained unconscious, and Kip just hoped upon hope that the old man hadn't lost more blood than he could spare. There was another worry—not his own torture; he'd have to deal with that when it came—no, it was Mara.

She had long since stopped crying. He suspected there just wasn't any more left in her at that moment. Her uncle's pain had damaged her, and the pain of her friends was just salt in the wound. At that moment, looking at the loss in her eyes, Kip didn't much care if someone was listening.

"Hey, now," he murmured. "Look at me."

Mara turned and gazed miserably into his eyes, her face and eyes all red and puffy, her eyes deadened, dulled with her emotional pain. He shifted slightly against his bonds to better face her, and then he smiled reassuringly. "We're going to figure this out. I promise." There was a dry laugh from somewhere in the forest. Kip continued, "Seriously. We have made it through so much already, and there's so much left to do still. It doesn't end today."

"It might," she whispered.

Kip's heart ached to hear the hopelessness in her voice. *I hope never to hear that sadness in her voice again,* he thought. He pushed confidence into his own voice when he replied. "No, it won't. It can't. Fate brought you here to the realm of chaos, and all of us with you. We're not done until fate says we're done, and we're not done until your quest is completed."

Mara nodded miserably. "But they've hurt Teddy. They're hurting Finn. And they're going to hurt you," she whispered.

"Yeah, maybe, but mark my words: They will not get through me to you. This pain you feel knowing what's been done to us is the only pain you're going to feel tonight."

Kip looked into Mara's eyes, ready to tell her goodbye, ready to tell her what he'd been holding in for over a year with her, but as he inhaled to begin, the screams died away and the laughing in the forest grew louder. Finn was dragged back into the clearing by cackling and jeering captors, and Kip turned to see blood running down the sides of Finn's face and neck, disappearing to glisten in the chainmail. Mara cried out in horror, but Kip hissed for silence. They tied Finn back up to the tree as the giant strode in once more, turning quickly to face Mara and Kip.

"Alright, now is time for the little one," he said, rubbing his hands together in anticipation as his men untied Kip. Before leaving the clearing, he turned back to Mara and added, "Don't worry, young lady. We'll be back for you soon enough."

No, no you really won't, Kip thought fervently.

"So," the giant began, sitting on a stump in front of Kip after the gnome had been thrown to the ground. "So, my men tell me that you had some nice words for that girl just now. Told her how we weren't going to hurt her. That you wouldn't let that happen. Touching. Touching. But misguided."

The giant stood and walked around. "I mean, how kind of you to give her a little hope that she might not meet a grisly end here in these woods. She'll be so surprised when her turn comes and her little knight in dingy scale mail isn't there to protect her. Oh, to see the look on her face. I cannot wait."

"Well, you're just going to have to," Kip said.

"Yes, yes, maybe. But not too long, I think." The giant looked Kip up and down. "Not much of you here to play with is there?"

"Yeah, boss, it won't take long at all to break this one," someone jeered from behind Kip.

"Now, now," the giant said. "Let's give him the benefit of the doubt, Jeff. I'm sure we'd all want our goblin brethren to outlast any pain, despite their size."

"Yeah," came a throaty voice from behind Kip. "It wasn't one of *our* kind who slipped and told them our secrets!"

There was a tussle, and a crazed woman charged the goblin before the giant rose and whistled sharply, glaring at the creature behind Kip. "Now then!" he barked. "We have a task at hand here that cannot be completed without a certain level of professionalism. Do you want them to think we're heathens?" After scattered murmurs, the giant nodded curtly and sat back down on the stump in front of Kip.

"Your blue companion there was broken by fear, did you know?" he said, sliding his duster to the side and drawing his revolver, watching Kip intently for any reaction. "You see, your blue friend was afraid of this little thing. He's just blue, you see, not a real sea elf—well, not anymore anyway." His companions chuckled. The giant poked Kip's ear with the barrel of his revolver a few times and said, "No more pointy ears, you see. There's no point to that blue man. No fight. No fire. So, we rounded his ears so no one would ever mistake him for a sea elf. Now he's just … blue."

Oh, Finn, Kip thought miserably. He shrugged in what he hoped was a noncommittal way. "Well, I guess it's good that gnomes don't have such reputations," he said.

"Hmm, yes. Though your reputation is a lot like what your friend's turned out to be, and it's no fun to hurt someone who can't take any of it. No fun at all." The giant holstered his gun and slipped a small knife out of his boot, sighing. "I guess since you're small we can start small, but I promise I'll take my time."

He brought the tip of the knife up to Kip's leg and ran the blade lightly down his thigh, just enough to make a shallow cut. He continued in this way, making small slices in Kip's legs, shredding his pants, but doing little, stinging damage instead of real damage. He dug a little deeper with his second pass, and Kip was finding it difficult to remain stubbornly silent. Unlike Finn, although he was a trained soldier with too many scars to count, he hadn't really had any experience with torture. And there's a big difference between pain in battle and pain when you're just sitting and waiting for it to come.

"What's all this then?" A giant man, much larger than the giant in charge, appeared from the depths of the forest. He strode into the camp with an air of great authority, and Kip was surprised to see a complete change in all the captors around him. The torturer sheathed his small knife and stood at attention, bowing respectfully to the newcomer.

"Captain, we weren't expecting you," the smaller giant said.

"Clearly." The captain leered down at the other giant and then to Kip. "What's this?"

"Uh, this is one of our prisoners," the other giant stammered. "You see, we captured the reavers in Fear and we brought them here to question them so—"

"The Great Harbinger is not interested in questioning them," the captain snapped. "Dispose of this. I have news to bring you from the capitol." The smaller giant nodded meekly and approached Kip, who squeaked and went limp, flopping to the ground. The captain laughed once, sharply, and then added, "Never mind, just leave him there for now."

He beckoned for the others to gather around him, and they obeyed, leaving Kip with one human guard. Kip slowed his breathing. If he was going to pretend to faint to keep them from killing him immediately, he would have to sell it well to buy himself any time at all. He breathed evenly and listened intently as the captain began.

Chapter Fourteen

Fight and Flight

The Great Harbinger was ready, the giant explained. Through the hooting and cackling, Kip strained to hear without being noticed. The captain paused, for effect, surely—he knew what treasured information he possessed.

"Settle, settle," he growled. "Yes, yes, the Great Harbinger is ready to begin the spread of chaos to other lands. Despite *their* feeble attempts to delay us, we are ready."

Someone kicked Kip in the back of the head, and the crowd cackled. He did his best to lie still. *You'll get yours, buddy,* he thought.

"What's the plan, then, Captain?" came a raspy voice, likely a goblin.

"Well … we have eliminated our only threat, so in two full turnings of the moon, we will all gather. The Great Harbinger will lay out plans for our bright future, and we will make final preparations to begin building our ships," the captain explained.

"The moon will rise as the reign of chaos comes to fruition," a woman said wistfully.

"Where will it all happen?"

There was a pause and a rustling of papers, and then the captain said, "The Harbinger's symbol can only be seen by firelight."

Of course, Kip thought. Gingerly, he opened his eyes the tiniest bit and risked a glance. The captain stood over the campfire with the others gathered around him. Kip could just barely make out a reddish glowing symbol before someone moved behind him and he snapped his eyes closed again and tried to burn the image into his mind.

"Oi!" shouted his sentry. "Dontcha think before revealing the location of our Great Harbinger, we should get rid of the gnome?"

"He's out cold, George," someone called back. "What harm could he do?"

"No, no, he's right. Best be safe," the captain said. "Go tie him back up. George, was it? We can deal with him and his friends later."

"And the girl!"

There was a buzz of agreement as George picked Kip up and dragged him back to his tree. It took all of Kip's effort to keep himself calm, and he almost grinned when George groaned at the deadweight. *Good.*

Mara cried out in relief when she saw the guard return with Kip. He didn't have any immediately visible injuries like Finn or Teddy, and that was surely the best she could hope for. The guard threw Kip unceremoniously against the tree and tied him up, grumbling and cursing about how heavy the gnome was for a little guy. When he was done, he kicked Kip once for good measure and spat before turning away.

"Barbarian!" Mara shouted angrily.

The guard stopped and slowly turned. "You'll see just how much when our business is done and we come back for *you,*" he jeered. Then he turned and was gone.

Kip slowly opened his eyes and smiled at her. "It's alright, Mara. We're going to be alright."

"How can you say that? What did they do to you? Did they cut off any of your fingers?" she burst.

"No, no, someone came before they really started in on me, so they never got the chance," Kip replied. "But we need to find a way out of here now, before they come back for you." Mara nodded, gulping back tears. Kip continued, "How have they been?" He nodded to the other men, who both sat unmoving.

"Not good," she whispered miserably. "Not good at all. Both have been out cold for a while now. Teddy I'm sure has lost a lot of blood, and Finn—" Her lip quivered for a moment before she choked, "I don't know how he's ever going to recover from this."

"He will, and so will Teddy. You have to believe that. Now, have you been able to loosen your ropes at all?"

She shook her head. "The movies always make it seem so simple. There's always a jagged nail or something, and they get out in minutes, just in time to get the bad guy at a pivotal moment." She sighed, laying her head back against the tree. "Sometimes I wish the movies were true."

"This would be the best time for it, too, since they're all occupied and we're all here," Kip murmured, tilting back to do the same.

As if fate had just been waiting for them to catch up, a wolf howled in the distance. Kip and Mara snapped to look at each other. "That's it!" they whispered. Mara made a bird call—as light and inconspicuous as she could. She repeated the call a few times before a giant, brown owl came to rest on her leg, talons digging into her flesh. She winced.

Why are you calling into the forest, dwarf? the owl asked.

"We are in need of help, great owl," Mara replied. "I thank you for coming to our aid."

I cannot free you from these bonds.

"No … but you can find someone who can."

Time passed so slowly after the owl flew away. Mara tensed at every rustle and loud sound that made its way to them from the enemy camp. Finally, a rustle and a familiar yip came from a different direction. The owl glided into the clearing, and Keena dogged quickly behind, crashing into Mara and covering her excitedly with kisses.

"Shh. Quiet, Keena. I'm glad you're okay, too, but we need to get out of here now, before the bad guys come back," she whispered. She looked around for the owl, but he was gone. She turned back to Keena. "Can you chew Mama out of these ropes?" she asked.

Keena plodded around to the back of the tree, made a few small noises in effort, and the rope slackened around Mara's wrists. She was free. Keena ran next to free Kip, and then Finn, and then Teddy. Mara ran first to Teddy and grabbed one of his butchered hands. It had been wrapped, but not tightly. The bandage was sopping with blood.

No time for this now, she thought. Blessing the stupidity that prompted their enemy to take their supplies only to leave them in a pile at the center of their little prison, Mara strode to the pile and grabbed her father's dagger. She quickly hiked up her chainmail and quilted shirt and cropped off the bottom half of her undershirt. Carefully but quickly, she made tourniquets and stemmed the flow of Teddy's wounds.

When she returned to the supply pile to load up to leave, Kip stood there with Finn. The elf stood on his own, but his eyes had no light in them, and his face was blank. Kip had clearly done the same thing Mara had—Finn's head was now wrapped tightly with a piece of brown cloth. Finn muttered incomprehensibly, and Mara's thoughts raced to those who'd been tortured to insanity. All she could make out were "ship" and "burned." Kip just shook his head once, and he and Mara began to load up supplies.

"Neither of these two will be able to carry anything on their own," Kip murmured as he picked up Finn's dirks.

"Then we'll travel light," Mara replied. Surveying their supplies once, she added, "All we need are the basic weapons. We can leave the crossbows. Collect weapons and take my pack so we can try to bandage these two properly. Do you think he can follow behind?" Mara tipped her head to gesture toward Finn.

"I don't know. We'll have to try. It will probably take the both of us to get Teddy away from here without dragging him."

Mara paused for a moment and looked back at her tree. "Get him ready to go," she said quickly. Kip turned and returned Finn's dirks to their sheaths, and Mara did the same with Teddy's sword. Then, she went back to her tree and gathered some of the rope from her bindings. Wordlessly, she walked over to Finn and looped the rope around his waist, tying it tightly. Then she retrieved Kip's spear and pressed it into Finn's hands.

"What are you—" Kip began.

"Keena!" Mara whispered sharply. Her pup hurried over to her side. "I need you to lead him with us, okay? I'm going to tie this rope around you, and you have to pull him along, even if he doesn't want to follow you. That's the only way to keep him safe. Do you understand?"

Keena bobbed her head and stood beside Finn, while Mara looped the rope around her neck and chest and tied it. Then she and Kip each wrapped an arm around Teddy to heft him to their shoulders, and they walked out into the darkness of the forest, Keena trailing behind while Finn followed without seeing.

They trudged through the forest until the sun was coming up, and they found themselves along the coast. There were a few places along the beach where they might hide, so Mara and Kip lay Teddy down there. He had stirred a few times, but he still hadn't woken. Turning to Keena, Mara pulled out her dagger and cut her free from Finn, who Kip led to sit by Teddy as Mara knelt beside Keena and blinked back tears.

What's wrong, Mama? Keena asked.

"I have to ask you to do something, Keena. Something big," Mara said miserably.

What is it, Mama?

Mara turned to glance at Kip before replying, "They destroyed our little boat, Keena. We can't sail back to the island. We need Ashroot to come get us so we can save Teddy and Finn."

"You can't—" Kip began.

Keena stretched her wings slightly and tilted her head. She knew what her mama meant.

"Keena, I need you to fly back to Questhaven and bring Ashroot back to us on the raft so we can get back there. Can you do that for me?" Mara asked.

Keena bobbed her head and rubbed affectionately against Mara, licking away her tears. *I love Mama,* she said.

"I love you, too, my Keena Keena," Mara replied. "Be safe and come back to us."

Without another word, Keena plodded down the beach, flapping her wings. Once she had enough speed, she lifted steadily up into the sky and flapped away across the sea.

When Mara stood and turned, tears streaming down her face, Kip pulled her into a tight hug. "What do we do next?" he asked gently.

"These two can't wait," she said quietly. She squeezed Kip and pressed her cheek to the top of his head before looking miserably over at her uncle.

Teddy's face was darkened with the heat of a fever, and blood was seeping through Finn's bandages. She sighed and wiped her face. "Kip, will you go collect some firewood? We're going to need heat if we're going to help these two."

Kip nodded and retreated out into the forest to do as bidden. Mara went first to Teddy, opening her bag and rifling through to assess her supplies. Needle and thread. That was something. They had a basic antibiotic ointment and the pain-relieving poultice, but that was it. They would have to make do with what they had until they could make it back to their camp, but Teddy, at least, couldn't make it that long, and Mara just hoped they could make him last a little longer if they did what they could immediately. He'd just lost so much blood, and Ambergrove didn't have the technology for a transfusion. Teddy would just need to have the will to urge his body on.

Kip returned shortly and built a small fire up against the cliff face to hide it from immediate view. Judging Finn's wounds to at least be the easiest dealt with, Mara pulled her father's dagger from her boot once more and pressed the tip into the coals.

"I'm going to need your help with this," she said, staring into the flame.

Kip knelt beside her and rested a hand on her shoulder. "I know," he said softly.

Mara stood and put together a makeshift spit, stringing two of their waterskins above the flame. As her tools heated, Mara went over to where Finn sat. At least his eyes were now closed. She shuddered to think how he'd react just then to someone coming at his ears with a knife. She unwrapped his head and surveyed his ears. They'd been completely rounded. Dried blood was matted into his hair and all over his ears, so she began by pulling it back. She shucked off her chainmail and quilted shirt and ripped off part of a sleeve to use to pull Finn's hair back out of the way. Then she ripped another piece to use as a washcloth, loosened Finn's waterskin, and began to dab with the watery cloth to clean up his now-purpling skin.

"It's ready," Kip called.

Mara slowly lay Finn down on his back and knelt up at his head as Kip brought one of the hot waterskins from the fire. "Sit on top of him and press down on his shoulders," she ordered.

Kip did as bidden, and Mara accepted the waterskin before turning to Finn, whose eyes were still closed. "I'm so sorry about this, friend," she said quietly. She unstopped the waterskin and poured some of the hot water on his wounds. He barely stirred as the hot liquid seeped over his ears and opened what of the wounds had been closed. That would have to do for now to sterilize, so she could do what needed to be done next.

As Mara stood and strode back to the campfire, Kip stuffed Finn's mouth with a piece of cloth. "Can't have you screaming when we do this, can we?" he said.

Finn was stirring just a little when Mara returned to his side with the red-hot dagger. His eyes snapped open and widened as she knelt beside him once more and took a deep breath. With a small squeak, and Kip's help, she held his head as steady as she could with one hand and pressed the hot blade to his ear.

Finn had fainted after Mara successfully cauterized the first ear, so it was a bit easier to do the second. He'd still seemed to be in shock, but his muffled screams, while painful to hear, had given Mara hope that he might be able to heal over time after the horror that had been done to him. Kip applied the pain-numbing poultice generously to Finn's ears as Mara returned to the fire.

She wasted no time moving to Teddy's wounds. The time it had taken to cauterize Finn's ears had brought the water in the second skin to a boil, and she risked burning her hands to ensure that her needle and thread were sterilized.

They sat Teddy up against the cliff face and Kip braced his full body against the forest dwarf as Mara got to work. She cleaned his wounds thoroughly and used her dagger as best she could to carve away some of the loose skin. Perhaps it was just because carving into bone was difficult, but Mara silently thanked the torturer for taking Teddy's fingers at the knuckles so she wouldn't have to try to remove bone as well. His two little fingers on his left hand had been severed at the base, and they'd taken the first two digits of his pinky and the first digit of the next finger on his right hand.

Thankfully, she had enough to work with to patch him up well with the resources available. She packed a layer of ointment into the cleaned wounds and stitched Teddy up. He thrashed a little under Kip's weight, but he'd ultimately lost too much blood to put up much of a fight. Once she'd finished stitching him up, Mara rubbed the pain-numbing poultice on Teddy's maimed hands and wrapped them tightly with the last pieces of Kip's shirt.

The worst dealt with, Kip removed Finn's chainmail and cleaned his burns, and Mara cleaned Teddy's burns and cuts. Only when they had been seen to did Kip's legs begin to shake. As he sat and Mara finally got a good look at him, she scolded him for hiding his injuries. Not up for a fight, he allowed her to slice his shredded pants off at the knee. She peeled the ruined material away from his thighs and used some of the remaining water—now warm rather than boiling—to clean up his cuts. They weren't deep enough to require stitching, and they didn't have any more material to use that wasn't dirty or already in use, so she applied some poultice to seal them as best she could, and Kip rolled the remainder of his shorts up to keep them from rubbing.

By this time, Mara could feel her eyes getting heavy, but there was one more thing that needed to be done. She and Kip pulled Finn over to lay beside Teddy, and she piled all the quilted shirts on top of Teddy and laid the warm waterskins up against his sides. All they could do for Teddy now was try to cook out his fever. Mara lay on her uncle's opposite side so she and Finn would share their body heat with him, and Kip sat cross-legged at her side, keeping dutiful watch as Mara's eyes fluttered closed.

Mara woke some time later to Kip's hand resting on her bare stomach. He shook her gently. "Mara, Teddy is awake. Mara, wake up," he said.

She turned and looked over into her uncle's smiling face. "Teddy!" she cried, throwing an arm around him and squeezing. He groaned. "Sorry, sorry, sorry!"

"It's alright, Mara," he said weakly.

She felt his cheek. He still had the fever, but he wasn't as hot as he had been. "How do you feel?" she asked.

"What a question," Kip said.

Teddy laughed softly and groaned again. "Better. I'm feeling ... better. Not my best, but I think I'll be okay."

"Of course, you will," Kip said. "Once you have some rest and time."

Teddy turned and peered at Finn's sleeping form. "Wh-what did they do to the kid?" he asked.

Mara sat up and looked at Finn, but it was Kip who answered. "They rounded his ears. They told me about it when they brought me in to start in on me. They said he wasn't a real sea elf because he was afraid of their gun, so they made sure he wouldn't be mistaken for a sea elf."

Teddy closed his eyes and swore. He shook his head. "Unbelievable to do something like that to him. I can handle life with a few missing fingers, but they stole a part of him."

"I know," Mara whispered.

Kip placed a reassuring hand on her shoulder. "We'll help him through it though. None of us are alone."

"That's ... right ..." Teddy said slowly, drifting off again to sleep.

Mara turned to Kip. "It's your turn now for some rest," she said. "I'll take the next watch. You sleep now." Kip took Mara's place beside Teddy without argument, and Mara watched over her men until the day turned to darkness.

Days passed without much change. Finn woke a few times a day, but he refused to speak or eat, and he was back to sleep shortly after. On the third day, while out hunting, Kip found the plant they'd used for the healing tea that had saved Mara's life after the gauntlet. Due to careful brewing and steady administering, Teddy's fever finally broke. Soon, Teddy was awake and speaking, though he was still too weakened from the blood loss to stand.

Mara and Kip redressed Finn and Teddy's wounds twice a day, washing the bandages in the sea so they could be used again. The cauterization had taken nicely, so they mostly added more poultice to the skin and rewrapped Finn's head to keep him from touching his ears in the times he briefly woke. Teddy's pinky had blackened over time, and Mara had been concerned it would need to be amputated, but a few doses of the tea and consistent application of ointment appeared to be the right combination to bring the green back into his skin.

When both men seemed to be out of the woods, Mara's concern then shifted to Keena. She'd only flown for short bursts up to that point, and her wings had been covered for much of the time they had been raiding in Chaosland. What if they weren't strong enough to get her all the way across the sea? Kip had been doing a good job of distracting Mara at these times. When she went silent and her face scrunched up, he'd make a crack about her shirt—now a sleeveless crop top—and she would fire back about his lack of shirt altogether, and they would often go wade knee-deep in the shallow water for a bit before returning to one duty or another.

Kip's lack of shirt was distracting in another way as well. It had been quite a long time since she'd seen his torso in full. Their first excursion into Fear had added to his scars, and he'd picked up a few more in the past few months, but his torso was covered in them. Mara wondered, not for the first time, what could possibly have happened to her gentle soldier in his time as a guard to cause such lasting pains. She didn't ask, and he didn't offer. This was for the best, as they already had enough pain on their hands.

Mara often gazed out across the sea when it was her turn to keep watch. She pondered what had happened to her men, and she worried about where Keena had gone and if she'd even make it to Questhaven.

"She will," came a voice from behind her.

Mara turned and saw Teddy's eyes were open. "Did I say it out loud again?" she asked.

Her uncle shook his head weakly. "Nah, I can just tell."

"It was unfair of me to put so much on her," Mara said quietly, looking back out across the sea. "I haven't let her use her wings for months, and then I told her to fly further than she's ever flown. By herself."

"Sometimes these things are necessary."

"Making poor decisions and risking the lives of the people you love?" Mara scoffed. "Like how I should have spoken up and told that giant that I was the leader and not you? Like how I should have been the one to be lying there with lost fingers and—"

There was surprising force behind his arm as Teddy shoved her and made her tip over to the ground. She looked at him and saw tears in his eyes. He spoke severely, "Don't you *ever* think that what happened to us was your fault. Had you spoken up and said that you were the leader, me and both of those boys would have denied it. There is nothing that we wouldn't have done to keep them from getting to you. You're our lass as well as our leader."

"It's true," Kip said quietly, rolling over to look at her.

"You should be sleeping," she said.

"Yeah, maybe. But what bad luck would it be for you to have your turmoil when the rest of us were asleep and couldn't shake some sense into you?" Kip retorted.

Teddy laughed and then groaned at the strain to his weakened body. He sighed and then added, "Like I said, you're our lass, and we're behind you—in front of you when need be—and you're doing the right things. We'd tell you if you were making poor decisions." He smiled and reached out to pat her on the leg.

"It's true," Kip repeated. "And Keena will be okay. Sometimes you just know things because you believe in them, Dragonwolf."

The two men nodded to each other, and then Kip rolled back over, and Teddy closed his eyes, leaving Mara once more staring across at the emptiness of the horizon.

Two weeks into their vigil on the beach, Mara was keeping a night watch. She listened to the animal sounds from the nearby forest and watched the moonlight rippling over the water ahead. The rippling grew stronger and stronger, and Mara peered out across the water, looking for the source of the disruption. After a few moments, a large shape came into view, and Mara heard splashing as it neared them. She reached back a hand to pat Kip awake and ended up smacking him unceremoniously in the face a few times instead. He sat up with a grumble, and she pointed when he looked at her.

"What is that?" he whispered.

"I'm not sure. It's way too large to be Ashroot or Keena. It may be an enemy ship of some kind."

They both stood silently. Kip hefted his spear, Mara picked up her bow and nocked an arrow, and they waited. When the form came into view, it wasn't a maraudering ship or monsters, but someone else entirely.

"Is that ..." Kip began.

Mara threw her bow to the beach and splashed as far as she could out into the shallow waters. "Fang!" she cried. "It's so good to see you!" She gave the giant wolf a quick hug—at least as much as she could reach—before she noticed what he bore.

A harness had been tied around him, and he had swum all the way there pulling the old raft behind. He growled as Mara gave him space. *It is good to find you well, forest dwarf,* he said. *The little one was worried about you.*

"Keena? Did Keena make it to you okay? She wasn't hurt, was she? And what about Ash? Why didn't she come along?" Mara asked quickly.

"Let him get to land first!" Kip called. He waded out to the shallows and helped Fang haul the raft up onto the bank. The wolf shook some of the water off and laid down on the beach with a sigh.

Been swimming for days, he said. *Need some rest before we head back to the den.* He huffed. *Little one is okay. Your kin has become family to my pups in these past few moons, and we would not risk her trying to cross the seas on her own. Not to this bad place—especially when you have kept her from it for so long. She worried herself sick when Keena came back without you. They comfort each other at your den and await our return.* He yawned, bearing a great cavern of sharp teeth. *I will rest, and then ... we will ... head back home ...* Fang drifted off to sleep.

The next morning, Kip and Mara loaded Teddy, Finn, and the supplies onto the raft, and Fang pulled them across the sea and back to Questhaven. It had been nearly half a year since they had landed in Chaosland, and as they neared their island camp, Mara could feel the darkness slipping away. They had survived, and they would make it back to their camp. They would be able to tend to Teddy and Finn there before they headed out again, though she had no idea where they might start.

The current took them safely to their island, and when the moon was highest in the sky, Mara could just make out Ashroot and Keena on the beach. When she turned to Kip, she found that he was looking not at their friends but up at the bright moon. She was about to ask him what he was thinking about when she heard loud flapping, and a happy Keena crashed into her, licking every part of her she could reach.

Chapter Fifteen

The Head of the Snake

Fang pulled the raft right up onto the beach, jostling and waking up Finn and Teddy and causing Kip to fall off into the shallows. Ashroot scurried over to the raft, grinning ear to ear and pulling Mara into a tight hug.

"Oh, Ash! I missed you so much!" Mara exclaimed. "It's been way to long away!"

"I missed you, too, and I was so worried when Keena came, I didn't know what to do. Are … uh …" Ashroot fell silent as she looked at the men behind Mara.

Finn remained silent, but Mara had assured herself that it had just been a few weeks, and he would begin to work through it and come back to them once he had some time to rest in Questhaven. Ashroot clearly did not share this opinion. She saw a man—still a boy, really—bandaged and broken. He didn't even look at Keena as she excitedly circled him. Ashroot turned to look at Teddy, who grinned back at her.

"You know what would warm this little blood of mine?" he asked. "A bit of supper from you, Ashroot. Do you think you could whip something up for us?"

"Of course! Right away, Teddy!" Ashroot replied quickly. She gave Mara a final squeeze before running back toward the main tent.

Mara rounded on Teddy. "What did you do that for?" she demanded.

"Just look at him," Teddy said, gesturing to Finn. "Or him. Or me," he added pointing to sopping-wet Kip before raising a bandaged hand. "We've just come from a hard few days at sea, and we're as worse for wear as we could possibly be right now. She doesn't need to see this."

"I agree," Kip added, splashing back up to the raft.

"Now, one of you take Finn here back to his tent. If he's feeling up to it, he can say hello to Ashroot in the morning. And I just need someone to help me to the dinner table, so I can put on a smile for her and reassure her that all is well," Teddy explained.

I will be happy to take you to the tent, Fang growled. *If this harness can be removed, I will take you and return to my family for the night.*

Mara cut Fang loose while Kip helped Teddy to stand and walk over to the wolf. Then Kip gathered their supplies, and Mara took Finn's hand and led him back to his tent, while Keena trotted behind. When she was sure she was out of earshot, she ventured, "I can't imagine what you've been through, Finn. I can't. But you don't have to face this pain alone. You can talk to us. We're here for you whenever you need us. But it's okay to not be okay."

Mara fell silent and walked quietly beside Finn until they reached his tent. Outside the opening, he paused. He looked at Mara, straight into her eyes, finally seeing someone for the first time in days. He opened his mouth, and when he spoke, his voice was a whisper. "I will never be okay again," he rasped. Then he stepped into the tent and closed the flap behind him.

Finn's armor lay in a crinkled heap on the ground in his tent. He kept his eyes closed so he wouldn't have to look at it. So he wouldn't see his blue-skinned hands. There was no solution, because when he closed his eyes what he saw instead was a gun. He was bitter. He was broken. More than he had ever been in his life. He'd hated his mother for the way she raised him. He'd hated his people for what they had become. But he'd still always been a sea elf. That life was all he'd ever known.

What kind of sea elf is afraid? the giant had jeered. The words echoed in his butchered ears.

I don't know what kind, Finn thought miserably. He wrapped a hand around the bullet necklace Kip had carved for him. He'd kept the thing around his neck, concealed under his clothes, since the gnome had made it for him, but he didn't want anyone to know that. He'd already shown so much weakness.

With one sharp yank, he snapped the cord that held it around his neck and tossed the stupid thing onto the pile of armor. He slammed his hands to the sides of his head to try to press out the bad thoughts and bit back a cry of anguish. Quietly cursing to himself, he unwrapped the binding on his ears and tossed it to the growing pile, before wrenching the lid off the pain-numbing poultice and mashing a generous amount on his ears.

Who am I now? What *am I now?* Finn asked himself. *A sea elf wouldn't do what I do or feel what I feel. What do I do now?*

He curled up into a ball on his bed and stared at nothing until sleep overtook him.

It took a few days before they could get Finn to leave his tent again. Teddy said the best thing for him was to leave him be. His ears had healed well enough to do without bandages, and his chest burns were coming along fine on their own, so Mara had just left a jar of poultice in his tent for him to apply himself. The only one who wouldn't leave him be was Ashroot. Where Mara and Kip had been unsuccessful in getting him to eat, Ashroot had refused to budge, bringing food to his tent and nagging at him until he gave in and just ate it, like a mother to a picky toddler. In addition to bringing him real meals, she also brought pickles for him, and the greatest change was when he finally started eating them. Eventually, he did begin to eat without being forced, but they still left him to his own devices.

With the wider range of supplies in Questhaven, Mara had been able to get Teddy's hands healing much more quickly, and the mixture of foods and teas—and the lack of stress—had brought much of his strength back. Kip brought him Mara's crutch after the first week, and Teddy made his way around fine on his own, though he was quick to comment that he'd told them already that they would need the crutches again. Mara was not amused.

Keena, boldened by her solo flight across the sea, had taken to flying around everywhere. Mara was a little sad to find that her pup didn't want to spend time with her, but she really wasn't much of a pup anymore. Over the months in Chaosland, Keena had grown to the size of a large dog, but the freedom, open space, and regular wing exercise seemed to give her quite the growth spurt. Every time Mara saw her, she was bigger, until one day she couldn't fit herself into Mara's tent. But it wasn't until Mara awoke to laughing one morning and found Teddy leaning on his crutch watching Kip take Keena for a ride that Mara realized her baby had grown to the size of a small pony. Keena's mother had been about draft horse size—like Moon—and until that moment, Mara hadn't thought about how big Keena would one day be.

Kip turned to look at Mara, letting go of Keena's fur to make a sweeping gesture, and he was promptly cast off into the dirt. "Ah, that's okay. You'll get bigger, dragonwolf, and then we'll see who tames who!" he said, tussling with Keena as if she were a younger sibling.

Mara stretched, yawned, and moved to stand beside Teddy. "How long have they been doing this?" she asked.

"Ah, not long," Teddy replied. "Keena told me that she was going to throw him as soon as you got up. She's enjoying growing up, you know."

"They grow so fast."

"Too right! Before long, she'll be bigger than Fang!" Teddy paused, then added, "You know, we won't be able to disguise her as a dog anymore when we go back to Chaosland. She's practically a horse now."

"I know," Mara replied quietly. "The thing is, I don't even know what we'll do now. We have to go back, but it feels like we're worse off than when we started. Finn is absolutely traumatized, and you'll have to learn to use your hands again before we do anything. They know more about us now, and they tricked us once already. And Swish …" Mara sniffled.

"Aye, I know. Swish is gone, and that was a great injustice. But you know as well as I do that we did make his life better. And, sure, we're down, but we're not done. This Great Harbinger does have a weakness, and we will find it."

"I suppose. First we have to find *him*."

"No … first we have to find *us*—the new us—and then we'll face what chaos brings."

They didn't speak again about Chaosland for a few days. As the days passed, Kip became more irritable and driven, and none of them could really figure out why. Finn had begun to emerge from his tent, though always with a makeshift bandana covering his ears. Teddy had embraced being down to almost seven fingers. Having partial fingers on his sword hand allowed him to use his sword more or less the same as he used to, so he only really had difficulty holding things when he was used to having more fingers for stability. Ashroot had come a long way from bursting into tears the first time she handed Teddy a bowl of soup and it fell right through his fingers.

Finally, one morning while they all sat around the table in the main tent for breakfast, Kip looked up at the fading moon and sighed with his whole body. He slammed his fork to the table and said, "Alright, that's it. I can't wait any longer."

He stood and strode away to his tent, leaving the others baffled. "Can't wait any longer for bed, I guess," Teddy said before sticking his tongue out in concentration to use knife and fork at once.

Kip returned quickly with a pile of papers and a kaleidoscope. "Okay, listen," he said. "I know that there's still a lot of recovery ahead of us, and no one is ready to talk about what happened that night or what we're going to do now, but time is running out, and we need to talk about it."

Finn flinched.

"What is it you have a mind to talk about?" Teddy asked slowly, glancing at Finn.

"We don't need to talk about what they did to either of you," Kip replied quickly, also looking at Finn, whose face had turned a pale, powdery blue. "We just need to talk about what *I* heard and what that means for all of us."

"What you *heard*?" Teddy asked.

"*Yes,* what I heard. They were taunting me about … other stuff, and they were just about to get started when another giant arrived. A captain. With orders from their leader!"

"What?" Mara asked. "And they just told you everything?"

"Well, no, not exactly," Kip stammered.

"Why haven't you said anything before now?" she pressed, panic seeping into her voice.

"W-well, I didn't think it was the best time before with—well, everything—but soon it will be too late," he replied nervously.

Teddy set his knife and fork down on the table. "Right, Kip, you'd best tell us everything," he said.

Kip launched into the story of how he'd pretended to faint and they'd just left him there while they talked about their plans. He relayed everything he heard. "So, you see, their Great Harbinger is supposed to be at this secret meeting place *one month* from now so the army will all have their orders to spread chaos throughout Ambergrove."

Teddy stroked his beard. "If only we knew where they'd be."

Kip sighed deeply and picked up the kaleidoscope, waving it in the air.

"You know where this is all taking place?" Mara asked.

"They brought out a map and pointed to the thing on the map. It was a symbol we hadn't seen before on any of our maps, but that's the symbol of the boss's location. I was able to sneak a peek of the thing before they hit me a few times and brought me back." Kip's crazed manner really reminded Mara of a conspiracy theorist with a web of yarn behind him.

Mara glanced briefly at Teddy, who offered, "Okay, so then what?"

Kip spread the map across the center of the table, pushing away the plates in his path. He pointed. "Here is where the leader is going to be. I kept running it through in my head to make sure I wouldn't forget, and I marked it on the map as soon as I had one. Here, look." Kip tapped the kaleidoscope at Teddy's hand.

Teddy took it and peered at the area Kip had marked. It was a copse of trees just outside of a city. "Tombstone," Teddy read. "Fitting."

He handed the kaleidoscope to Mara, who got her own look. "But it isn't Tombstone," she said quietly. "That was the old name for it. The new name is just … Death." She slowly looked up and was going to pass the kaleidoscope to Finn, but he seemed much more interested in picking his food to tiny pieces with his fork than anything they could possibly be doing. She cleared her throat. "So, the leader will be in Tombstone in a month?" she asked Kip.

Kip nodded, glancing at Finn. They wouldn't mention death again with Finn in such a state.

"We can still make it up there in time if we set sail with *Harrgalti* soon," she replied.

"Aye," Teddy said. "This will be our best shot at this Great Harbinger, and if we fail, it may mean that the long arm of chaos will spread to our homes. To Aeunna."

"We can't let that happen," Mara said fervently, clenching a fist and slamming it on the table for emphasis.

"No, we can't," Kip said. "And that's why we can't wait until everyone is up to their best. It may be too late then."

Mara glanced quickly at Finn. It was no use. None of them were prepared for a venture like this, but they had to do it anyway. It was reckless, sure, but what other choice did they have? "What will we do, then?" she asked.

The table was silent for a moment before Teddy said, "Well, you're the boss, Mara."

She peered at the map, checking some of the surrounding areas before beginning, "We'd be no use with ranged weapons. We'd need to go in with all we have, prepared to face it head-on. We could make final preparations and leave in a couple days. That will leave us enough time to sail up to here," she pointed at the map, "so we'll be able to catch them there." She looked around the table before adding quietly, "This will be our last stand."

Kip slowly sank into his seat. Teddy said, "This is what it was always leading up to. Aeun told you this would be your trial, and we've been at it nearly a year to get to this point. It's time."

"Someone has to die for a Ranger trial to be completed," Ashroot whispered.

Someone has to die. Mara looked around the table. *No. No, it can't be now. Not yet. I'm not ready to lose someone,* she thought.

"Well, there's no avoiding it," Teddy said, rising and standing on his own. "If one of us is about to go down fighting, we need to make the best of the time we have here and now," he added fervently. "I'm going to go to Gylden Grotto for one last thing before we head out. I'll be back tomorrow morning at the latest. We can be ready to leave by the next morning."

Teddy stood abruptly and walked to his tent. He was only in there a few moments, returning to the table to quickly say his goodbyes and to have Ashroot call for Fang to help him push *Harrgalti* back into the water. He didn't seem to have anything with him, but when he made one last check, Mara saw him pat his chest. It wasn't something to get; it was something to send. He had one more thing he needed to do.

Awhile later, Mara found herself looking out across the water in the direction of Gylden Grotto. She didn't even hear it when Keena approached and pressed her head into her hand. She gasped and then murmured, "Oh, hey, Keena."

What's wrong, Mama? she asked.

"Well, you were just a little pup when I met with the goddess Aeun, but she gave me a job to do. I had to defeat this bad person in Chaosland and rid the world of the rule of chaos. The problem with that is … well, in order for the trial to be completed, someone who came along has to die." Mara sat down in the sand and clenched her fists, squishing mounds of sand into them.

Who? Who has to die? Keena asked.

Mara sighed and threw a fistful of sand at the water. "I don't know. Not me, I guess, but someone."

Teddy's going to die? Keena whined.

A dagger to the heart. Teddy. Teddy might die. They were finally at the point when Teddy might die. "Maybe not. It may be one of the others."

Finn? … Kip? Keena whined.

Finn. Finn who had already been broken and lost more than anyone is meant to lose. How could he lose his life after everything else? And Kip? Kip who had Loli to return to. Kip who she … who she might … "I don't know what to do, Keena."

Keena sat silently for a moment and then whined, *If the fancy island lady said it will happen, it will. You just need to love them before it happens, so they know.*

"You're right, Keena. Of course, you are," Mara replied. "You know, you've grown up so fast."

I have? I'm not as big as Moon or Fang, Keena replied.

"No, no, you're not, but your mother was. If she was as big as Swish or as Moon, then you should get there someday." Mara felt a sharp pang of sadness again remembering their dear horse friend.

Keena spread out her wings and peered at them. *Maybe I can be like horse friend,* she said.

"Sure, you can!" Mara replied, thinking of Kip trying to ride her.

You and me can fly together then, Mama, she said excitedly. *When this is all over and I'm big like Moon.*

"I'd like that, Keena." Mara grinned at the idea of flying through the skies on Keena's back, but there was something else she needed to do first. Mara sighed and stood. "If we don't have much time left together, I need to spend these next few days making sure our last memories together are good ones. I just have to figure out where to start." She looked back at her pup. "What will you be doing, Keena Keena?"

The big wolves have more to teach me before we leave again. I will spend all the time I can with them, Keena replied.

Mara smiled. "Off you go then, big girl."

Mara hugged Keena tightly around the neck, and then headed back toward the camp. She had no idea where she would begin. How could she decide who to spend a happy moment with first? Who to say goodbye to first? As she neared the main tent, she saw Ashroot collecting dishes. She scanned the area further. She couldn't see Kip. Ashroot would be first then. Mara was just about to call out to her friend when she noticed movement out of the corner of her eye. Off at the edge of camp, Finn was heading into the lightening forest.

Finn. Finn will be first, then, she thought. *If he is going to have any hope of surviving, I have to remind him who he is, and I have to do it now.* She quickened her pace to be sure she wouldn't lose sight of him, and then she followed Finn into the trees.

Chapter Sixteen

A Time for Friends

Finn walked with a purpose. This was good, because he had lost all purpose in recent weeks, but Mara was having trouble keeping up. Just as she thought she might lose him, he stopped abruptly and sat on the ground. Mara approached quietly, noticing that the ground around him was stained with old blood. As she came up to his side, she moved slowly and deliberately, settling herself to sit on the ground next to him.

They sat in silence for a while. Mara didn't want to push him by speaking first, so she let him sit and stare at the ground while she kept him company. Finn passed the time by plucking individual blades of grass. Finally, he asked, "Do you remember what happened here, Mara?"

Even if she hadn't, they'd done precious little out in this island, so it wouldn't have taken much to narrow it down. "This is where you, Keena, and I fought the goblins and saved Moon and her pups," she replied.

"Yes ... yes, we saw someone in need, and we helped them. We jumped out of these bushes without fear of the consequences, and we protected strangers just because they needed protecting," Finn told the ground. "That—that was the last time I truly felt like a sea elf, Mara," he said quietly.

"What do you mean?"

"What do I mean?" he shouted, glaring up and into the forest. "What do I mean? I mean I wasn't *afraid*. I didn't want to run. I didn't flinch. I just went. I went into battle and acted like any one of my people would. It was the last time I was brave. Strong. Before we went to the forbidden lands and got *shot!* Before I began to fear a tiny piece of metal and what it might do to me! Before I *proved* that I-I wasn't— I'm not—" Finn slowly reached a hand up to his ear.

It was Mara's turn to pull up blades of grass as she searched for the right words. "You've never been a traditional sea elf, Finn," she ventured. When he didn't reply, she added, "A traditional sea elf would never have come along with me, and sometimes it's good to not be like them. No one else would have had the courage to stand up, alone, for what he believed in when it meant standing against his entire civilization."

"It doesn't take courage to run, Mara. That's what I did."

"That's not entirely true. Sometimes it does take courage to run. It takes courage to try to escape a terrible situation you find yourself in, because you know what the consequences will be if they catch you. It takes courage to run *toward* something you believe in—to jump headfirst into the abyss and hope that everything will turn out okay."

"I suppose," Finn murmured.

Mara laid a reassuring hand on Finn's leg, and rested it there until he looked up at her. "Regardless of what you believe, Finn, it's not your ears that made you who you are. You were fated to be the sea elf for this trial. Not because of your ears or because you were this great, fearless, impossible man. You came because you are different. You believed in something different."

Finn shifted awkwardly.

"Who you truly are has nothing to do with what you were born or what you're expected to be. Even some of the most fearless men on Earth are afraid of getting shot. There's no shame in it. You pushed through your fears when we needed you to, but that doesn't mean you weren't still afraid—and that doesn't mean you didn't have every right to be. Those who captured us were impossibly cruel. They took your ears because they thought that would break you. They just wanted to tear you apart. Don't let them, Finn."

He looked up at Mara, and she could see his eyes were burning with the effort to hold back tears. "What do I do, Mara?" he whispered.

"You *fight,*" she replied fervently. "Dark times sometimes win. That's the way of it. You will never forget what was done to you—nor should you be expected to—but you can keep it from poisoning who you are by fighting it when it does come."

She had no idea if Ambergrove understood notions like depression and posttraumatic stress. Perhaps if they did, they had another name for it. Darkness was universal, at least in some aspects. Finn, at least, appeared to be heartened by it. What had happened to him in the past months would haunt him forever, but how he handled it would determine the remainder of his entire life, and she would not let herself be responsible for ruining it.

When she looked up, Finn met her gaze. "Thank you, Mara. You're a true friend," he said.

"No need. That's what friends are for. And you've become a dear friend in this year I've known you," she replied, somewhat awkwardly. She cleared her throat. "Tell you what. You and I need to do something together. Something nice, as friends, before we head off and face whatever we're facing." Finn nodded slowly. She continued, "What is it you've always wanted to do?"

He stood and paced slowly around the small clearing, brows furrowed, hands clasped behind him as he walked. After a few moments, he stopped and turned abruptly to look at her, then shook his head and turned to resume his pacing, mumbling, "Never mind, it's silly."

"Tell me," she pressed, standing. "What is it?"

"Well …" He shifted awkwardly. "All my life, it's been duty after duty. Pain after pain. It has always been hard for me to understand your willingness to laugh at even the smallest things. You seem to find joy in so many little things. And I …" He paused and touched one of his ears. "Uh … well, even before this, I've never been in a situation where I've felt truly free and having fun. I-I've never … *played* … before. And I'd just like to play around—to do something that's just fun—a-at least once," he managed.

Her jaw dropped, and she quickly snapped it shut. She wracked her brain, but it was useless. He'd never played with them. He'd been mildly amused, sure, but that was about it. How could he have lived such a life that being maimed was just another of a lifetime of blows? "Definitely!" she said, a little too loudly. "We can definitely have some fun. What did you have in mind?"

He kicked at the dirt and looked around thoughtfully. "Uh … I don't know. How about something you know? Something from Earth?"

Mara scratched her arm absently, and her hand came to rest on her little pink and blue bracelet. *Kara*. "I have just the thing!" she exclaimed. "Just let me get a few things together first, okay?"

"Okay," he replied.

She turned excitedly toward the camp but stopped when she reached the edge of the clearing. She turned. "Are you good?" she asked.

Finn nodded, and Mara turned and strode off into the forest, on a hunt for Kip.

Kip awoke to Mara tapping on his feet. He'd been napping, rather well, in a secluded part of the beach. "Mm-what is it? What's going on?" he asked sleepily, as he blinked Mara into view.

"I need your help with something. Something important," she said fervently.

He bolted up in alarm. "What? What is it?"

She knelt beside him and rested a hand on his arm. "You and I are going to get a game together."

Kip rolled his eyes and fell back into the sand with a sigh. "A game? That's what's so important?" he asked.

"It's for Finn," she said quietly.

Kip opened an eye and peered at her. "Okay, then, what do you want me to do?"

"I'm in need of your woodcarving skills," she replied.

Kip sat up again and gestured for her to explain.

"Uh . . . um . . ." Mara hunted around for a stick, and then drew a shape in the sand beside him. "Two of these," she said. "Solid and smooth here. I'm sure Ash has a crate or something you can work with."

Kip nodded. "Alright, so when do you need these?" Mara looked at him and grinned. He sighed. "Oh, so you mean now."

"Yes, please," she said brightly. "Thanks so much, Kip. I mean it. I owe you."

She tapped his arm again and made to stand, but he clasped a hand around her wrist. "Uh, hang on, Mara," he said. She sat. He continued awkwardly, "I, well, I was wondering if you would do me the honor of spending the afternoon with me tomorrow. Just the two of us."

Mara's brows raised. "Oh! Uh, yeah. Yeah, I will," she replied. "What do you have in mind?"

"I'll be helping Teddy with loading in the morning. Then afterward I just have some things I'd like to show you before we leave," he said cryptically.

"Yeah, yeah, that sounds fun. It will be a nice thing to do tomorrow, for sure," she said.

Kip stood and patted her shoulder. "Good, then it's a date," he said. He turned and headed back up to the camp without another word.

While Kip crafted one piece, Mara went back to the forest to hunt for the remaining items. Thankfully, Ambergrove still contained similar plant life to what she grew up with. She called out triumphantly when she found the tree she was looking for. Quickly, she gathered as many of the solid walnuts as she could find. Then, she found some long, broad leaves and a few twigs to serve her other purposes. Grinning, she headed back to the camp.

When she got to the main tent, she found Kip at the table, carving what she'd asked while Ashroot looked on. When she saw Mara, her friend grinned and stood. "Mara! Can I talk to you for a moment?" Ashroot asked.

"Uh … sure!" Mara replied. She dumped her spoils on the table beside Kip, who picked up a walnut and chucked it at her when it rolled across his work. She turned to Kip. "Ow—hey. Have you seen Finn?" she asked.

"He went off with Moon a little bit ago," Ashroot interjected. "He said they were going to talk about something, and he'd be back by suppertime for whatever it was you had planned."

"That should be good for him. Then I'll take care of this in a little bit," Mara replied. "Come on, let's go."

Ashroot led Mara on a walk down the beach, strolling out of Kip's earshot before she began, "I haven't been able to spend very much time with you since we got here and you all started going to the forbidden lands."

"I know, Ash, and I miss that. I miss our talks," Mara replied.

"That's how I feel, too," Ashroot replied. "So, I hoped that maybe you and I could just talk like we used to today, before you go off again."

Mara stopped walking and looked at her friend. "Before *I* go off again?"

"Well, yeah, I mean ... I thought—"

"No, no, you're right, Ash. At least a bit. We're not going to leave you here on the island this time, but I still don't want you coming to Chaosland with us. I promised your dad that I would keep you safe, and the forbidden lands should still be forbidden for you."

Ashroot nodded and gestured for her to sit. "I miss him, you know?" she said softly, as they settled on the ground together.

"I know. I see my dad so much in Teddy, and it was a blessing to be able to see his statue in Nimeda, but I miss him so much. And I wonder how he's doing, and Kara. It's almost her birthday now, I think." Mara looked at her friend and cleared her throat, continuing, "Tell me, Ash, what was your favorite thing you and your dad did together?"

"My favorite? Hmm ... there are so many fond memories."

Ashroot's mother had died when she was a cub, killed by a wild boar while she was out gathering berries. Mapleleaf was all she had. Well, not all. The bearkin were a closeknit community, and they had all had a hand in raising her. The loss of her mother did, however, leave Mapleleaf very protective of her. It was a marvel to say the least that he ever allowed her to collect berries on her own, much less go on an adventure far from home.

Ashroot clicked her claws. "Well, there is one thing," she said thoughtfully.

"What?"

"Well, my da and I always used to cook together."

"Naturally." The first thing Mara learned about the bearkin was that they loved to cook.

"Yeah, naturally. But there was one thing I liked most because of the way we had to make it," Ashroot continued.

"How did you make it?"

"It took two of us to make, so it was something we were always able to do truly together, instead of him doing it while I watched or me doing it while he supervised." She paused, and her lip curled into her bear smile. "It was something he called Forest's Delight," she said.

"I don't think we've—"

"No, we haven't had it before," Ashroot added quickly. "It requires small amounts of specific ingredients, and they don't grow in the scale necessary to make it for all Aeunna."

"Oh." Mara frowned. "So why does it take two to make?"

"Well, it has to be cooked at a high temperature to bring out the flavors of some of the ingredients, and the ingredients are added in increments, gradually. If something is added too quickly, it will lump together, and the flavor won't spread through the whole dish. If it's not stirred constantly, it will burn," she explained.

"So, one of you needs to add the ingredients and one of you needs to stir."

"Not just stir, though," Ashroot said, raising a paw. "There's a specific pattern and pace to the stir."

"I see." Mara absently scratched her chest, then ran a hand along her first scar from Ambergrove. She would not have made it out of Aeunna without Ashroot's help. She turned back to her friend and ventured, "Well, can the supplies be found in any forest?"

"Usually, yes. They are common enough ingredients. They just are not typically abundant," Ashroot replied.

"Well, then, why don't you and I make it together?" Mara asked. "I'm not much of a cook myself, but I could add the ingredients with your instruction, at least, and that will bring a little bit of family here for you. What do you think?"

Ashroot closed her eyes briefly. When she opened them again, they were watery. "That would be lovely, Mara," she said. She wiped her eyes with a paw and looked at Mara in mild alarm. "But if we're going to make it, I'll need to get everything for it right now. It will take a little while to cook," she said.

"Go, then. Go." Mara grinned. "I'll finish making this game for Finn and then you and I can make this for supper."

Ashroot nodded, and they both stood. The bearkin gave her friend one quick, fierce hug and scurried into the main tent for a basket. *Check*, Mara thought. She would have fun with Finn, and she would cook with Ashroot, and both of them would have happy memories to carry them into the events that were about to unfold. She just had to cross her fingers and hope that all went to plan.

When Mara entered the main tent, Kip was about halfway done with his task. She opened her mouth to speak, but he held up a hand.

"If you want me to get these things done today, you'll need to give me some peace to do my work," he said. He reached up a finger to his lips and grinned when Mara rolled her eyes and sighed.

"Scoot over, at least, so I can do what I'm planning to do," she said, elbowing him playfully until he grabbed his things and moved to the end of the table with a dramatic groan.

She got to work. First, she gathered up all the walnuts and piled them into a small bowl, which she set at the end of the table. Then, she took her dad's dagger out of her boot and began strategically slicing the giant leaves. When Ashroot returned a few hours later with her spoils, Mara had just finally gotten everything to hold together like she'd intended it to.

She smiled at her friend and rubbed her hands together. "What's first, boss?" she asked.

Ashroot set the basket down on the end of the table opposite Kip. "First, we prepare the ingredients."

Mara followed her friend's commands as they worked to prepare their supper. They laughed as they went about their work and periodically tossed ingredients at Kip. Mara sliced and diced as best she could, and Ashroot kindly praised her for the effort. Mara didn't realize this was because Mapleleaf had done the same when Ashroot had first tried to make this dish, and the bearkin was remembering her father more and more as they worked. Her actual work was nothing to be praised.

Ashroot prepared the fire, and they got to work actually cooking. Determined to make this the best it could possibly be, so it was a positive experience for Ashroot, Mara drowned out everything else and focused on making sure she did her part well and listened to her friend. Ashroot's lip curled, and she smiled the whole time they were cooking. When Ashroot deemed it ready and they took it off the fire to place it in the middle of the table, they found Kip watching them, his task completed, and Finn sitting opposite him, inspecting the new additions to the table while he slowly ate some pickles—more as a comfort than anything else. Mara understood that. Cheese had the same effect for her.

Mara set the table for supper, and they all tried the special meal, Forest's Delight. It was delicious. Earthy and savory while still having small bursts of sweetness. They ate in silence, but for pleasure sounds—a true compliment to the cook—and Ashroot's eyes were watery the entire time. When the pot was scraped clean, all their bowls were empty, and each of them had leaned back to stretch their full stomachs, Kip was the first to speak.

"Mmm ... well, now, are you ready to see what Mara has up her sleeve with all this?" he asked Finn, gesturing vaguely to the rest of the table. "Because I sure am."

"Me too!" Ashroot added.

"That's it, then," Kip replied. He and Ashroot cleared the table as Mara began to explain the game to Finn.

Finn looked down at the instrument Mara handed him. "What did you say this was?" he asked.

"A paddle. It's to hit the ball with—or, well, the walnut," Mara explained.

"And I hit it across the table?"

"Yeah, yeah, *but* you have to be sure to bounce it once," she tapped the table, "on the other side of this ... net." Mara gestured to her makeshift leaf wall. "And then I hit it back to you, and we keep going back and forth. If you don't hit it back to me, then I win," she explained.

Finn looked across the table and raised a brow. "What did you say this was called again?"

"Ping pong," she said brightly. She looked at each of the confused faces in turn. "Let's just try it and you can see if you like it. Just so you know, though, I have never met anyone who didn't enjoy a friendly game of ping pong, even if they were bad at it—and that includes my posh sister, Sara," Mara added. "Here, I'll serve to you first."

Kip and Ashroot pulled chairs back to what Mara determined was a safe distance, and they sat and watched as the game began slowly. Thankfully, the walnuts had just the right amount of bounce. She hit the first walnut to Finn, and it bounced off the table and to the ground.

"So, you have to swing the paddle and hit the walnut back across to me," Mara said patiently. "Let's try it again."

She slowly and deliberately hit walnuts across to Finn, and he did start swinging at them, but it was a delayed reaction—kind of like her old cat when he tried to catch a toy. After quite a few tries, Finn hit it back to her, but when she hit it back to him he'd forgotten what he was supposed to do. She hit it to him again, and slowly they went back, forth, back, forth, back . . .

"Aha!" Finn cried. His face was scrunched up in concentration, but he was holding his own at a modest pace.

"Are you ready to turn up the heat?" Mara asked, hitting the walnut back to him.

"What?" Finn asked, barely hitting it back in his distraction.

"Yeah, what?" Kip asked.

"Faster! Go faster! Show her who's boss!" Ashroot called, winking at Mara when she turned to her friend and gave her a look of mock betrayal.

Finn nodded, and the real game began. Soon, they were playing the game like any group of friends on Earth. Finn hooted when he beat Mara—though she was sure he knew she'd let him—and they ended up doing best of five. Mara laid the friendly banter on thick, and by the time he beat her, he was grinning ear to ear.

Keena had heard the ruckus from further inland and came to investigate. A side game for her became running and fetching runaway walnuts as they disappeared into the darkness. Kip took a turn against Finn, and by the time they tied up two-two, they were all laughing and both men were developing their own forms of trash talk.

"I'll keep it in the middle for you since your arms are too short to reach both ends of the table!" Finn jeered, hitting the walnut to Kip.

"On the contrary, my spindly friend, I have the power behind my swing that your wiry arms just can't match. Power beats spread!" Kip called, swinging the paddle hard and splitting the walnut slightly as he hit it back to Finn.

"Well, I can move faster with my long hair working like a sail. What do you have?"

"A glorious beard that keeps my face cool, so I can stay focused to destroy you!" Kip growled.

Ashroot fell on the ground laughing, and Mara laughed so hard she snorted and teared up. The game continued until Kip lost valiantly and dramatically to Finn.

When it was Ashroot's turn, she struggled to hold the small paddle in her claws, so she and Finn played a friendly game rather than a competitive one. Keena ran around the table, whipping her tail excitedly, and they didn't stop until they heard horn blasts coming from the coast signaling that Teddy had returned and was ready for some help with the ship.

As they all headed down the beach to meet Teddy, Finn caught Mara's shirt sleeve and pulled her back. When she turned to him, he was smiling. "I can't stop doing this," he said, gesturing to the smile. "I want to thank you, Mara. You gave me an experience I've never had before in my life, and I'm grateful to you for that."

Mara pulled her friend into a tight hug and said, "I'm so glad."

Today has been quite successful, she thought. *Ash had a nice time, and she got to remember a fond experience she used to have with her dad. And Finn . . .* Mara's face fell. She could hardly bear to think it. If Finn was the one to die on this trial, at least he got the chance to have a little fun. She looked up across the beach and met Teddy's knowing eyes. *Two down, two to go.*

Chapter Seventeen

A Time for Love

Teddy's mind raced as he steered *Harrgalti* into the docks at Gylden Grotto. He had a mission, and he walked like one possessed into Hodd's hall. The burly dwarf looked up and grinned when he saw his forest kin.

"Tederen! What brings you back this time? Food? Weapons? Armor?" Hodd asked.

Teddy drew a folded-up letter from his shirt. "Something a little more personal," he said.

"Ah." Hodd took the letter from Teddy and called to another dwarf to ready a messenger. He turned back to Teddy and waved the letter slightly, as if he were testing its weight. "It's a little light, Tederen. You don't have more for your lady after so long?"

"With what's in this one, everything else would just be noise," Teddy said gravely.

"Are you coming to your final stand?"

Teddy nodded. "We believe so."

"So, this is your goodbye for your lifemate," Hodd replied.

"No, no … I don't do that," Teddy grumbled.

He'd never been surprised to hear all the goodbyes from the women, but the leader of a village of mining dwarves speaking of it was a surprise. Hodd didn't press further. Teddy sat in relative silence, waiting impatiently for the messenger dwarf to return. It was taking far too long. There wasn't time left to dally in such a way. Just as Teddy was about to demand Hodd take action, the messenger dwarf scurried back to the hall, breathing heavily.

"I am very sorry, sir. I was searching for something else for our forest kin and was delayed," the dwarf panted. "Another letter."

"There wasn't another from me. Hodd there has the last one," Teddy said.

"No, no. Not *from* you, *for* you," the dwarf explained.

No. Don't you dare give me hope. Could it be possible that after all this time reaching out for her, she'd finally been able to reach back?

The dwarf stretched a hand out toward Teddy and showed him a tattered envelope with *My Dearest Teddy* written on one side in a familiar scrawl. His breath caught in his chest and time stood still. A hand jostled Teddy into focus, and he saw Hodd smiling in front of him.

"Don't you worry," the mining dwarf said. "We'll get this one to her. You take that one and head on back to the Dragonwolf." As Teddy turned to leave, Hodd shouted, "And good luck!"

Teddy quickly gathered the remaining minor supplies he needed and set sail back to Questhaven as soon as he could. Once he was in open waters, he set the pin in the wheel and sat to read Freya's letter. When he was done, he tucked the letter into his shirt and returned to the helm, sobbing for the remainder of the journey back to Questhaven. As the beach came into view, he strode down to the hold for one last item. When he found it balled up in the storeroom, he smiled and wiped the tears from his eyes before returning to the deck and blowing his horn.

When they each woke the following morning, they began packing for their long journey north. Teddy said they should plan to return to Questhaven no matter the outcome, so they just packed up certain items. All they would need to do before heading out the next day would be to load up the bunks when they got out of them. Mara helped Ashroot to pack the kitchen items up while the men carted supplies back and forth to *Harrgalti*.

The ship was loaded by midmorning, and Mara had gone back to her tent to do a last once-over before meeting Kip for their mysterious outing, when Teddy stepped into her tent.

"Uncle Teddy! What are you doing in— What is that?" she asked.

Teddy held up a blue mass and motioned for Mara to sit. She obeyed slowly. "This is your trial dress, Mara. I think you should wear it for your date today," he said.

"I don't need to wear something fancy. I was just going to— Wait, what?" Her eyes widened. "What do you mean, date?" she squeaked.

"Oh, Aeun's locks." Teddy sighed and rubbed his bald head nervously. "You didn't realize it was a date? The boy said he specifically said 'date.'"

"He *told* you?" Mara shrieked. "I mean, yeah, he said 'it's a date,' but I didn't think he knew what that meant. Wait, how do you know what that means? It's a date!" Mara's face turned crimson, and she covered it with her hands.

"We know what dates are, Mara," Teddy said. "It's not really a complicated concept. Haven't you been on a date before?" Mara split a finger to peer at him before covering her face again. Teddy winced. "Oh," he said quietly.

"What am I supposed to do, Teddy? I don't know how to do any of this! What do I—"

"Now, listen," Teddy said sharply. "You're making too much of it. You and the boy enjoy each other's company. You're great friends. All you need to do is be yourself and enjoy your time with him. … Oh, and wear this dress," he ordered, dropping the thing playfully over her head.

"But I—" she began. Teddy held up a hand. "Okay," she murmured.

"Don't forget the *enjoying* part," Teddy said. He winked, waved, and left her in the tent, staring blankly at the mess in her lap.

A short while later, Kip called to her from outside her tent, and she emerged. When she did, he swore. She had only worn this dress twice before. The first was before she met Kip, and the second was when she had just completed the gauntlet and it was all she could wear—and he'd been distracted at that time by the thought of losing her, so he hadn't really paid attention. He sure was now.

The dress Freya had made was in a deep blue with light blue accents and intricate embroidery. Mara had a light blue shirt and pants to wear underneath, but the shirt still had a low enough neckline to show her entire scar from the Great Silver Bear. She still wore her bracelets, but she had removed her bracer for the date. Her father's dagger was tucked in its place in her boot. Her hair was the real spectacle. She'd put real effort into it. She made sure to brush out every tangle, and she used some tubelike items she'd found on *Harrgalti*, some water, and some gentle heat from Keena to make and use a serviceable form of curlers. Now, her beautiful, russet hair cascaded down her back—the first time she'd worn it down since coming to Ambergrove.

Kip shook his head to clear it. "You look beautiful," he told her softly. After an awkward pause, he cleared his throat and held up a basket. "I've got some things for a picnic here," he said. "Also, I'd like you to bring your Polar Oid with you. There's something you're going to want to see."

Squinting at Kip suspiciously, Mara retreated into her tent, grabbed her camera, and surrendered it to Kip to add to his basket. Then she took his offered arm and followed him out of the camp and into the forest. Kip remained silent as he led her through a part of the forest she hadn't seen before, telling her he wanted her to take it all in.

They looped around the northern part of the island until they came to a clearing in the forest. "Here we are!" he said triumphantly.

Mara looked out at the sight. The surrounding trees seemed to all be some willow variety, so it was beautiful, but otherwise it was just a grove. She had expected more—to be camera-worthy at least. She glanced at Kip. "It's great!" she said kindly.

Kip threw his head back and laughed. When he looked back at her, his brown eyes twinkled. "No, it's not!" he cackled. "Nice try, though. No, no, the real sight can only be seen from this side. Come on, close your eyes."

Mara did as she was bidden, and Kip led her forward. He stopped her, and she heard a rustle as he set down the basket and returned to her side. "Okay, now … open them," he said.

When Mara opened her eyes, she gasped, and she blinked a few times to take it all in. Steam was rising up from a hot spring. She'd thought that the ground in front of them had been flat, but this spring was just hidden by a small cliff face. A waterfall emerged from it, flowing from some underground stream. That and the beautiful, blue flowers and willow canopy surrounding it made for quite a magical sight. Kip pressed something into her hand. Her camera.

She took a picture and shook her head in disbelief. "This is amazing, Kip. How did you know about this place?" she asked.

"I found it our first night here," he explained. "I just didn't put it on your maps when I made them, because I was saving this place for this moment—if we ever had it."

He retreated to a mossy rock by the edge of the spring and patted the spot beside him before removing his boots, rolling up his pants, and dipping his toes in the spring. Mara moved to sit next to him, putting the camera back in the basket, and did the same. They sat in silence for a moment before Mara ventured, "So, you said you'd been planning for this moment. What moment is that?"

"Uh … well …" he began awkwardly. "Why don't we get to that later? What do you want to talk about?" he asked.

"Hmm …" she considered Kip's face for a moment, trying to figure out what topic might distract them both, because he seemed to be about as nervous as she was. "Tell me about young Kip," she said finally. "What were things like growing up, and how were things with you and Loli?"

Kip smiled and launched into his tale. He'd lived all his life in the Big Hill before Mara came. He and his sister were orphans, as far as they knew, so they always stuck together. Kina was always more interested in adventures—and trouble—so he was usually cleaning up her messes. Mara had guessed correctly in her estimate of his age. He became a guard in his early teens and worked for a handful of years before Mara came. He was just a few years older than her, but he had been raising a sister and serving in the army while Mara had been putting off math homework and whining about wanting a cellphone.

In his time as a soldier, he used his influence to get Kina out of the biggest scrape of any gnome. She'd fallen in love with a mining dwarf and gotten pregnant. Gnomes and mining dwarves don't get along, and it was an unforgiveable offense. It soon turned sour on her end when the man abandoned her and the baby, so Kip had a hand in raising young Loli. He learned various skills from the other guards over the years, and they'd given him pointers on parenting. Loli was as much his son as anyone's. And then he lost him.

"That was the darkest day of my life," Kip said. "I thought Kina had just gotten into some minor scrape somewhere. I never imagined she was in the caves with little Loli."

Mara patted Kip's arm tenderly, and he cleared his throat. "Anyway, we don't need to be talking about sad things today. It's a beautiful day, and we're in a beautiful place," he said, grinning and looking Mara up and down. "Let's have lunch."

Their lunch was simple, but pleasant, and after lunch, it was Mara's turn to tell Kip about her childhood. She told him what life was like on Earth and how divided her family was. She told him about the fun she'd have with her dad and with Kara, and she told him about the days leading up to the last day she saw them, before she trailed off and went silent.

"What is it with us and the sad moments?" Kip asked. He tried to lighten the mood by throwing his hands up dramatically, and Mara laughed when he almost lost his balance and toppled into the spring.

"Careful!" she said, grabbing his arms. When he had settled, her hands lingered, and Kip covered one of them with his own.

"Mara, there's something I wanted to talk to you about," he said softly, looking down at her hand in his.

"Of course," she said reassuringly.

He sighed deeply and looked up at her. "Okay," he began. "Now, just let me get all of this out while I can, alright?"

Mara nodded.

Kip held her hands gently in front of him, took a deep breath, and shakily asked, "Do you remember the day we met?"

Mara nodded.

"You had come for your trial, and I was just one of the guards then. When I met you, to be honest, I thought that you were going to turn out to be some kind of fraud. I didn't believe you would go into the caves—"

"Yeah, especially when you scolded me for doing nothing while you all stood there," Mara interjected. Kip gave her a disapproving glance. "Sorry, no interruptions," she said.

He smiled to himself. "No, I didn't expect you to go in. What's more, I really didn't expect you to come back out. I was too afraid to defy the chief and go into the caves against his will, but you went. And when you came out all covered in spider goo, and leading my family behind you … why, you were the most beautiful woman in the world in that moment."

Kip cheeks darkened, and Mara could feel the heat in her own as she asked, "Really?"

He chuckled. "Really. You're the most beautiful in those times. When you're working on something or fighting for something. Your passion and your heart just shine in your face like your own inner fire blazing bright." He paused for a moment, then said, "I really thought that it was just a phase of some kind, but it wasn't. We spent the cold days and nights on watch and fought the kraken together, and every time I saw you, this feeling just grew and grew."

"What feeling?" she asked, hoping, wishing, but not daring it to be true.

Kip looked deep into her eyes and whispered, "I have loved you more and more each day since the moment you came out of that cave. I-I love you, Mara. I do, and I have." Mara opened her mouth to speak, but he shook his head. "Just let me get this all out while I can," he repeated. He took a deep breath. "I don't know if I have shown you properly this past year just how I feel, but I want you to know without a doubt that I love you. I love the sound of your laugh. I love the way you scrunch up your nose when you're mad. I love the way you care for all of us who chose to come on this journey with you. I love how your eyes light up when you play that game you like. I love how you fearlessly strode into the gauntlet all those months ago, and how you refused to kill the elf woman even though it might mean that you would fail. I love everything about you, Mara. I can only hope that you feel for me as I do for you, because I have some more things I want to say, but I want to check first."

Mara had been holding her breath to keep from interrupting him, but now a maniacal laugh burst out of her, taking Kip by surprise.

"Does that mean you … don't?" he asked, unable to hide the hurt in his voice.

She shook her head fervently and answered quickly, "No, no, no! No—Sorry, yes! Let me start again." She took a breath. "Ash and I talked about this before we even faced the kraken, and I talked to my grandma about it when we were in Nimeda, and I've talked to Teddy too. I guess Finn might feel a little left out," she said. Kip just stared at her. "Sorry, sorry!" she continued, wondering where her brain had gone and why it refused to communicate with her mouth. "I mean, yes, Kip, I . . . I love you too."

Kip's face spread into a wide grin, and his eyes glistened. "G-great! That's great!" he managed.

Mara nodded excitedly. "I've been trying to tone it down because, well, I didn't think you could possibly feel the same way, and because I wanted to make sure that I didn't distract you or something and get you hurt," she explained.

Kip threw his head back and laughed. "Me too!" he cried. He pulled his hands out of Mara's and plunged them into the picnic basket, pulling out a small, wrapped item. "Then that means I can keep on going with this," he said happily.

Mara motioned that she would be silent, adjusted to give him her full attention, and clasped her hands in her lap, grinning ear to ear.

Kip cleared his throat. "Okay, so I've been wanting to carve something for you just to show you how I feel about you," he said. Mara gently touched her necklace. He continued, "Yes, I made you that before the gauntlet, because I panicked and wanted to make sure you had something before you went in there, but I also wanted to do something else."

He chuckled to himself for a moment before continuing, "I also talked to Teddy." They grinned at each other briefly. Shaking his head awkwardly, Kip went on, "I asked him about Earth and what a token from your world would be for something like this, and he told me, so I made one for you." He took a deep breath. "First, I wanted it to be something strong, protective. Something that would protect you and would symbolize that for you. So, I talked to your grandmother about the sgiath trees, and she let me take a branch from one, so I had something to work with."

Nimeda, she thought. *Whatever this is, he's been planning it for almost a year. How can this be?*

He opened the wrapped item and reached a hand out to show it to her. It was a ring, carved from the wood of a sgiath tree. Carved into this ring was the same symbol from the necklace Kip had given her, along with some knots and leaves, and opposite the symbol were two tiny, crossed weapons—a hammer and an axe. Mara blinked back tears as Kip went on.

"Teddy said that rings are the big thing on Earth, and that they're given at various times when you're in love until you become lifemates. So, this is my promise for you. I love you, Mara, and if you accept this ring, then we are making a promise to each other that we will no longer ignore this love, and that when this is all over … we might build a life together," he finished quietly. "Do you accept it?"

Mara nodded. "I definitely accept!" she cried, throwing her arms around him.

It was too much. Too wild. She caused them both to fall off-balance and topple into the hot spring. She squeaked in surprise, and he cried out. Then they both laughed, and she hugged him again. He had the ring securely in his hand when they fell, and now he held it out, ready to slip it on her finger. "Uh … which one is it?" he asked.

She held out a hand and pointed at her ring finger, and he slipped it on. To his surprise, she then pulled out of his grip and splashed to the edge of the spring. She returned to him with the camera in hand and showed him how to help her hold it out so they could take a picture of themselves together. She pressed her cheek against his and smiled brightly. After taking the picture, she checked it to make sure they were both in it—it was actually a great picture—and then she returned camera and photo to the basket and swam back over to him.

When she got back to him, she couldn't look at him. She didn't know what to say, so she decided instead to play. She splashed Kip with the water and trudged out of the spring and up to the cliff. "Fire in the hole!" she cried, jumping from the cliff and cannonballing into the water.

After she jumped, she realized that he probably didn't know what she meant, but when she resurfaced, she found he was no longer in the water. She looked around to see him sneakily running up to the cliff himself. "Whatever you just said!" he cried, jumping off the cliff.

They played until they were too exhausted to keep playing, and then they swam in silence for a while, just holding onto each other awkwardly like they were dancing—like young lovers do on their first date. They floated in the warm water before settling on a rock near the waterfall, Mara wrapped in Kip's arms. She giggled, and her giggle turned into a laugh as she lay her head back to rest on his chest.

"What? What is it?" he asked gently.

"Do you remember the last time we swam together?" she asked, turning to look at him.

He laughed. "Yeah, you had just sailed through the Dragon's Teeth, and we were celebrating before going to see Aeun," he replied.

"And you picked me up and threw me into the water!"

"Oh, you mean this?" he asked, sweeping his hands under her like a baby and tossing her up in the air in the center of the pool.

She squealed as she splashed back down into the water, and then she laughed and splashed him back. "That's one of my favorite memories," she said, grinning.

Kip floated toward her and wrapped her in his arms, his face inches from hers. "I think it's time for a new memory," he whispered. "Don't you?"

She nodded, and her heart hammered as he leaned in slowly and pressed his lips to hers.

That night Mara lay awake in her tent. Soon after the kiss—her very first—Keena had burst into the clearing, and, not realizing there was a cliff until it was too late, skidded off it and splashed into the water next to them. They'd played with her for a bit, but the romantic moment was over, so soon they packed everything up and headed back to camp.

They'd stayed out way later than Mara thought, and Keena made little puffs of fire to light their way. Soon, she'd really be able to breathe fire. As soon as they made it to camp, Keena pulled Mara playfully to her tent, so she barely had the chance to look back and smile at Kip before he disappeared from view. Now, Keena was curled up outside her tent and snoring while Mara stared up into the dark with one hand on her necklace and the other on her ring finger.

Who could have imagined what this day would be? she thought. It had been her very first date, and that was her very first kiss. She really had no idea what was so great about kisses until that point. Now, all she wanted to do was go kiss him again. Kip. Her Kip. Her Kip who *loved* her and wanted to build a life with her when this was all over.

When it was over. When they survived it. Mara closed her eyes and sighed. *He will make it home to Loli. He will make it home with me. He and I will build a life together full of love and family. I will make sure of it,* she vowed silently. When she opened her eyes again, she blinked rapidly for a moment, sure she was imagining a green glow filling her tent and dimming. She was more tired than she thought.

Soon they would sail to meet this Great Harbinger, and the only thing Mara knew was that the more time she spent with her companions the surer she was that the loss of any of them would devastate her completely. She hadn't even had the chance to spend some time with her uncle yet, and he, one of the last family members she had left, who reminded her so much of the father she lost, would surely be the hardest to bear.

Chapter Eighteen

A Time for Family

Mara woke the following morning with one goal in mind—by the time they made it back on land, she would have spent some one-on-one time with Teddy. In short order, they loaded their supplies and prepared to say their final goodbyes to the wolves. The pups were still asleep, so only Fang and Moon came to the beach to see them off.

After a very tearful farewell from Ashroot, Mara was last to say her goodbye. "I cannot thank you enough for all you have done for us—for Ash—in the months that we've been on this island. You are true friends, and I hope that when we all see you again, we will be victorious," she said.

You may be, Moon replied, *but not all of you will return.*

"What?" Mara asked. "How do you know that?"

The small one told us of the path that lies ahead, Fang said. *What awaits you is dark and unforgiving. The time has come for one of your band to pay the price for success. I can feel this in the wind. May it carry you to success and bring you back to us on your way home to your people.*

Farewell, dragonwolf dwarf, and good luck, Moon added.

Teddy's hands rested on her shoulders and steered her onto the boat. Uneasy, she watched the wolves fade into the distance as Finn took the helm and guided *Harrgalti* to open waters, murmuring something about favorable winds.

Finn projected it to take a month for them to make it to their destination, so they would be arriving with just enough time to make the final trek to where the leader would be. The month was proving to be difficult, as every time Mara tried to get some time alone with Teddy, he had a new excuse. After two weeks, Mara had enough. When it was her turn to keep watch with Finn, Kip took her place, and she followed Teddy below deck.

"What is it, Mara?" he asked.

"Why are you avoiding me?" She crossed her arms and waited for some denial, but it didn't come.

"Because you're trying to check me off your list, and I've told you already that you're not doing any of that, Mara."

"We— What?"

Teddy turned and crossed his own arms. "When you were facing each and every one of your trials, and you wanted to have a little chat beforehand, what did I say?"

"But this is—"

"What did I say?" he repeated.

Mara sighed. "You said not to say goodbye because that was giving up, so to just go do it and come back."

"Well, there you go." He sat on his bunk.

"But this is different, Teddy."

"Oh? How so?"

"It's not giving up if you know for sure someone is going to die!" she cried, throwing her hands in the air.

"That may be true, but does going around and being sad about it help anyone?" he asked.

"Well, no, but—"

"No. So, I don't want to do that," he said matter-of-factly.

Mara sank to her own bunk and sat silently for a moment before quietly saying, "Then why did you spend every waking moment with Freya before we left on this journey? How is this any different?"

The silence stretched on between them. Finally, Teddy sighed. "I see your point. I do. That is still a bit different," he said. "She is my lifemate after all."

"And I'm your niece," Mara said. "I lost so much of my family, Teddy. You, Freya, and my grandmother are the only family I have left."

Teddy glared into the middle distance, sighing. He ran a hand across his bald head and then slowly scratched his beard. He grumbled something Mara couldn't hear.

"What was that, Teddy?" she asked.

"Okay, but no mushy stuff, alright?" he conceded grumpily.

Mara grinned.

The watch schedules were switched around so she could spend some time with Teddy before they landed. Mara was careful to just spend time with him and not mention anything about death, the trial, or the future. For a while. But she was far too determined to say what she had to say to every single one of her companions to take that rule lying down.

Keena, Ashroot, and Mara sat together in the galley. Before long, Keena would be too large to fit down there. For now, at least, they plotted under the guise of preparing lunch while the men all worked on deck.

"What are you going to do?" Ashroot asked.

"I don't really know," Mara replied. "He's so stubborn about all of this."

Family time is important, Mama, Keena whined.

"I know, Keena Keena," Mara replied, scratching her pup behind the ear. "I know, and you are all my family. Ash, you're like my sister, and Keena, you're my baby girl."

She looked down at the ring on her finger. *And Kip may be my lifemate,* she thought.

Ashroot smiled at Mara and patted her arm across the table. "Yes, but you've had time with us. All of us together, even, while Teddy was off on his special trip to Gylden Grotto," she reasoned.

You said you needed to spend time with everyone before we go to face what the island lady said. We're almost there, Keena said.

Mara sighed and rubbed her face. "I know we're almost there, but I don't know how I can get him where he can't just run away from me or refuse to talk to me."

A loud sniff came from behind them, followed by a few more dramatic sniffs for emphasis. "Nope," Kip said, standing in the doorway. "Doesn't smell like sandwiches." Sniff. "Doesn't smell like foods." Sniff. "Smells like … a *plot.*" He turned to Mara and grinned.

"Yes, yes, it's a plot," she said, laughing. "How are you going to help?"

"Any way you need me to, my love," he replied. His eyes twinkled.

Near the start of the fourth week, Mara cornered Teddy again, this time in the galley. With Kip's offer of help, Mara and Teddy were "accidentally" barricaded in with some crates. Teddy plopped into a chair and bonked his head dramatically on the table a few times before Mara slid into the seat across from him.

"I know you don't want to do this, Teddy, but I need to," she said in earnest.

He stopped banging, and she heard a muffled, "Well? I'm listening."

"Um … okay then," she replied. She cleared her throat and began, "Uncle Teddy, from the first moment I arrived here, you have been there for me. Literally, when I woke up here, yours was the first face I saw. You were there for me, and you taught me so much already. You're my family, and I know how important family is. I thought I lost mine. I lost my dad. You know how it feels to lose him."

Teddy grumbled something against the table.

"What?"

He shook his head.

She sighed and continued, "You changed my life, Teddy. I know you don't want to hear any of this, but I wouldn't be who I am or where I am without you, and I need you to know that I appreciate your love, and I love you so, so much, Teddy. If anything happens to you, I—"

"STOP," he ordered, clearly and loudly. He raised his head, rubbed his face, scratched his beard, and sighed before saying anything else, and when he spoke, his voice was soft. "She insisted too," he said.

"What?" Mara asked quietly.

"Freya insisted too. On saying goodbye." He sighed. "I told her then, and I told her again when I went to Gylden Grotto that we couldn't say goodbye."

"Gylden Grotto?" Mara asked incredulously. "What do you mean?"

He slowly reached a hand into his jacket and pulled out a piece of paper. He set it on the table between them, and Mara could make out *My Dearest Teddy* on the outside. He had finally gotten one of Freya's letters.

"But I thought you said that she couldn't reach you?" Mara asked. "You said you sent her letters, but you could never get any replies."

"That's true. We were never in one place long enough for a letter to get to her and for her to send a reply before we left again. But when we came here, we were," he said. He paused and looked at her before adding, "You can read it. I don't mind."

Slowly, Mara picked up the letter and read:

> *My Dearest Teddy,*
>
> *I am so glad to hear that you have found somewhere safe to camp for now. It has been so long since I heard from you, I feared the worst. I don't know how long I may be able to reach you here, and I want to be sure to say everything I want to say, just in case this is the only letter that makes it through.*
>
> *I love you so much, forest man. From the moment I arrived in Ambergrove and learned about forest dwarves. From the moment I saw you after your morning train. The old trainer had thrown you for a loop, do you remember? Some trick about teaching you how to do something after you tried to figure it out yourself, and you were so mad! You did the same to Mara when you first taught her.*
>
> *I remember bringing little Toren into the world and how you loved him, and I remember the pain in your eyes when we discovered we could never have one of our own. I wish I could have given that to you. I wish I would have a piece of you in them after you're gone. I don't know if this trial will be it for you, and I know what you say about not saying goodbyes. I just hope that if I am to lose you that Mara is still able to find her way home. She's my part of you. She's the daughter you never had and I never got the chance to warm to. When you come home, we'll be a real family. The kind of family that neither one of us was able to have.*
>
> *You just have to come home to me.*

Do you remember our wedding day? I do. I remember Rhodi made me a beautiful, blue dress and you wore ceremonial robes Aengar insisted on. Little Toren wanted to play his favorite game even if we weren't properly dressed, so we did. It was always so hard for you to say no to him. Almost as hard as it is to play in a dress instead of pants! I hope I have the chance to play Bullfrog's Hunt with you one more time. Maybe with Mara's kids. It's always more fun with kids.

I have so many happy memories of you, my love. And not all of them ended with me towel-whipping you, though you did teach Toren how to get me back.

I'm rambling now. I know I am, but I just can't bring myself to stop. I just want to write and write about senseless things. Old times, things that are happening as I write, and the future I want to have with you. We had many years together, but I want so many more. Ending this letter seems so final. And if they are my last words to you, I don't know what I want them to be. I do understand why you always said not to say goodbye, and it's not for the reasons you gave.

Goodbyes are hard. They're the end. It's the knowledge that there may be no more hellos or goodnights or good mornings. No more listening to you snore (I never thought I would miss it so much!). No more being in your arms. No more growing old together. No more.

I hope there will be. I hope to look up one day and find you standing in front of me. But now it's time for that goodbye. Know that I love you, dear Tederen, with everything in my heart. You were the one who turned this strange new place into a home, and there is no home without you.

Goodbye, my love. Goodbye for now. If you are to be taken from me during Mara's trial, and I have to wait until the end of my life to be in your arms again, just know that I long for that day with all my heart. Until then.

I love you.
Your Freya

Mara blinked rapidly and pinched herself to keep from crying. She could not cry with Teddy sitting there across from her. She cleared her throat and managed, "So did you send her a letter when you went to Gylden Grotto?"

He nodded curtly.

She slowly folded the letter back up and slid it to him across the table. "Uh … what's Bullfrog's Hunt?" she asked awkwardly.

Teddy took the letter, returned it to his jacket, and chuckled softly. "Toren's favorite game. It's actually a game that Aengar made up—back when he was young and fun."

"Fun?" Mara asked, raising a brow. "Aengar?"

"Oh, it happened," Teddy replied. Mara looked at him in disbelief, but he just nodded.

She shook her head. "What's the game?"

Teddy leaned back in his chair and stroked his beard. "Well, the first thing to know is there's no winning or losing. Aengar usually lost at games, you see, so this was a way to keep it fun for everyone," he explained.

"Okay, so it's a game for Aengar and for small children who are bad at everything. Got it." Mara snorted.

Teddy nodded. "Pretty much."

"Why do you have to play it with pants?" Mara asked, laughing.

Teddy chuckled. "You see, some of it involves being able to climb to high places or move very fast, and it's just easier to do with pants."

Mara leaned forward. "Tell me how to play."

It seemed to Mara to be a hybrid between leapfrog, tag, and hide-and-seek, only it seemed the worse you were at those other things, the better you were at Bullfrog's Hunt. The game started with a leapfrog scenario. Whoever couldn't leap over the person in front of them was the bullfrog, because it was bull that they were a frog—Teddy came up with that portion, and for that he was very proud.

The bullfrog then had to hunt for the other players. The trick was that they needed to go hide somewhere, so the bullfrog could find them without having to run very fast to catch them when they ran away, but the bullfrog didn't have to find everyone. The first one the bullfrog found became the new bullfrog, and they all had to go hide again. You couldn't be bullfrog twice in one game, so everyone had a turn to play every part, and there were no winners or losers.

When Teddy explained this all to Mara, she immediately banged on the barricaded door until Finn and Kip let them out. Kip burst in and hollered, "What's wrong?"

"We need to play a game," Mara replied, grinning.

Ashroot decided to take the helm and keep watch while they played. The bearkins' size and shape affected the enjoyability of a game that was based on agility—even if the standards were low. Funnily enough, Teddy was the first bullfrog, because each of the rest of them had leapt with all their might—even Kip—and Teddy's old knees wouldn't do the job after not being used that way in so many years.

They scattered. Finn ran below deck and climbed up on top of some crates in the hold. Kip ran behind him and hid in a cabinet in the galley. Mara took an unorthodox approach, lassoing the tail of *Harrgalti*, so Teddy couldn't reach the rope to pull her up, and launching herself off the back of the ship.

As she spat and sputtered, Teddy guffawed and shouted, "Poor gamesmanship!" before clambering down the steps after the boys.

A few minutes later, they all stuck their heads out over the bulwark and laughed at her. They worked together to haul her back up, and the game continued. They played it to completion—twice—and then it was time for someone to take over for Ashroot so she could make their meal. Kip took the helm and Mara and Teddy walked to the bow together and sat.

"Thank you for this," Teddy said, still panting a little.

"For what?" she asked innocently.

"You know what. Same thing you did with all the others. Show them a good time—a time they needed—just in case they don't make it back. I appreciate it. I do," he said. He cleared his throat and continued, "You know that I've thought of you as a daughter since I first laid eyes on you. I'm very proud of you and all you have done. Don't forget that. Remember how important your family is, and … that we love you." He kissed her on the forehead, patted her leg, and then stood and headed down below deck.

Mara's eyes widened in panic and her mind raced. *No. No. NO!* she thought. *Teddy just said goodbye.*

Mara had little chance to panic about the signs of Teddy's surrender before the upper coast of Chaosland was in view—in the shadow of the Dragon's Teeth, of all places. It seemed right that they would end up back there. They solemnly gathered their belongings, but only the essentials, and dressed for battle. Mara packed the basic supplies in her pack and grabbed her axe. They weren't hiding anymore. Today, they were true Ambergrovians.

Mara pursed her lips when Teddy donned only his leather jerkin. He didn't get new chainmail from Gylden Grotto, and she hadn't mentioned it. They hadn't replaced the crossbows, agreeing that for this they would not work that way, so this would have to be fine too. They each wore and bore what made them feel safest, because it was their last stand. When they were ready, they all headed to the deck to say their goodbyes to a tearful Ashroot.

"It'll be okay, Ash," Mara assured her. "We'll win this fight. We have to."

Mara hugged her friend, squeezing tightly for a moment before letting go, and then Kip and Finn hugged the bearkin as well. When it was Teddy's turn, he knelt in front of her.

"Ashroot, you may not be coming into the thick of it, but your job is important. Sail the ship out a safe distance into open water and stay there. Listen for a horn to sound. If you do not hear from us in five days, leave this place. The morning current should take you back to Port Albatross if you head east and follow the coast. Are we clear?" he asked.

Ashroot nodded.

"Very well. Stay strong, bearkin," Teddy replied, patting Ashroot on the shoulder and straightening. He turned to the others. "Time to go."

Chapter Nineteen

One Must Die

A gloom settled over them as they journeyed toward the location Kip had marked on his map. Due in part to the danger of the area—further north than they had ever been—and also to the fact that they were heading toward Death, they walked in relative silence, alert and watchful.

The name was apt for this area, and they found themselves wishing they had packed more provisions. All the grass was yellowed as far as the eye could see. In the forested areas they passed, the undergrowth was poisonous or dead. The water in the streams was blackened. It was too dangerous to have Keena fly over and look for resources. They couldn't risk someone seeing her in the heart of enemy territory. Their saving grace was the enemies they passed along the way. Because the Great Harbinger was gathering the army, small clusters of soldiers all journeyed the same way they did.

When they met their first enemies, they hid in the bushes a safe distance from the enemy camp while Teddy advised, "The head of the snake is what matters at this point. We don't have the time or food to fight everyone we meet."

"You're right, though. We need food," Kip replied.

The plan was simple. Mara would make an animal sound in the distance to draw them away from their camp. In the daylight, they wouldn't leave a sentry. Then, when they returned to find their food gone, they would assume it was done by animals. A little while later, Mara and her companions were again heading toward their destination, but this time digging through packs of food.

They continued this way for a few hours before nearing their destination and becoming more cautious. Finally, they spotted a patrol and carriage on the road. Four men surrounded the carriage, all giants.

"That has to be the Great Harbinger," Mara whispered harshly from their refuge in the bushes.

"Agreed," Teddy replied.

Up here, the patrols had never had anything to fear from their raids. Whether they were still on alert in the southern parts of Chaosland, Mara didn't know, but here the guns were holstered. Here, they had a slight advantage. They didn't have time for discussion. They quickly got into position, Mara and Finn circled to the front, Teddy and Kip took the rear, and they charged.

"To arms!" shouted one of the giants.

It was too late. Before he had even closed his hand around his revolver, Mara swung her axe, and his arm fell to the ground at his feet. In moments, her giant was defeated. Finn had a little more trouble beside her. His giant had drawn his rifle instead of his revolver, and he was now blocking Finn's blows with it as if it were a staff. Mara growled and charged, ducking her head down and ramming her shoulder into the giant's side. He fell—out of shock more than force—and Finn finished him and nodded to Mara in thanks.

All four companions met at the carriage doors, Teddy and Kip on one side and Finn and Mara on the other, just as someone was starting to open Mara's side. Finn reached the door first and slammed it shut. He poked his dirk through the covered window and said, "Now you're going to come out here nice and quietlike, and my friend is going to have a little chat with you. Is that understood?"

"Y-yes," came a small voice.

Finn swung the door open, and a tiny, female goblin gingerly hopped down. She was positively shaking with fear. Mara sighed and rested her axe on the ground. "This is not the Great Harbinger," she said.

"The Great H-harbinger?" the goblin asked. She shook her head fervently. "No, no."

"Who are you then?" Finn demanded.

"I-I am a recordkeeper," the goblin stammered. "The Great Harbinger wanted someone small for this task, and that small person is me."

"What records do you keep?" Teddy asked.

The goblin whimpered but didn't answer.

"Tell us," Finn ordered.

"You really don't have a choice," Mara added.

"Everything," she squeaked. "S-supply lists, population, schedules ..."

"Where is it?" Teddy asked.

The goblin raised a shaky hand and pointed inside the carriage, and Teddy and Kip poked their heads inside. "Mara, here!" Kip called.

Finn kept his dirks trained on the goblin as Mara turned and looked for herself. The carriage was filled to the brim with books. There was only a tiny seat open, just enough space for the goblin to sit. Mara opened the nearest book and gasped, flipping hungrily through it. "This has everything!" she cried.

Finn strode over to her and peered over her shoulder. "What do you mean by everything?"

Mara turned to look at her friend, book in hand. "I mean that this has— Finn, look out!" she shrieked.

The goblin had a small dagger raised and pointed at Finn's back. Finn whipped around, and the dagger plunged into his left side. He roared and grabbed the goblin's hand, pulled the dagger out of his body, and pressed it into her chest with her own hand. She fell to the ground, and so did he.

Mara dropped the book and fell to Finn's side as Teddy and Kip met them. Teddy flipped Finn's chainmail shirt up and pressed a hand against the wound. Finn grimaced and panted. *Not like this,* Mara pleaded. *Please not like this.*

"Is he going to be okay?" she asked Teddy.

Teddy pressed into the skin and slowly nodded. "Yes, it was lucky. The blade just made it through the chinks in the armor, but she didn't have enough strength to press in too deeply to repair."

The goblin coughed behind them, and they turned. When she spoke, her voice was a raspy wheeze. "You will never win. The Great Harbinger has power you cannot defeat. You ... cannot ... kill ... chaos ..." Her breathing rattled to a stop, and her eyes glazed over.

Mara and Teddy shared a look, and then Finn groaned.

"We need to get him out of the open, so you can patch him up," Kip said.

They drug the giants and the goblin into the bushes and led the carriage into the woods, making camp at a safe distance, so they could tend to Finn.

Teddy cleaned and stitched up Finn's wound while Mara and Kip rifled through the carriage. They found ledgers of all kinds, detailing the Great Harbinger's plans for the future. Mara determined there would be no point in them trying to read everything before they found the Great Harbinger, so they instead began to restack the books to leave more space in the carriage.

"Mara, look at this," Kip called.

He held a piece of paper with a broken seal. Orders, it seemed, like they had found before. "What does it say?" she asked.

He handed it to her. She read:

> *Recordkeeper, these guards will take you to the edge of the forest, where Death is in view. From there, you will head north from the large boulder and turn west at the fallen horse. This will bring you to my camp. Come on the last night before the moon is full. I will be waiting.*
>
> *—Great Harbinger*

She handed it back to Kip. "Another trap?" she asked.

"I don't see how it could be. They didn't know we might come up here. It doesn't make sense for this carriage to have been placed here just for us," he replied.

"That's where the leader will be, then," Mara marveled. She looked up at the darkening sky.

"Tonight," Kip said quietly. "We need to get moving."

"In Finn's condition …"

"Finn will be patched up in a minute, thanks," Finn called over to them. He winced as Teddy pulled a stitch tight. "If we need to go now, we need to go now."

"Just one more stitch," Teddy added, looking pointedly at Mara.

Mara turned and looked at Keena, trotting around the wagon and trying to talk to the carriage horse. Mara slowly approached her. When Keena looked at her, the dragonwolf's eyes twinkled and her tail wagged. *Yes, Mama?* Keena asked.

"I have a big job for you, Keena Keena," Mara said seriously.

Keena sat obediently and waited. *Like flying to get wolf friend,* she replied.

Mara nodded. "There's a lot of important stuff here in this carriage. We're going to need it all when we get back." She paused, hoping that Keena wouldn't realize that she was being given a typical keep-the-kid-busy job. "I need you to stay here and protect the carriage until we get back. Can you do that for me?" she asked.

Keena nodded excitedly and began to bound around, wagging her tail. *I can help! I can help!* she woofed.

Mara grinned and returned to Teddy just as he was finished with Finn's wound and bandaging him up. They both turned to look at her. She met each man's gaze, met Kip's, and turned back to the excited Keena. That was it. They just had a little further to walk, and they would meet the Great Harbinger. Mara gave Keena one last hug goodbye—as did Kip and Finn—and then they gathered their weapons and grimly followed the road toward Death, Mara dreading whose it would be.

They made it to the edge of the forest as dusk was just starting to settle. Mara took a deep breath and turned at the boulder. The others followed her silently, alert and listening for any sign of their enemy. They met the fallen horse—quite literally a horse statue that had been partially destroyed and whose head had fallen—and Mara turned and met each of her companions' eyes briefly before continuing on.

One foot in front of the other. When the moon was high in the sky, they saw the warm, flickering glow of firelight in the distance. The leader's camp. Mara pointed. Slowly, they each drew their weapons and crept toward the light, ducking behind tree trunks. They scouted the area and were, however, surprised to find that there was no one. No guards, no patrol, no soldiers of any kind. Just one lone figure sitting on a downed tree by the campfire with a rifle in their lap.

Mara turned and looked at Teddy. He nodded and jerked his head in the direction of the camp. Nowhere to go but forward. He lay a hand on her shoulder, and she felt Kip briefly grasp and squeeze her hand, before both of their hands fell away, and she was left with the impossible move. She stepped forward into the firelight.

The figure did not move. In the light, Mara could see an average human-sized figure wearing a duster and a wide-brimmed hat that hid their features. Mara walked forward, no longer trying to sneak, and her companions looped around at her sides. Kip was on her left, Finn on her right, and Teddy looped furthest forward on the other side of Finn. Once they made it into full view of the campfire, Mara stopped and cleared her throat.

"Are you the Great Harbinger?" she asked.

A voice filled the clearing—a raspy, female voice, like that of a heavy smoker. "Now what kind of leader would I be if I answered that question?" the woman asked.

"But you *have* just answered it," Finn said.

The woman paused. "And so I have."

"The leader of this dark movement is a *woman*?" Finn asked incredulously.

Growing up with a mother like his, you'd think Finn would have more respect for the power of evil women, Mara thought.

"That's why the patrol responded when Teddy said 'Haeyla,'" Kip murmured. "She's not just the mother of chaos—she's the mother of *this* chaos."

"Ah, it is funny you would mention that, actually," the woman said. "I am the mother of many chaoses."

"And what does that mean?" Mara spat.

"I am the mother of a boy named after the great god of chaos. A boy who was prevented from reaching his true calling by the people around him," she said waspishly.

Teddy inhaled sharply.

"What does that mean?" Finn growled.

"It means," the woman began slowly, "that I am the mother of Toren, a foolish boy who was taken in by the silly views of the forest dwarves instead of awakening his chaos. He abandoned his calling, and he abandoned *me* for the sake of some foolish dream." Her voice raised to a shout as she cried. "And so I ask you!"

She lifted her head slightly and looked right at Teddy and then to Mara. Her father's grey eyes looked back at her, twinkling in the woman's greenish face. Teddy swore and cried out, and the woman grinned. "Hello, *brother.* Hello, *granddaughter,*" she spat. She paused, staring wickedly at Teddy's horrified face. "How's my son been?"

Keena sat by the carriage and peered into the darkness. Her mama had given her a job to do, and she was going to make sure that nobody messed with the important thing. Soon after her friends and her mama had gone away into the forest and left her in charge, she heard voices. Bad voices.

She sneaked behind bushes with her wings tucked up close to her to make herself smaller. The carriage was a bit off the road, but they were still close. On the road was a wagon with two little, yellow creatures in it. They were going to go past the carriage. What if they saw it? She had to be sure to do a good job. She had to protect the important thing.

Keena circled around the wagon, like she'd seen Mama do. When the wagon slowed and the yellow men looked into the woods in the direction of the carriage, Keena pounced, brandishing her claws before the yellow men could get their angry metal. She pushed them off the wagon and coughed. A small puff of fire burst from her mouth and lit one of the yellow men's sleeves.

She tried harder, and the fire was bigger, but the yellow men started to scramble away and reach for their angry metal. She worried they would get away or they would get her with the angry metal, so she took a deep breath and yelled at them with all her might. A great burst of fire came out of her mouth and held until she closed her mouth again.

Keena looked around her and yipped happily to the horses that pulled the wagon, to the sky, to the yellow men that were no longer yellow, and to herself, as she pranced around in a circle and wagged her tail. She led the horses and wagon back to the carriage, head held high, victorious.

The silence in the leader's camp was deafening. Whipping to look to Teddy and back to the woman, Mara cried, "Your son? Your *son?*" It was unbelievable. *Impossible. Unfair. It cannot be!* she thought. *After all this time, this is . . . and I'm supposed to . . .*

"Hello, Gaele," Teddy hissed. "You're looking terrible, as always."

"Terrible?" she asked. Gaele threw her head back and cackled. "I was nothing in Aeunna. Nothing but the mother of the next Ranger, a silly boy. No, no, here— here I am glorious. I am the Great Harbinger, and I will lead my people to a bright, new world! . . . Oh, and I go by Haeyla now."

"Fitting," Teddy said. The hatred in his voice was a blade all its own.

"That's fine, brother, you don't have to call me by my chosen name. You won't be calling me for long anyway," she said, leaning back in her seat and crossing her legs.

"What's that supposed to mean?" Finn challenged.

"It means," she raised her rifle with one hand and rested it on the log beside her, "that I never go anywhere unguarded." She paused and raised her brows significantly. "It means that you are at this moment surrounded by my loyal followers who will take you all down as soon as I give the word—if I give it." She grinned, turning to Mara, and continued, "At this time, I am still hoping we can have a chat and move forward in a way that's satisfying for everyone."

Mara shifted uneasily and looked around. She couldn't see anyone in the woods. They hadn't seen anyone when they'd come up either, but Gaele's men may have moved in after. There was no choice. They would have to talk to her and see where they ended up. They were a step behind again. She'd known who they were all along, and they'd been brought here. Mara lowered her axe and rested the head on the ground.

"Fine," she said, "We can talk."

"Excellent," Gaele said, smirking.

Kip lowered his hammer and rested its head on the ground, and Teddy stabbed his sword in the ground angrily. Only Finn still stood at the ready, glaring across the campfire at Gaele.

"Very well," Gaele grumbled. "It is your choice—though be warned, if you attack me, you will not make it very far. And I hear you have a great fear of guns." She stared into his eyes and then slowly swept a loose hair behind her ear. Finn faltered, his face fell, and he slowly lowered his dirks. Gaele grinned. "That's what I thought."

Mara couldn't believe the cruelty. *How could she even have known about that? What else could she know?*

"What is it that you want, Gaele?" Teddy growled.

"What I want?" she asked innocently, turning to her brother. "What I want is to tell my granddaughter a story, hear from her in return, and give her a proposition."

"Get on with it, then!" Kip spat.

Gaele turned to Kip. "Ooh, you're a feisty little one, aren't you?" She raised her hands in mock surrender. "Very well, very well. First, granddaughter—"

"Don't call me that," Mara hissed.

"Fine. *Mara,* what has my dear brother told you about me?" she asked.

"He told me that you ran off with a human because you wanted to make chaos wherever you went. My dad was just a tool for you to be able to spread your poisonous ideals. When he kept you from corrupting my dad, you left. I guess you came here and decided to build your evil empire all your own," Mara said coldly.

Gaele gasped a little too dramatically. "How untrue!" she said. "No wonder you came to me ready for battle!" She laughed. "No, no, dear. Let me tell you the real story."

Gaele removed her hat, and Mara held back a gasp when she could see the woman more fully. She had the same russet hair as the rest of the family, and Mara understood why her dad had selected Green for their Earth surname. Although her skin wasn't as green as Teddy's, it was a pale greenish hue—she almost looked sickly. Gaele put on a warm face, but where the flickering light showed other wrinkles, there were no laugh lines. There was no warmth to her face except the light from the fire. Mara steeled herself as the woman began her tale.

"You see, Tederen and I grew up without our parents. He quite poorly tried his hand at raising me until some foolish, human girl came into our village after arriving from Earth." Teddy's knuckles lightened as he tightened them on his sword hilt. "Freya was so amazing, you see—well, you've surely met her, Mara. She was a needy one. And then I saw it: Humanity. Humans are the most chaotic creatures of all, and the humans from Earth had a unique knack for pulling out all the chaos in the world. So, I went to find my own human. I couldn't let Tederen have everything, you see."

"Of course not," Teddy grumbled.

Gaele ignored him, focusing on Mara. "So, I went to a human village nearby, hoping to find a human man. I met one named Dakota, but he already had his heart set on some other woman. I settled for the first one who paid me any mind. I never even got his name. He left me high and dry once he found out I was with child, so I was forced to crawl back to my brother and his wonderful new life. You see, no matter what he did, he always got the good things, and no matter what I did, I always got the bad things."

"You think maybe that was because I didn't seek out bad things like you did?" Teddy asked.

"No, it was because you were the golden boy, and I was shunned for wanting to do something different. An outcast among my own people," she replied dramatically.

"And then what?" Mara asked. "How long has your envy of Teddy been making you do terrible things?"

"Envy?" she asked. "No, I didn't want what Teddy had—I wanted something better."

"And better was a child?" Kip asked.

"Well, considering that he took mine for his own, I would say yes," Gaele replied.

"That wasn't—" Teddy began.

"Anyway!" Gaele cut in loudly, "I came back with a child and a plan for a bright future for him. I nearly died giving birth to him, you know. And in those moments of near-death, I was visited by Haeyla and Toren. They told me of a prophecy the Oracle was too frightened to pass along. The flipside of your prophecy, Mara." She looked at her granddaughter and smiled pleasantly.

"And what prophecy was that?" Mara asked, eyes hard.

Gaele grinned. "The world would fall into chaos when an Aeunnan and a human had a child of chaos, and when the chaos began, it would be led by the mother who calls herself Haeyla. I was their chosen! I named my son Toren—a child of chaos in name—and I've chosen the name Haeyla for myself."

"It's not a prophecy if it's your choice, Gaele!" Teddy shouted.

"Haven't you ever heard that you make your own fate?" she snapped. "They called to me, and I answered. I became their agent then to be the great harbinger of chaos to cleanse the world!"

"So, you became this Great Harbinger when you were still in Aeunna?" Mara asked incredulously.

Gaele leaned back. "Well, not exactly," she said. "I began gradually, devoting myself to my new calling and passing my teachings on to my son. But my *brother*," she glared at Teddy, "wouldn't have that, so I ended up running away with the intent of returning with my new followers to reclaim my son—the son my brother took from me out of hand. All I wanted was my family then, to come with me on my grand destiny, and that's all I want now."

"Join you?" Mara shrieked. "You want me to join you? You know *my* destiny is to defeat you, right?"

"But you won't," Gaele hissed. "Not here, not today. Do you know why?"

Mara glared at her and shook her head defiantly.

"Because there is power in chaos, Mara!" Gaele shouted. "Because at the slightest snap of my fingers, I can take everyone here away from you and leave you nothing and no one … but me. You'd have no choice but to warm to me then, granddaughter."

"You think killing people I love will make me join you? You're mad."

Gaele jumped up and shrieked, pointing at Teddy, "Well if I'm mad, *he's* the one who made me that way! Who abandoned me because of a woman? Who threw my life into chaos? Who didn't try to find me when I ran away? Who. Took. My. Son?" With every question, she jabbed her finger at Teddy. "I embraced the only family who was there for me! I embraced the cause that empowered me! And I will empower others like me by bringing down the broken society we live in and ushering in the new rule of chaos. MY RULE!" she roared.

No one spoke. Teddy shook his head at his sister, and she strode back to her log and plopped down, sighing with her whole body. Mara shifted, uncertain, and then asked, "How do I figure into all of this?"

Gaele looked up at her and grinned wolfishly. "You're my legacy," she said. "I lost my son, but I still need my family to carry on my work. To be the new line of world leaders. With you at my side, we could bring the rule of chaos to all corners of Ambergrove. Join me, and together we can do anything."

Mara hung her head for a moment, trying to process. She stared blankly at her axe hilt, and her vision blurred. When it refocused, she saw something else entirely. She saw the wolf's head of her dragonwolf axe sinking into the dirt. She saw the glistening of the firelight on the pommel of her father's dagger. She saw the hammer and axe crossing on her ring. She saw her bracelets—one from her father and one from her sister. She saw her bracer, given to her as a promise so long ago when she wasn't sure what to believe. About Ambergrove. About herself.

"No," she said fervently.

"No?" Gaele hissed.

Mara looked up at Gaele and pressed her axe into the ground before striding forward. "No, Gaele! No, I will not follow you. I cannot be who you want me to be. You are not, have never been, and will never be my family. My family is here, and in Aeunna, and in Nimeda, and far, far, away on Earth, living peaceful lives forever away from you. I will not turn on them. I will not turn on all the goodness I have been taught my entire life. I will *not* be sucked in by your own hatred of your life or your empty promises."

Mara strode back to her axe and wrenched it out of the ground, shaking the head for Gaele to see. "This is who I am! I am the Dragonwolf of Aeunna, a Ranger who will put the needs of the world above all else. I was tasked with defeating you and your whole evil plot, and somehow that's what I'm going to do. You cannot sway me, Gaele. No matter what you think of me or of the world, *I am my father's daughter,* and I will stop you."

The forest went silent but for Mara's panting. Gaele just looked at her, and when she spoke, her voice was impossibly calm. "Oh?" she asked.

"Yes!" Mara spat.

"Well then, I suppose it's settled," Gaele said quietly. "When you look back on this day and think me a monster, just know that it was you who drove me to this."

She paused, looking to each of Mara's companions in turn. Kip met her gaze defiantly, Finn would not meet it, and Teddy only looked at Mara, who was shaking with the effort to remain firm and confident. Gaele stood slowly and picked up her rifle like a walking stick before turning back to Mara.

"I failed, Mara," she said. "I failed to awaken the chaos in my son. I didn't know then how to do it. I know now. When I was most alone, the chaos burned in me like a fire. When I thought I could not handle any more pain, the chaos came to take that pain away. I will show you pain, Mara. I will show you a life that is not worth living. Loss that you could never imagine. I will show you your worst fears … and you will be glad to see me then." She paused. "Are you ready, Mara?"

Gaele took a single step forward, looking around the clearing once more. All raised their weapons now, ready to make their final stand. Ready to fight for the cause that had brought them so far from home. The hatred in Gaele's eyes when she looked at her brother was mirrored in his own. The disgust when she looked at Finn, shaking with fear but still ready to fight, Mara knew he felt in his heart too. When Gaele's gaze skipped over Mara to Kip, the gnome shifted, taking a step to the side to place himself between Mara and her grandmother. It was the smallest of movements, hardly perceptible. But it was enough.

Gaele's lips spread into a terrible grin, and she raised her hands. "It's time, Mara, to awaken the chaos in you. You will know pain, and you will embrace the chaos one way or another." Amplifying her voice, she added, "And I, too, have *little* men who would do anything to protect me."

She clapped once.

The sound was impossibly amplified, drowned out by the terrible echo of a gunshot. Mara turned to look for the source of the sound, of the danger, and watched in horror as Kip crumpled to the ground.

Chapter Twenty

The Wheel Turns

A bloodcurdling scream echoed through the forest. Gaele turned and ran, disappearing into the darkness. No more shots were fired. None were needed. Her point had been proven and the damage was done. It all happened so fast. There was no time to fight. No time to defend. Just a split second, and everything changed.

Mara rushed to Kip to check for his injury, to see if she could save him, unable to breathe or stop her own screams. He was still. Blood poured from the side of his head and his eyes were already darkening with death. Mara threw back her head and screamed harder, and her screams turned into wailing sobs. Kip was dead.

Arms gripped her from behind and tried to pull her away. She clutched onto Kip until green hands wrenched her hands away, and she turned to where her uncle knelt beside her and buried her face in his chest. She dimly heard him yelling, "No, Finn, don't! Mara needs us."

She did need them. All of them. The injustice of it poured out of her like the tears streaming down her face as she cried, "It's not fair, Teddy! It's not f-fair! I'm supposed to be able to say goodbye. That's how it always is in the stories. Everyone always gets that. Always. But h-he's just *gone*! He's gone, Teddy, and I couldn't do anything. I didn't even get to say goodbye!" She wailed and flung herself down onto Kip's chest.

"I know, Mara. I know," Teddy said softly, "But we have to go now. It isn't safe here, and I can't carry you both."

"Come on, Mara," Finn whispered. He hefted her to her feet and placed his arms on her shoulders, trying to steer her away. She pulled against him, reaching down to pick up Kip's hammer before allowing Finn to guide her out of the clearing. Teddy followed close behind, scanning around one last time for his sister, but she was long gone.

Finn led them to where they had stashed the carriage just a few hours earlier. Keena wagged her tail at them when they approached, excited to show them that she'd protected the carriage, and got them a wagon, and found some horse friends. She sniffed the air as Teddy neared her with Kip in his arms, and her tail stilled. It was a new blow for Mara to hear her pup's heartbroken whimper at seeing Kip. Teddy gently laid Kip in the wagon, and Finn led Mara up to sit beside him. Then the two men silently transferred the records from the carriage to the wagon, Teddy hopped up front to drive, and Finn climbed into the back. He placed himself between her and Kip's body so she wouldn't have to see it. Teddy urged the horses forward and ordered Keena to fly back to *Harrgalti* for Ashroot.

Ashroot met them at the coast as soon as they arrived. Keena had prepared her for the news, but she was still shocked at the sight of Kip's lifeless body, and she fell to the ground and cried. Mara was in a daze. She allowed Finn to steer her to sit on the ground, and then Keena lay around her to keep her company while Teddy and Finn got to work dismantling the wagon to create a funeral raft. They would not bury him in that dark place; they would set him free to sail to his final rest.

Mara stared out across the water, disgusted and disbelieving. Kip was gone, and it was her fault. She brought him to this evil place. He was protecting her, and for that, he was killed. Killed. They wouldn't build a life together in Aeunna. She wouldn't bring him back to see Loli. She had promised, and she had failed.

Numbly, she stood and staggered to where Kip lay at the edge of the water, and she began to clean his face. She used a shell to scoop water over him and to wash the dirt off, and she sliced off a piece of her shirt to wrap around his head to cover the wound. Teddy had already closed his eyes, so for a moment, she could imagine Kip was only sleeping.

"I'm so sorry, Kip," she said quietly. "I wish you were just sleeping. Or I was. I wish I could have taken your place. I promised that I would bring you back to Loli. I swore I would. But I'm just not strong enough. How do I even say goodbye?" She rested her left hand on his face and tears filled her eyes again as she saw his ring on her finger.

Mara reached up her other hand, enclosed the necklace he'd made for her inside it, and yanked. The cord snapped, and she lowered her hand and tied the necklace around Kip's neck, sniffling.

Mara heard footsteps and Teddy's voice behind her. "Do you know what that means?" he asked quietly.

"I don't know what anything means," she whispered.

He knelt beside her and held the necklace up so she could see it clearly. "This is a bindrune," he explained. "They're made of a combination of runes—symbols of the gods—to help the user."

Mara shook her head miserably.

"No, really," Teddy said gently. "You two have been bonded to each other for a long time. See here," he traced an n-shape, "is a symbol of strength. All strength. When he gave you this, Kip was trying to give you the strength to face any obstacle and to carry on." He traced a crooked cross shape and continued, "This is a symbol of determination. Whatever you needed or wanted to do, this keeps you on the path to do it."

Mara sniffled and asked, "What else is there?"

Teddy traced M and B next. "These are the symbols of Aeun and Baerk—the forest dwarf goddess and the gnome god. This was to bind you two together," he said softly.

Her lip quivered, and she shook her head. "Not for long," she whispered.

"No, no, Mara. Forever," Teddy said. He traced the last symbol—a square tipped on its point. "This is love, Mara. Not a fleeting love, but a deep, forever love that is stronger than the earth itself. He loved you so much, Mara, and that kind of love lingers long after someone is gone."

Teddy rested a hand on Mara's shoulder, and she turned and leaned into him, once again sobbing into his chest until she could sob no more.

Just as the sun began to rise, Teddy and Finn settled Kip on the raft to send him out to sea. Mara stood knee-deep in the water beside them and straightened the necklace around Kip's neck. She rested her hand on his cheek one last time and bent to kiss him lightly on the forehead before returning to the beach. She passed Keena trotting out into the shallow water with something in her mouth and turned to see the pup drop one of Kip's wooden toys on the raft by his hand, nudge the hand gently, and lick him before turning and following Mara back to the beach. Teddy and Finn pushed the raft outward, and it began to float away with the early tide.

When the men met Mara, Keena, and Ashroot on the beach, they all stood silently at the edge of the water. Teddy accepted a bow and arrows with cloth-wrapped tips from Ashroot, who also held a small torch. She was the first to speak.

"Thank you, Kip, for being my friend from the very day we met," she said.

Finn cleared his throat. "Thank you, Kip, for telling me what I needed to hear, even if I didn't know it, for helping me through the dark … and for having fun with me."

Mara looked at Teddy. Tears streamed down his face and disappeared into his beard. "Thank you for treating me like a father this past year. I would have been proud to call you my son," he said quietly.

Teddy looked down and sniffled, and Mara took a deep breath. "Thank you for the love you showed me. I will wait until the end of my life to be in your arms again. I long for that day with all my heart. Goodbye, my love. Goodbye for now."

Teddy glanced at her, no doubt knowing this came directly from Freya's goodbye to him, and then he nocked the arrow and lit the tip. The raft had already floated a good distance away, so he took a deep breath, drew, and fired. A few moments later, they could see the glow of the flames.

"Goodbye, my son," Teddy whispered.

Mara caressed her ring absently as she watched the raft fade away, vowing silently that this would not be the end. When Keena let out a mournful howl, it all became too much, and Mara collapsed to the ground. As the raft disappeared into the distance, a green light flickered on the horizon, and he was gone.

"What do we do now?" Ashroot asked quietly.

Teddy rubbed his beard and choked, "Head back to Questhaven. Rebuild. Try again. We brought back records that may help us find her again. We just have to hope that we can defeat her."

"She's all alone, now, isn't she?" Mara spat. Her blood boiled as she turned to look at them. "I will never join her, so her plan to have a legacy has failed. I will defeat her, one way or another, and rid the world of her poison. For Ambergrove. For Aeunna. For Kip." She turned back to glare across the water as silent tears continued to steam down her face.

"We'd best get started then," Finn said.

Mara rose to her feet and nodded once, determined.

Gaele sat on a log by her campfire. She'd returned immediately when she saw a white flash, and she sent all her men away when she realized what that light truly meant. She spent a little time setting up a show while a young woman lay unconscious on the ground beside her. She removed her duster, took a stone from the ground, and hit herself with it on the face and arms. Next, she took a small, curved blade from her duster pocket and made shallow cuts as well.

She hoped she was a grisly sight. She slapped her cheeks a few times and tried to force her face to soften. Slowly, she knelt down and bent over the unconscious young woman and gently roused her from her sleep. The young woman blinked rapidly as Gaele helped her to sit up, and the old woman bit her lip to hold back a triumphant smile. What the girl saw was a face of utmost concern.

"Gently, gently, dear," Gaele said to the girl. "Oh, you've had quite a journey, haven't you?"

The girl had appeared at the camp as if by magic, just as Gaele had been making her escape and her granddaughter and her companions were retreating. It was fate, plain and clear, and she would have the upper hand this time. That the others would be gone and leave this one here just for her—with no knowledge of them at all.

"Y-yeah, I have," the girl said. She ran a hand through her russet hair and looked around wildly. The girl turned to Gaele and added, "Wait, uh, this isn't right. Dad said that I would go to my family when I got here. Where's …" She looked around. "Where's Mara?"

Gaele scrunched her face and her eyes watered. "Oh, dear, you're her younger sister, aren't you? Another daughter of Toren's?"

"Yeah," Kara replied slowly. "How do you know that?"

"I'm your grandmother, dear," Gaele replied kindly, patting the girl's cheek.

Kara grew lightheaded and fell back into Gaele's arms. "B-but where's Mara?" she asked.

"Here, dear, sit up and drink this," Gaele ordered, propping her against a log and handing her a waterskin. Kara took it and drank a sip. Gaele sighed dramatically and said, "Oh, dear. You do come to family when you come to Ambergrove from Earth. Very good of my son to tell you that. But your family here is a little broken, you see?" She shook her head and made a show of being overwhelmed.

"Broken? Broken how?" Kara squeaked, her eyes widening.

"Well, as I'm sure you know, not all family has your best interests at heart, my dear, and, well, I've lost your sister to a bad influence," Gaele said miserably.

"Lost?" Kara cried, jumping up. "What do you mean, she's lost?"

Gaele buried her head in her hands and plucked an eyelash to make the tears flow when she looked back up at her granddaughter. "A grandma loves her babies," she choked. "And I loved Mara. I thought she loved being here with me, but, well … my brother is an evil, evil man, my dear."

"Evil?" Kara squeaked.

"Oh, yes, very. See this?" Gaele showed her granddaughter her bruised and bloodied arms.

Kara gasped. "He did this to you?"

Gaele nodded pitifully and pointed to Kip's dried blood on the ground to indicate where and how severely she'd been hurt. "This and more—and Mara helped him!" She paused for effect, delighting in the horror on the girl's face as she looked at the blood on the ground. She continued gravely, "Ambergrove has changed her, my dear. She turned on her family, and I fear she's lost to us forever!"

Kara dropped the waterskin and knelt to give the old woman a hug. Gaele smiled into her granddaughter's russet hair as the girl said, "That's awful, grandmother! I can't believe it. I can't imagine what you must be feeling after being betrayed by your own family." Kara squeezed the hug tighter and trembled.

"Oh, oh, yes. It is a great evil to turn on one's family!" Gaele cried. She scrunched up her face and held the girl at arm's length, sniffling and staring soulfully into her eyes. "Y-you won't turn on your family, will you?" she asked.

The confusion and hurt in Kara's eyes was muddied by tears, and the girl shook her head defiantly. As her grandmother pulled her back into a tight hug, Kara said, "No, grandmother. No, I won't."

CPSIA information can be obtained
at www.ICGtesting.com
Printed in the USA
BVHW042154280223
659432BV00009B/89